George Birkbeck Norman Hill, Dante Gabriel Rossetti

Letters of Dante Gabriel Rossetti to William Allingham

1854-1870

George Birkbeck Norman Hill, Dante Gabriel Rossetti

Letters of Dante Gabriel Rossetti to William Allingham
1854-1870

ISBN/EAN: 9783337137854

Printed in Europe, USA, Canada, Australia, Japan

Cover: Foto ©Andreas Hilbeck / pixelio.de

More available books at **www.hansebooks.com**

Letters
of
Dante Gabriel Rossetti
to William Allingham
1854~1870

BY

GEORGE BIRKBECK HILL, D.C.L., LL.D.

HONORARY FELLOW OF PEMBROKE COLLEGE, OXFORD

EDITOR OF BOSWELL'S "LIFE OF JOHNSON," ETC.

London

T. FISHER UNWIN

PATERNOSTER SQUARE

1897

PREFACE

" THE best of all Rossetti's letters, so far as hitherto
published, are those to William Allingham, printed
by Dr. Birkbeck Hill in the *Atlantic Monthly* for
1896." Such is the judgment passed by Dr. Garnett
in his article on Dante Gabriel Rossetti in the *Dictionary of National Biography*. Though the editor
of the American magazine was liberal in the space
which he allowed me, nevertheless in my four papers
it was only a selection, though a large selection, that
I was able to give. In reading through the original
letters a second time this summer I was surprised
to find how much of necessity had been omitted that
in point of interest was scarcely inferior to what had
been inserted. All these passages I am including
in the present volume, with the exception of one or
two which might, it was thought, give pain either
to those criticised by Rossetti or to their surviving
friends. Were I, however, to print all that he
wrote little fault could be found with it on the score
of severity. In these letters, at all events, the
writer was not often harsh in his judgment of his
fellow-men.

The additions, both in the text and in the notes,

are so considerable that it will be found, I believe,
that the four articles have been increased to nearly
thrice their original size.

In writing my notes I have made great use of
the following works :— *The Letters and Memoir
of Dante Gabriel Rossetti*, by William Michael
Rossetti ; *Dante Gabriel Rossetti as Designer and
Writer*, by the same author ; *The Autobiography
of William Bell Scott ; The Life of Ford Madox
Brown*, by Ford H. Hüeffer ; *The Life of Anne
Gilchrist*, by H. H. Gilchrist, and three articles
in the *Contemporary Review* for 1886 by Holman
Hunt.

In the Introduction will be found an acknowledgment of my obligations to Mrs. Allingham, Mr. W.
M. Rossetti, and Mr. Arthur Hughes.   Without
their assistance my part of the work would have
been imperfect indeed.

For the illustrations and fac-similes I have to
thank Mrs. Allingham, Mr. G. F. Watts, R.A., Mr.
W. M. Rossetti, Mr. Arthur Hughes, Mr. J. G.
Kershaw, and Mr. C. Fairfax Murray.

G. B. H.

October 30, 1897.

TABLE OF CONTENTS

ILLUSTRATIONS

INTRODUCTION

LIFE seems to me strangely varied this sunny January day, as, sitting at my desk in the parlour of a pleasant villa on the outskirts of the little town of Alassio, I look beneath palm-trees upon the blue waters of the Mediterranean, and listen to the measured beat of the waves on the sandy shore. Lying open before me are copies of the letters which Dante Gabriel Rossetti wrote to his friend William Allingham. In the table drawer are copies of another set of letters, which, more than a century and a half ago, Swift wrote to an Irish country gentleman. This double correspondence, written by men wide as the poles asunder, I have brought from England to edit in Italy for readers on both sides of the Atlantic. Have I not good reason for finding a strange variety in life?

Delightful as is this spot where winter seems to have gone a-maying, yet it better suits a poet or a painter than an editor, who needs long shelves of books far more than trees laden with oranges and bushes weighed down with roses. From England and libraries I have been driven far away by weakness of health. In editing Rossetti's letters—that part of my twofold task to which I have turned first—I have had the help of friends at home. Mr. W. M. Rossetti has read a great part of the correspondence, and has furnished me with elucidatory notes. My old friend Mr. Arthur Hughes, of Eastside House, Kew Green, who, though not one of the seven Præraphaelite Brothers, lived in great intimacy with many of them, has let me draw on his reminiscences. More than forty years ago he was painting in Rossetti's studio ; his hand, happily, has lost none of its exquisite skill. Mrs. Allingham, whose pictures of English cottages. are not surpassed in refinement and in beauty by the best of her husband's verses, enables me to give a brief sketch of that graceful poet's uneventful life. He had made some beginning in writing his autobiography. From what he had written she sends me a few extracts. Some day, I am told, a memoir of him will be published. It will be delightful indeed if it contains the full records he kept of his long talks with Tennyson and Carlyle. Of Carlyle he saw much more than most of that great man's friends, for during some years scarcely a week went by in which they did not walk together. Strange to say, this intimacy has been passed over in total silence by Mr. Froude.   In the four volumes of his hero's Life there are sins of omission as well as of admission.

Allingham used to recount how Carlyle would sometimes begin by flatly contradicting him, and end by tacitly adopting what he had said.   One day the old man was describing his interview with the Queen at the Dean of Westminster's.   " She came sliding into the room," he said—"as if on wheels," exclaimed Allingham, interrupting him. " Not at all, Allingham," he gruffly replied.   A few days later his friend overheard him telling the story to Mr. Lecky.   " The Queen," he said, "came sliding into the room as if on wheels," and in that form he ever afterwards told it.   He used to add that he saw that he was expected to stand during the interview ; but that he took hold of a chair, and saying that Her Majesty would allow an old man to sit down, down he sat.

William Allingham was born at Ballyshannon, County Donegal, in March, 1824, of a good stock, for he was sprung from one of Cromwell's settlers. Of his birthplace he gives the following description : " The little old town where I was born has a voice of its own, low, solemn, persistent, humming through the air day and night, summer and winter.   Whenever I think of that town I seem to hear the voice. The river which makes it rolls over rocky ledges

into the tide.   Before spreads a great ocean in sun-
shine or storm ; behind stretches a many-islanded
lake.   On the south runs a wavy line of blue mountains ; and on the north, over green, rocky hills, rise
peaks of a more distant range.   The trees hide in
glens or cluster near the river ; grey rocks and
boulder lie scattered about the windy pastures.
The sky arches wide over all, giving room to multi-
tudes of stars by night and long processions of
clouds blown from the sea, but also, in the childish
memory where these pictures live, to deeps of
celestial blue in the endless days of summer.   An
odd, out-of-the-way little town ours, on the extreme
western verge of Europe ; our next neighbours,
sunset way, being citizens of the great new republic,
which indeed, to our imagination, seemed little, if
at all, farther off than England in the opposite
direction."

Of the cottage in which he spent most of his
childhood and youth he writes : " Opposite the hall
door a good-sized walnut-tree leaned its wrinkled
stem towards the house, and brushed some of the
second-story panes with its broad, fragrant leaves.
To sit at that little upper window when it was open
to a summer twilight, and the great tree rustled
gently, and sent one leafy spray so far that it even
touched my face, was an enchantment beyond all
telling.   Killarney, Switzerland, Venice, could not,

THE PURT, BALLYSHANNON.

(From a water-colour sketch by Mrs. Allingham.)

[To face page xx.

in later life, come near it. On three sides the cottage looked on flowers and branches, which I count as one of the fortunate chances of my childhood ; the sense of natural beauty thus receiving its due share of nourishment, and of a kind suitable to those early years."

Allingham's schooling was far too brief to satisfy his thirst for knowledge. He was scarcely fourteen, if indeed quite so old, when he was placed as a clerk in the town bank, of which his father was manager. The books which he had to keep for the next seven years were not those on which his heart was set. He was a great reader. Year after year he kept adding to the scanty stock of learning which he had brought from school, till in the end he had mastered Greek, Latin, French, and German. His father, proud though he was of his son's intelligence, had little sympathy with his constant craving for knowledge. In the bank manager's eyes it was not the scholar, but the thorough business man who ranked highest. From the counting-house the young poet at last succeeded in escaping. " Heart-sick of more than seven years of bank-clerking, I found a door suddenly opened, not into an ideal region or anything like one, but at least into a roadway of life somewhat less narrow and tedious than that in which I was plodding." A place had been found for him in the customs, as it was found for another and a greater dreamer on the other side of the Atlantic.

"In the spring of 1846 I gladly took leave for ever of discount ledgers and current accounts, and went to Belfast for two months' instruction in the duties of Principal Coast Officer of Customs, a tolerably well-sounding title, but which carried with it a salary of but £80 a year. I trudged daily about the docks and timber-yards, learning to measure logs, piles of planks, and, more troublesome, ships for tonnage ; indoors, part of the time practised customs book-keeping, and talked to the clerks about literature and poetry in a way that excited some astonishment, but on the whole, as I found at parting, a certain degree of curiosity and respect. I preached Tennyson to them. My spare time was mostly spent in reading and haunting booksellers' shops, where, I venture to say, I laid out a good deal more than most people, in proportion to my income, and managed to get glimpses of many books which I could not afford or did not care to buy. I enjoyed my new position, on the whole, without analysis, as a great improvement on the bank ; and for the rest, my inner mind was brimful of love and poetry, and usually all external things appeared trivial save in their relation to it. Yet I am reminded by old memoranda that there were sometimes overclouding anxieties : sometimes, but not very frequently, from lack of money ; more often from longing for culture, conversation, opportunity ; oftenest from fear of a sudden development of some form of lung disease, the seeds of which I supposed to be sown in my bodily constitution." This weakness he outgrew.

Having gone through his apprenticeship, he returned to Donegal, where he was stationed for some years. Close to his office he had a back room, where he kept all his books and where he read for hours together. Here, no doubt, he covered many a sheet of paper with verse. From Mr. Arthur Hughes I have the following account of the young poet :—

" D. G. R., and I think W. A. himself, told me, in the early days of our acquaintance, how, in remote Ballyshannon, where he was a clerk in the customs, in evening walks he would hear the Irish girls at their cottage doors singing old ballads, which he would pick up. If they were broken or incomplete, he would add to them or finish them ; if they were improper, he would refine them. He could not get them sung till he got the Dublin 'Catnach' of that day to print them, on long strips of blue paper, like old songs ; and if about the sea, with the old rough woodcut of a ship on the top. He either gave them away or they were sold in the neighbourhood. Then, in his evening walks, he had at last the pleasure of hearing some of his own ballads sung at the cottage doors by the crooning lasses, who were quite unaware that it was the author who was passing by."

He liked, his widow tells me, to see all sorts of people and all sides of life. He knew every cottage for twenty miles round Ballyshannon. When she visited the place with their children, after his death, "very many," she writes, "were the friendly greetings we had from folk who remembered him kindly." He sought for sympathy outside the narrow limits of this secluded spot. "I had," he says, "for literary correspondents, Leigh Hunt, George Gilfillan, and Samuel Ferguson, and for love correspondent F. [one of his cousins], whose handwriting always sent a thrill through me at the first glance and the fiftieth perusal." Gilfillan had not the good fortune to win the esteem of Coventry Patmore, who wrote to Allingham in 1850 :—" I hear that you have had the misfortune to be publicly praised by that coxcomb of coxcombs, Gilfillan." To Samuel Ferguson Allingham dedicated his *Laurence Bloomfield* with " admiration, gratitude, and love."

In June, 1847, he paid his first visit to London, and called on Leigh Hunt. " I was shown into his study, and had some minutes to look round at the bookcases, busts, old framed engravings, and to glance at some of the books on the table, diligently marked and noted in the well-known neatest of handwritings. Outside the window climbed a hop on its trellis. The door opened, and in came the *genius loci*, a tallish young old man, in dark dressing-gown and wide, turndown shirt collar, his copious iron-grey hair falling almost to the shoulders. The friendly brown eyes, a simple yet fine-toned voice, easy hand-pressure, gave me greeting as to one already well known to him. Our talk fell first on reason and instinct. He maintained (for argument's sake, I thought) that beasts may be equal or superior to men. He has a light earnestness of manner, a toleration for almost every possible different view from his own. I ask him about certain highly interesting men. ' Dickens, a pleasant fellow, very busy now, lives in an old house in Devonshire Terrace, Marylebone. Carlyle, I know him well. Browning lives at Peckham, because no one else does! He's a pleasant fellow, has few readers, and will be glad to find that you admire him (!!).'

" In 1850 I ventured to send my first volume of verse to Tennyson. I don't think he wrote to me, but I heard incidentally that he thought well of it; and during a subsequent visit to London (in 1852, perhaps) Coventry Patmore, to my boundless joy, proposed to take me to call on the great poet, then not long married, and living at Twickenham.

We were admitted, shown upstairs, and soon a tall
and swarthy man came in, with loose dark hair and
beard, very near-sighted ; shook hands cordially,
yet with a profound quietude of manner ; immediately afterwards asked us to stay to dine.   I
stayed.   He took up my volume of poems, which
bore tokens of much usage, saying, ' You can see it
has been read a good deal ! '   Then, turning the
pages, he asked, ' Do you dislike to hear your own
things read ? ' and, receiving a respectfully encouraging reply, read two of the *Æolian Harps*.
The rich, slow, solemn chant of his voice glorified
the little poems."

These two poems, which are included in Alling-
ham's *Day and Night Songs*, are mentioned by
Rossetti in one of his letters as among his favourites.
He too glorified his friend's verse by his recitation.
" I remember," writes Mr. Hughes, " before I knew
Allingham, Rossetti speaking of him to me and of
his poems, and reciting, as he only could, *The
Ruined Chapel*, beginning :—

> " ' By the shore a plot of ground
>   Clips a ruined chapel round,
>   Buttressed with a grassy mound,
>   Where day and night and day go by,
>   And bring no touch of human sound.'

He was the most splendid reciter of poetry, deep,

full, mellow, rich, so full of the merits of the poem and its music." Nevertheless, his recitation, fine though it was, must have been marred by one great defect ; the man who made " calm " rhyme with "arm" had no ear for one of the most beautiful sounds in the English language. Tennyson, to whom in early years he sent some of his poems in manuscript, found fault with these " cockney rhymes," though he himself had been guilty of them, and guilty of them in print. In the first version of *The Lady of Shalott* " river " rhymes with " lira."

As years went by, Allingham saw much more of the world and of those men of letters whose society he loved. In the course of his official duties he was moved first to one station and then to another in England. Twice he had an appointment in London. In 1870 he retired from the customs, being appointed sub-editor of *Fraser's Magazine* under Froude. He succeeded him as chief editor in 1874. In the same year he married. He died in 1889.

" He had," as Mr. W. M. Rossetti tells me, " a good critical judgment ; he was a man who could pounce on defects in a poem." Madox Brown described him as " keen and cutting." It will be seen in the course of these letters that Rossetti not only sought his criticism of his poetry, but often acknowledged its justice. Coventry Patmore was scarcely less eager to have his opinion, but was not so willing to submit to it. " You horrify me with your talk about pruning," he once wrote to his friend, who had found *The Angel in the House* somewhat too long. " You have marked for omission several of my pet passages." Early in their correspondence he described Allingham as " a grave and truthful character, combined with a strong and quick intelligence."

It is much to be regretted that of Allingham's letters to Rossetti not a single one has been preserved. The great painter was in the habit from time to time of clearing out his drawers by the simple method of destroying all their accumulations. The loss, however, is the less serious owing to Rossetti's admirable clearness as a letter writer. However thick may be the mist which in places covers his poetry, when he writes in prose his thoughts and the words in which they are set forth are as clear as day. It is time, however, to bring this introduction to an end, and allow him to speak for himself.

I.

CHATHAM PLACE,

[BLACKFRIARS BRIDGE],

Midnight 12½   {*Friday*   [*probably Spring*
                  {*Saturday*   *of* 1854].

DEAR ALLINGHAM,

Yea, unto 70 times 7!—and what a beast I was not to write all that time. And you to call after all on such a beast! And I to be absolutely prevented from being here just now in the daytime—as I am painting elsewhere.

Pray do come instead in the evening after 8,—or else write me word where we can meet. In a day or two I trust to be free. I will wait here for you to-morrow evening. But if impracticable to come, never mind keeping me in.

Yours affectionately,

D. G. R.

NOTE ON I.

Nathaniel Hawthorne recorded at Liverpool on February 23, 1854:—"There came to see me the other day a young gentleman with a moustache

2

and a blue cloak, who announced himself as William Allingham. His face was intelligent, dark, pleasing, and not at all John-Bullish. He said that he had been employed in the Customs in Ireland, and was now going to London to live by literature. His manners are good, and he appears to possess independence of mind." Allingham did not this time succeed in escaping from the counting-house into literature. Rossetti, writing from Hastings on May 25th of this same year, says :—" I heard from Millais yesterday, who tells me Allingham is going back to Ireland and the Customs."

II.

Saturday [probably spring of 1854].

DEAR ALLINGHAM,

We forgot, I believe, to settle last night whether we go to dinner at Mr. Marshall's, 85, Eaton Square, at 7 to-morrow. I am going. If you do not, will you write to him, or indeed in any case. Perhaps we had better go separately to avoid trouble in meeting.

Your D. G.

In turning your things over, will you keep an eye to that lost MS. of mine.

Let's call together on the Martins soon.

" Mr. Marshall was a millionaire from Leeds, who had a large estate in Cumberland." Rossetti wrote of him on May 15, 1856 :—" He is disposed to be very useful to me, I think, in purchasing my works, and also in very generously paying for them, as he always declares the prices I ask to be trifles."

III.

Monday, ½ past 6 o'clock.

[*April,* 1854.]

DEAR ALLINGHAM,

I suppose you are gone to bask in the Southon [*sic*] ray. I should follow, but feel very sick, and moreover have lunched late to-day with Ruskin. We read half the *Day and Night Songs* together, and I gave him the book. He was most delighted, and said some of it was heavenly.

I took Miss S. to Hastings, and Bessie P. behaved like a brick. I have told Ruskin of my pupil, and he yearneth. Perhaps I may come down on Anna Mary to-night, as I believe she leaves on Wednesday with Barbara S. I am going now to my family, and if you feel inclined to come down to 45, Upper A. St., we will go to the Hermitage together. Otherwise I am not sure of going.

Your G. D. R.

Notes on III.

On April 14th of this year, a few days before the date of this letter, Rossetti wrote to Madox Brown : "Mac Cracken sent my drawing [*Dante drawing an Angel in Memory of Beatrice*] to Ruskin, who the other day wrote me an incredible letter about it, remaining mine respectfully (!!), and wanting to call. I of course stroked him down in my answer, and yesterday he called. His manner was more agreeable than I had always expected. . . . He seems in a mood to make my fortune."

A few months later Ruskin wrote to Rossetti : "I forgot to say also that I really do covet your drawings as much as I covet Turner's ; only it is useless self-indulgence to buy Turner's, and useful self-indulgence to buy yours. Only I won't have them after they have been more than nine times rubbed entirely out—remember that."

Miss S. was Miss Siddal, with whom Rossetti had fallen in love so early as 1850, though it was not till 1860 that he married her. His brother has told us how her striking face and "coppery-golden hair" were discovered, as it were, by Deverell in a bonnet-shop. She sat to him, to Holman Hunt, and to Millais, but most of all to Rossetti. The following account was given me one day as I sat in the studio of Mr. Arthur Hughes, surrounded by some beautiful sketches he had lately taken on the coast of Cornwall :—

"Deverell accompanied his mother one day to a milliner's. Through an open door he saw a girl working with her needle ; he got his mother to ask her to sit to him. She was the future Mrs. Rossetti. Millais painted her for his Ophelia— wonderfully like her. She was tall and slender, with red coppery hair and bright consumptive complexion, though in these early years she had no striking signs of ill health. She was exceedingly quiet, speaking very little. She had read Tennyson, having first come to know something about him by finding one or two of his poems on a piece of paper which she brought home to her mother wrapped round a pat of butter. Rossetti taught her to draw. She used to be drawing while sitting to him. Her drawings were beautiful, but without force. They were feminine likenesses of his own."

Rossetti's pet names for her were Guggum, Guggums, or Gug. A child one day overheard him, as he stood before his easel, utter to himself over and over again the words, " Guggum, Guggum." "All the Ruskins were most delighted with Guggum," he wrote. " John Ruskin said she was a noble, glorious creature, and his father said by her look and manner she might have been a countess." Ruskin used to call her Ida.

Anna Mary was Miss Howitt (afterwards Mrs. Howitt-Watts). The Hermitage (Highgate Rise), her father's house, was swept away long ago.

Barbara S. was Barbara Leigh Smith (afterwards Madame Bodichon), by whose munificence was laid the foundation of Girton College, Cambridge, the first institution in which a university education was given to women. Rossetti wrote to his sister on November 8, 1853 :—" Ah, if you were only like Miss Barbara Smith! a young lady I meet at the Howitts', blessed with large rations of tin, fat, enthusiasm, and golden hair, who thinks nothing of climbing up a mountain in breeches, or wading through a stream in none, in the sacred name of pigment." " She was a most admirable woman," adds Mr. W. M. Rossetti, " full of noble zeal in every good cause, and endowed with a fine pictorial capacity."

Bessie P. was Miss Bessie Rayner Parkes, daughter of " Joe " Parkes, whom Carlyle hits off in his *Reminiscences* (vol. i. p. 254), afterwards Madame Belloc. In *A Passing World* she writes :—" Barbara Smith suggested the conception of Romola to George Eliot, who has thus sketched an immortal [?] portrait of her face and bearing in early youth."

Speaking of Rossetti at the time of his visit to Hastings, she says :—" There was about him in his youth a singular good breeding, enforced and cherished by all the women of his family. . . . I did not think his wife in the least like 'a countess,'" she adds ; " but she had an unworldly simplicity and purity of aspect which Rossetti has recorded in his pencil drawings of her face. Millais has also given this look in his Ophelia, for which she was the model. The expression of Beatrice [*Beata Beatrix*, now in the National Gallery] was not hers. . . . She had the look of one who read her Bible and said her prayers every night, which she probably did."

In 45, Upper Albany Street (now 166, Albany Street), Rossetti's father died. Here the painter, on the death of his wife, sought refuge for a time.

IV.

26th April, 1854.

My dear Allingham,

We lost my father to-day at ½-past 5. He had not, I think, felt much pain this day or two, but it has been a wearisome, protracted state of dull suffering, from which we cannot but feel in some sort happy at seeing him released.

I shall call on you soon, and meanwhile and ever am yours sincerely,

D. G. Rossetti.

Will you tell Mrs. Howitt, should you see her?

P.S. I have forgotten two or three times to remind you of your promise to write a word of introduction to Routledge for my cousin, Mr. Teodorico Rossetti.

Would you kindly do so, and send it me? It is merely to say that he has a MS., which he wants Routledge to look at, and advise him about, and of course buy if it is possible.

Notes on IV.

Dante Rossetti, a year before his father's death, sketched the old man as he sat at his desk deep in study. This striking likeness is reproduced in the Letters and Memoir. The son of an Italian blacksmith, early in life Gabriel Rossetti showed that he had that double gift by which his own son was to become famous, The painter's art, however, he neglected for poetry. His love of freedom, under the despotic Bourbons, brought his life into danger. After lying hid in Naples for three months of the spring of 1821, he escaped to Malta on an English man-of-war. There he was befriended by that witty versifier, Hookham Frere. "One of my vivid reminiscences," writes his son William, "is of the day when the death of Frere was announced to him, in 1846. With tears in his half-sightless eyes and the passionate fervour of a southern Italian, my father fell on his knees and exclaimed, 'Anima bella, benedetta sii tu, dovunque sei!' (Noble soul, blessed be thou wherever thou art!)" He settled in London, where he supported himself by teaching Italian. With all the fervour of a poet and the enthusiasm of an exiled patriot, he was, like Mazzini, a man of the strictest conduct. By hard work and thrift, aided by an excellent wife, he always kept his family in decent comfort, and never owed a penny to any man. "He put his heart into whatever he did." His learning was great, though his application of it was often fanciful. In the literature of the Middle Ages and the Renaissance he found far deeper meanings than had ever been dreamed of by the authors. As his little son looked over the woodcuts of some old volume, he would be awed by his father's declaration that it was a *libro sommamente mistico*—a book in the highest degree mystical. Freethinker though he was, nevertheless "for the moral and spiritual aspects of the Christian religion he had the deepest respect." In his early years he had been a famous improvisatore. Throughout life he was great in declamation and recitation. If on one side of his character he affected his son by sympathy, on another side he no less affected him by a spirit of antagonism. Of politics he and his brothers in exile talked far too much for the young painter. Of *gli Austriaci* (the Austrians) and *Luigi Filippo* (Louis Philippe) Dante Rossetti heard so much in his youth that he seems to have registered a vow "that he, at least, would leave Luigi Filippo and the other potentates of Europe and their ministers to take care of themselves." At all events, for the whole of his life, as regards current politics, he was a second Gallio—he cared for none of those things."

The old man bore his banishment the more easily "as he liked most things English—the national and individual liberty, the constitution, the people and their moral tone—though the British leaven of social Toryism was far from being to his taste. He also took very kindly to

the English coal fires. He would jocularly speak
of 'buying his climate at the coal merchant's.'"
Paralysis struck him in his closing years. Nevertheless, "he continued diligent in reading and
writing almost to the last day of his life. His
sufferings (often severe) were borne with patience
and courage (he had an ample stock of both
qualities), though not with that unemotional calm
which would have been foreign to his Italian nature.
He died firm-minded and placid, and glad to be
released, in the presence of all his family."

"Teodorico (or properly, Teodoro) Pietrocola,"
writes Mr. W. M. Rossetti, "who adopted the
compound surname of Pietrocola-Rossetti, came to
London in 1851, hoping to find an opening of
some kind ; but found nothing except semi-starva-
tion, which he bore with a cheerful constancy
touching to witness. In 1856 he returned to Italy,
and later on devoted himself to preaching evangelical Christianity, somewhat of the Vaudois type,
in Florence and elsewhere." One of his disciples
was Miss Francesca Alexander, who in her turn
had a great influence on Mr. Ruskin. "It is
hardly too much to say (writes Mr. W. G. Collingwood in his *Life of Ruskin*) that T. P. Rossetti
did for evangelical religion in Italy what Gabriel
Rossetti did for poetical art in England : he showed
the path to sincerity and simplicity. And Mr.
Ruskin, who had been driven away from Protes-
tantism by the Waldensian at Turin, and had
wandered through many realms of doubt, and

voyaged through strange seas of thought alone, found harbour at last with the disciple of a modern evangelist, the frequenter of the poor little meeting-house of outcast Italian Protestants."

V.

Tuesday [*May* 2, 1854].

MY DEAR ALLINGHAM,

I have heard from Miss Smith from near Hastings to-day about Miss Siddal, who, she seems to think, is worse, and she encloses a letter from Miss Parkes also tending to make me very uneasy. However, I have one of Lizzy's own (29th April, Miss Smith's being 1st May), which speaks of no change for the worse, so that I hope it may be a mistake. I shall go down to Hastings to-morrow after my father's funeral if possible, and should go to-day but for that. If, however, I should be quite unable to go to-morrow, I shall go Thursday. There seems to be some talk of getting her into a Sussex hospital till she can enter the Brompton.

I have called because I wish you would get those wood-blocks (at any rate 2 or 3) sent by Routledge *at once, if possible*, to 45, Upper Albany Street. If they come in time I will take them to Hastings,

otherwise they can be sent after me.   I have made
a sketch for one, and must set about them and
other slight things to raise tin.   You may depend
on my stopping the 30s. you lent me out of the
first money for you.   I am sorry to have broken
my promise last week, but will redeem it very soon.
I may perhaps call here again after going somewhere else now.   But write lest I should not be
able.

Your D. G. R.

Note on V.

The wood-blocks were for illustrations of Allingham's forthcoming *Day and Night Songs.*

VI.

Saturday [*May*, 1854].

My dear Allingham,

Feeling very anxious about poor Miss
Siddal I have just written to Wilkinson, begging
him either to write to me on the subject or appoint
an interview at his house, Tuesday or any day
after Wednesday.   I write this in case I should
not see you to-day, as I hope I shall be in till
6 or so, and almost sure to dine at the [*letter
imperfect*].

In case W. should appoint Thursday and so prevent our sitting, I am sure you will excuse and fix another.

Your D. G. R.

Note on VI.

For an account of Dr. Wilkinson see note on Letter XLVII.

VII.

5, High Street, Hastings,

[May, 1854.]

My dear Allingham,

I got here on Wednesday night, and am glad to tell you that I do not find Miss Siddal worse, either by her own account or in appearance. I should judge her, indeed, to be rather better, and she thinks so herself. Before leaving town I saw Wilkinson, who gave me some more powders for her, as well as the address of a Dr. Haile here, to whom he has also written about her. He thinks it very unadvisable that she should go into the Sussex Infirmary, or be shut up at all just now. I have written to him a minute account of her state from her own lips. Barbara and Anna Mary came over yesterday, and walked some time with us; and Lizzy did not seem overfatigued. Several ladies here are very attentive to her, and seem quite fond of her.   Her spirits are much better, and some of her worst symptoms have abated.

I trust the glorious weather which seems setting in now will do everything for her.   If you have any thoughts of a trip just now come here.   I am going with Miss S. to-morrow to spend the day at Roberts Bridge, some miles hence, where Barbara Smith is.

Thanks for the wood-blocks which I have brought with me.   I fear neither is large enough for the sketch I have made; but no doubt they will do for some of them.   Routledge's prescribed size will admit of a rather larger block.   I find Miss Siddal has made a sketch from *Clerk Saunders*, which promises to be beautiful when drawn on the wood. You shall hear again soon, if I stay here any time.

On the day of my father's funeral (at Highgate Cemetery) I heard from Ruskin. . . . He is leaving town till August about, and says he has given orders for all his works to be sent to me, so I suppose they are at my rooms now.   He asks me to correspond with him, which I shall try to do.

Do you still dine at the Belle *pas* Sauvage? I shall have no chance against you now any more.   Write soon.

D. G. R.

Thanks for what you say of the 30s. which I hope soon to send. Routledge, I suppose, will pay eventually for the blocks—otherwise I, and not you, ought to pay.

Notes on VII.

The first reference to Miss Siddal's ill-health Mr. W. M. Rossetti finds in a letter dated August 25, 1853. "The consumptive turn of her constitution became apparent; and from this time forth the letters about her are shadowed with sorrow which often deepens almost into despair."

Miss Smith lived at Scalands near Robertsbridge. William Howitt, who was a guest there in April, 1864, thus describes the place :—" The country is a hop-growing one, and is pleasantly diversified with hill, dale, and woods. The house stands on a hill in the midst of one of these woods. In the openings are various kennels of pointers, retrievers, and beagles, which are used in the shooting-season by Madame Bodichon's brothers. They give us plenty of dog-music. This property is three miles long, so we can range about without fear of trespass."

Madame Bodichon used to tell how Rossetti, noticing the ost-houses (the kilns in which the hops are dried) each with its tapering roof and vane at the top, innocently remarked, "What a devout people they seem to be, with a chapel to every farm-house !"

Writing to his brother during this visit he

described Scalands as "a stunning crib, but rather slow."

In another letter he says :—"Miss Smith has lent me Ruskin's *Lectures*, where there is only a slight, though very friendly mention of me." In the Addenda to the *Lectures on Architecture and Painting* Ruskin mentions him twice as follows :— "Not only can all the members of the [Præraphaelite] school compose a thousand times better than the men who pretend to look down upon them, but I question whether even the greatest men of old times possessed more exhaustless invention than either Millais or Rossetti. . . . As I was copying this sentence a pamphlet was put into my hand, written by a clergyman, denouncing 'Woe, woe, woe! to exceedingly young men of stubborn instincts, calling themselves Præraphaelites.' I thank God that the Præraphaelites *are* young, and that strength is still with them, and life, with all the war of it, still in front of them.   Yet Everett Millais is this year of the exact age at which Raphael painted the *Disputa*, his greatest work ; Rossetti and Hunt are both of them older still, nor is there one member of the body so young as Giotto, when he was chosen from among the painters of Italy to decorate the Vatican.   But Italy, in her great period, knew her great men and did not 'despise their youth.'   It is reserved for England to insult the strength of her noblest children—to wither their enthusiasm early into the bitterness of patient battle, and leave to those whom

she should have cherished and aided no hope but in
revolution, no refuge but in disdain."

"The Belle *pas* Sauvage" I shall explain in a
note on Letter IX.

VIII.

5, HIGH STREET, HASTINGS,

Friday [May, 1854].

MY DEAR ALLINGHAM,

A little note of yours inviting me to
breakfast on Tuesday last has just been sent on
to me here. I hope to be in London again soon,
though probably not to stay long, but must get
my things together and replenish my colour box,
&c. Hitherto I have been disgracefully idle here
—poor Miss Siddal even has done better than I
have, and I have no doubt when I come to town
I shall bring with me a wood-block which she
has begun beautifully. Her health varies a little,
but I think not very materially—in some things
she is better. Miss Smith continues to suggest
kind plans for her benefit, and has lately hit on
one which seems promising in some respects, of
which I can tell you when I see you, which I
shall do as soon as I reach London again. Lizzy
and I have been twice to a farm of Miss Smith's

near here, which is a stunning place. Miss S. as well as Miss Howitt have left here, and will both soon be in London again.

. . . . I am melancholy enough here sometimes, and shall be glad to discuss our concerns with you in London as soon as possible. Lizzy is a sweet companion, but the fear which the constant sight of her varying state suggests is much less pleasant to live with. She has just come in to breakfast. Goodbye.

Yours most sincerely,

D. G. ROSSETTI.

P.S.—Calder Campbell, who wrote to me the other day, begged me to say to you that he had called twice, once at Southampton Row and once at Queen Square, but in neither case had been able to make any one hear or come to the door. His number in University Street is 27. I believe he leaves town very soon.

NOTES ON VIII.

Rossetti's colour-box had to be replenished, as one of his letters shows, before he began *Found* on the canvas—that picture which he never lived to finish, though his life was prolonged for nearly thirty more years.

The plan of "the indefatigable and active Barbara" was for Miss Siddal's entering the Sanatorium in Harley Street, New Road, London, "where governesses and ladies of small means are taken in and cured." Miss Smith's relative "connected with the management of this place" was, Mr. W. M. Rossetti says, probably Miss Nightingale, who towards the close of the year was to set out for the Crimea.

"As my brother was growing up towards manhood," writes Mr. Rossetti "he became acquainted with Major Calder Campbell, an officer retired from the Indian army, and a rather prolific producer of verses and tales in annuals and magazines; an eminently amiable and kindly elderly bachelor, gossipy, and a little scandal-loving, who conceived a very high idea of my brother's powers. He must, I think, have been the first literary man familiar with the ups and downs of London publishing whom Rossetti knew. For a year or two my brother and I had an appointed weekly evening when we called upon Major Campbell in his quiet lodgings in University Street, Tottenham Court Road."

IX.

HASTINGS,

Monday, 26 *June*, 1854.

MY DEAR ALLINGHAM,

I am here again you see, but return immediately to London; so when you write again, write thither (Chatham Place). I shall not fail to keep up our correspondence. Miss S. returns with me for the present, till she can get her picture *en train* at any rate. I think she has certainly benefited a good deal by her stay in Hastings, and has done some more sketches from the ballads. She desires particularly to be remembered to you, and did so-several times when writing to me in London, which I always forgot to convey.

I should certainly have seen you in town before your exodus, if I had known in time. As it was, I only heard of your change of plan on Saturday evening at Munro's. The day before, perhaps, you heard that I called on you with the mighty Mac Cracken, who was in town for a few days, but we did not find you. What do you think of Mac coming to town on purpose to sell his Hunt, his Millais, his Brown, his Hughes, and several other pictures! He squeezed my arm with some pathos on communicating his purpose, and added that he should part with neither of mine. Full well he knows that the time to sell them is not come yet. The Brown he sold privately to White of Maddox Street. The rest he put into a sale at Christie's, after taking my advice as to the reserve he ought to put on the Hunt, which I fixed at 500 gs. It reached 300 in real biddings, after which Mac's touters ran it up to 430, trying to revive it, but of course it remains with him. The Millais did not reach his reserve, either, but he afterwards exchanged it with White for a small Turner. The Hughes sold for 67 gs., which really, though by no means a large price for it, surprised me, considering that the people in the sale-room must have heard of Hughes for the first time, though the auctioneer unblushingly described him as "a great artist, though a young one." I have no doubt, if Mac had put his pictures into the sale in good time, instead of adding them on at the last moment, they would all have gone at excellent prices.

Some of the pictures in the body of the sale went tremendously. Goodall's daub of *Raising the May-Pole* fetched (at least ostensibly) 850. I like Mac Crac pretty well enough, but he is quite different in appearance—of course—from my idea of him. My stern treatment of him was untempered by even a moment's weakness. I told him I had nothing whatever to show him, and that his picture was not begun, which placed us at once on a perfect understanding. He seems hard up.

If I were to send you one of those Australian paragraphs about Woolner and the statue do you think you could get it in anywhere with or without a short accessory, puff of your own? Millais

and I have both besieged Eastlake, and Millais
and Dickinson Mulready. Dyce will be written
to by one of us. Hannay is going to get a
paragraph in somewhere, and I think of trying
for the same sort of thing with Masson and
Patmore, or any one else who seems likely.
Hannay was in town the other day, and I am
going down to Barnet on Friday to see him, and
take a walk to Saint Albans. He is looking much
better than I have seen him look for a year or
two, and had just parted with the copyright of
his Lectures to Bogue for 50 in addition to the
50 he got first.

I hope my next letter will have more news and
be a longer one. There are dense fogs of heat
here now, through which sea and sky loom as
one wall, with the webbed craft creeping on it
like flies, or standing there as if they would drop
off dead. I wander over the baked cliffs, seeking
rest and finding none. And it will be even worse
in London. I shall become like the Messer
Brunetto of the "cotto aspetto," which, by the
bye, Carlyle bestows upon Sordello instead! It
is doing him almost as shabby a turn as
Browning's.

The crier is just going up this street and moaning out notices of sale. Why cannot one put all
one's plagues and the skeletons of one's house

into his hands, and tell them and sell them "without reserve"? Perhaps they would suit somebody at least except this horrid fork of a pen! I went to the Belle S. the other day, and was smiled on by the cordial stunner, who came in on purpose in a lilac walking costume. *I am quite certain she does not regret* you *at all.*

Your D. G. R.

[*On the envelope.*]

P.S.—Nous pouvons vous envoyer L'Athenæum chaque semaine, si vous voulez. Soyez certain qu'une certaine petite affaire de £ s. d. n'est pas oubliée.

Notes on IX.

Of White the picture-dealer Madox Brown has the following entries in his diary : "*Jany.* 27, 1856. On Monday White called, but did not like the *Hayfield*—said the hay was pink, and he had never seen such.—*Thursday.* After much moaning over my brick-dusty colour he took off *King Lear* for £20. —*March* 6. Called on Gabriel. I saw a lot of his works gathered there from Ruskin's and others, as a bait to induce Old White to come and buy his works."

Rossetti's humorous sallies against Francis MacCracken must not be taken too seriously. "He really liked him," says Mr. W. M. Rossetti, "and had reason for doing so." This Belfast shipping-agent "was a profound believer in the 'graduate,' as he termed Ruskin. He was always hard up for money, but he was devoted to Præ-raphaelitism." In 1852 he bought Madox Brown's *Wickliffe*, giving for it £63 together with a picture by Dighton, "which," says Brown, "I sold for £8 10s."

The following letter with which Mr. Holman Hunt has honoured me gives an account of his doings with MacCracken.

DRAYCOTT LODGE, FULHAM,
February 27, 1896.

DEAR MR. BIRKBECK HILL,

I trust that I am not now too late—although so very much so, owing to a variety of causes—in giving you the information you desired. The only picture that Mr. MacCracken bought of me was *The Two Gentlemen of Verona*. It was painted in 1850–51, and was assailed by the critics in the R.A., together with works by Millais, in the most violent manner, until Ruskin came forward quite unexpectedly and assailed the critics, to the lasting confusion of one or two of the craft. The picture did not, however, sell in London, and I sent it to Liverpool, when again it was attacked most acrimoniously; but the committee of the exhibition, to my surprise, ended by giving me the £50 prize awarded to the best picture in the exhibition, and yet it did not sell there.; but from Belfast Mr. MacC. wrote, saying he very much wanted to get to Liverpool to see it. He could not, however, get away, and at last asked whether I would take a painting by young Danby as payment for £50 or £60 of the price, which was, I think, £157. (It might, however, have been 200 guineas.) Eventually I agreed, and he paid me the money, part in installments of £10 at the time.

The picture was bought at Christie's by Sir T. Fairbairn for 500 guineas, and he sold it about eight years since for £1,000 to the Birmingham Art Gallery, where it now is.

I am yours ever truly,
W. HOLMAN HUNT.

MacCracken, as will be seen later on, made another attempt to sell the picture, but in vain. The day of the great Præraphaelite painter was still in its dawn. It was, no doubt, some years later that Sir T. Fairbairn made his purchase.

Mr. Hunt, speaking of the sale of this picture in the *Contemporary Review* for May, 1886, says :— " When the dates for payment came, a letter invariably arrived proposing to give instead of money further paintings, so that the transaction became a continual torment to me."

From Rossetti MacCracken bought the *Ecce Ancilla Domini*, which had been exhibited three years earlier, and had been returned unsold. Its price was only £50. In 1886 it was added to the London National Gallery at the cost of £840. For Mr. Arthur Hughes's *Ophelia* he had undertaken to give sixty guineas. He gave in reality thirty guineas and two small pictures by Wilson, a painter at that time of no account, though highly esteemed now. Unfortunately, the young Præraphaelite could not bide his time, and had to turn his pictures into cash. Being sent to the leading art auctioneers, they were sold for five pounds. At *Ophelia* Mr. Hughes had been long working, when one day Alexander Munro, a young sculptor, burst into his studio, with most of the Præraphaelites at his back. Deverell found fault with a bat flying across the stream, but Rossetti warmly defended it, as " one of the finest things in the picture." " He always was," Mr. Hughes tells me, " most generous in his admiration ; anything that he did not like he hated as heartily. His manners were fascinating, enthusiastic, and generous."

" I remember," writes Mrs. Howitt, " one of the most distinguished [of the P.R.B.] asking us, as he had no banker, to cash a cheque for £14, given him by a Manchester gentleman for a small oil-painting."

Madox Brown, writing of the Academy of 1851, says :—" Goodall is excessive in all that is low and to the public taste."

For " Woolner and the statue " see a note on the next letter.

" James Hannay," writes Mr. W. M. Rossetti, " was a bright and cherished figure in the literary Bohemia of those days ; my brother and I had known him since 1850 or earlier. He was in early youth a naval officer ; but, while still young, he took to authorship, and published various sketches and novels connected with sea-life. He was busy with reviewing, comic writing, and journalism ; a fluent, witty, and telling speaker in private and in public, taking with great zest, as the years lapsed, to whatsoever savoured of High Toryism, whether in politics or in the minor matters of genealogy and heraldry. Ultimately he obtained an appointment as British Consul in Barcelona ; and there he died, in middle age, very suddenly, in 1873."

Coventry Patmore, speaking of Rossetti's "extraordinary faculty for seeing objects in such a fierce light of imagination as very few poets have been able to throw upon external things," continues :—
"He can be forgiven for spoiling a tender lyric by a stanza such as this, which seems scratched with an adamantine pen upon a slab of agate :—

> 'But the sea stands spread
> As one wall with the flat skies,
> Where the lean black craft, like flies,
> Seem well-nigh stagnated,
> Soon to drop off dead.' "

This stanza of *Even So* finds its first sketch—by no means a rough one—in Rossetti's description of the " dense fogs of heat " at Hastings.

Carlyle, in his third lecture on *Heroes and Hero-Worship*, spoke of "that poor Sordello with the *cotto aspetto*, 'face *baked*,' referring to a celebrated passage in Dante's *Inferno* (canto xv. line 26). It was not Sordello, but Brunetti Latini whom the poet described. This error ran through the early editions of the Lectures, but was corrected in the later.   Mr. W. M. Rossetti tells me that " the suggestion that Browning did a shabby turn to Sordello by writing the poem is of course mere chaff; for Rossetti, in all those years, half worshipped the poem, and thrust it down everybody's throat."

He used often to dine at the Bell Savage Inn on Ludgate Hill.   " As for the Bell Savage," writes Addison in the *Spectator*, No. 28, " which is the sign of a savage man standing by a bell, I was formerly very much puzzled upon the conceit of it, till I accidentally fell into the reading of an old romance translated out of the French ; which gives an account of a very beautiful woman who was found in a wilderness, and is called in the French *La Belle Sauvage ;* and is everywhere translated by our countrymen the Bell Savage."   By Pennant's time the sign was disused.   Mr. W. M. Rossetti has no doubt that " the cordial stunner " was a waitress with whom his brother had an innocent flirtation.   " In these early days," writes Mr. Holman Hunt, " with all his headstrongness and a certain want of consideration, Rossetti's life within was untainted to an exemplary degree, and he worthily rejoiced in the poetic atmosphere of the sacred and spiritual dreams that then encircled him, however some of his noisy demonstrations at the time might hinder this from being recognised by a hasty judgment."

X.

Sunday [*Endorsed July* 24, 1854].

DEAR ALLINGHAM,

I have been waiting to write until I could see Cayley who has my MS. translations (*i.e.*, such as are copied of them—*cetera desunt*, that is, are not decent), in order that I might send them on to you at the same time as this letter. Not that my writing now implies that I have had vision of Cayley (a fair type of *Divine Comedy*)—of course you can guess that—but merely that every day after dinner it has seemed a very long way from the B. S. to Chancery Lane, and that my interview with the great unshaved seeming no nearer, I may as well write at once, trusting very soon nevertheless to get hold of the Poems and send them, as I should much like to have your dictum, and especially any suggestions of yours, which I wish you would mark on the margin, regardless of the original Italian, as I can always compare what you suggest with that, and see if it be compatible. I am still hoping to get them out as soon as possible, and think I should include the *Vita Nuova* of Dante, which I translated some 5 years ago, and which would only want some revision. Title perhaps thus : *Italian Lyrical Poetry of the First Epoch from Ciullo d'Alcamo to D. Alighieri* (1197–1300) ;

translated in the original metres, including Dante's *Vita Nuova* or autobiography of his youth.

Can you think of any better title? or is this too long?

Maclennan (whom you once met at my rooms) visited Cambridge with my brother the other day, and at some gathering there they met Macmillan, the publisher, to whom Maclennan spoke of my translations, which he expressed every good disposition to publish. He also said he had some time been wishing to propose to Millais, Hunt, and me to illustrate a Life of Christ.

My original poems are all (or all the best) in an aboriginal state, being beginnings, though some of them very long beginnings, and not one, I think, fairly copied. Moreover, I am always hoping to finish those I like, and know they would have no chance if shown to you unfinished, as I am sure they would not please you in that state, and then I should feel disgusted with them. This is the sheer truth. Of short pieces I have seldom or never done anything tolerable, except perhaps sonnets ; but if I can find any which I think in any sense legible, I will send them with the translations. I wish, if you write anything you care to show, you would reciprocate, as you may be sure I care to see. As a grand installment I send you the Mac Crac sonnet : it hangs over him as yet like the sword of Damocles. I dare say you remember Tennyson's sonnet, *The Kraken:* it is in the MS. book of mine you have by you,— so compare.

MAC·CRACKEN.

Getting his pictures, like his supper, cheap,
Far, far away in Belfast by the sea,
His scaly, one-eyed, uninvaded sleep
Mac Cracken sleepeth. While the P. R. B.
Must keep the shady side, he walks a swell
Through spungings of perennial growth and height;
And far away in Belfast out of sight,
By many an open do and secret sell
Fresh daubers he makes shift to scarify,
And fleece with pliant sheers the slumb'ring green.
There he has lied, though aged, and will lie,
Fattening on ill-got pictures in his sleep,
Till some Pre-Raphael prove for him too deep.
Then once by Hunt and Ruskin to be seen
Insolvent he shall turn, and in the Queen's Bench die.

You'll find it very close to the original—as well as to fact.

I'll add my last sonnet, made two days ago, though at the risk of seeming trivial after the stern reality of the above :—

As when two men have loved a woman well,
    Each hating each; and all in all, deceit;
    Since not for either this straight marriage-sheet
And the long pauses of this wedding-bell;
But o'er her grave, the night and day dispel
    At last their feud forlorn, with cold and heat;
    Nor other than dear friends to death may fleet
The two lives left which most of her can tell:
So separate hopes, that in a soul had wooed

> The one same Peace, strove with each other long;
> And Peace before their faces, perish'd since;
> So from that soul, in mindful brotherhood,
> (When silence may not be) sometimes they throng
> Through high-streets and at many dusty inns.

But my sonnets are not generally finished till I see them again after forgetting them, and this is only 2 days old.

But now about friends. Outside your letter you tell me to tell you something of Woolner, and I cannot recollect whether I mentioned to you that he had written up [*sic*] touching a statue for which he was competing there, or rather which he stood every chance of getting without competition, until the people determined to ask Eastlake, Dyce, and Mulready about his competency. I have been to Eastlake to see about it, and Millais has written to all three. Between us I think Eastlake is safe, Mulready has not answered either Millais or Dickinson, who also wrote (but he knew Woolner in England, and I know liked him personally, though I do not think he ever saw any work of his); and Dyce has answered Millais that he cannot remember W.'s works but wants to see some. The Wordsworth group is therefore going to be sent to the Royal Academy, that Dyce may see it there. Dyce and Eastlake were both among those members of the Committee who were named in that letter which Woolner got on the occasion of the

Wordsworth job, as having stuck out to the last in favour of W.'s model; but it is very possible they did not know his name, as I suppose the competition was anonymous. Thus far as yet about this. Woolner is very probably now on his way to England. I will send you his letter, if you write me that you did not see it, of which I am uncertain.

Hunt has written Millais another letter at last; the first since his second to me, months ago. It was sent to me by M., but I had to send it on to Lear, or would have let you have it, as it is full of curious depths and difficulties in style and matter, and contains an account of his penetrating to the central chamber of the Pyramids. He is at Jerusalem now, where he has taken a house, and seems in great ravishment, so I suppose he is not likely to be back yet. Have you seen the lying dullness of that ass Waagen, anent the Light of the World, in *Times* last week? There is a still more incredible paragraph, amounting to blasphemy, in yesterday's *Athenæum*, which you will see soon. I hope you got the last one.

I spent two or three days at Ridge, near Barnet, with Hannay lately, where he is staying at his father's, and will remain probably for some months. His babe has grown quite beautiful, and I saw him put in a tub in a very vigorous state. Hannay and I walked to St. Albans, and saw Bacon's tomb, the Cathedral, &c. We purported writing to you jointly thence after dinner, but somehow out of the fulness of the stomach the speech wouldn't come. *Satire and Satirists* is out.

I hav'n't seen much lately of Munro, but hope he will come to-morrow evening when Collins and Stephens are to come too. I wish you had met Collins.

Hughes, I think, is in the country again—at Burnham. What a capital sketch of *one*, though not the best of your face's phases, Hughes did before you left! I suppose it must supersede, for posterity, that railway portrait, which was so decidedly *en train*. I trust certainly to join Hughes in at any rate one of the illustrations of *Day and Night Songs*, of which I hope his and mine will be worthy—else there is nothing so much spoils a good book as an attempt to embody its ideas, only going halfway. Is *Saint Margaret's Eve* to be in? That would be illustratable. By the bye, Miss S. has made a splendid design from that *Sister Helen* of mine. Those she did at Hastings for the old ballads illustrate *The Lass of Lochryan* and *The Gay Goss Hawk*, but they are only first sketches. As to all you say about her and the hospital, etc., I think just at present, at any rate, she had better keep out, as she has made a design

PORTRAIT OF W. ALLINGHAM.

(By Arthur Hughes.)

[To face page 34.

which is practicable for her to paint quietly at my rooms, having convinced herself that nothing which involved her moving constantly from place to place is possible at present. She will begin it now at once, and try at least whether it is possible to carry it on without increased danger to her health. The subject is the *Nativity*, designed in a most lovely and original way. For my own part, the more I think of the B.H. [Brompton Hospital] for her, the more I become convinced that when left there to brood over her inactivity, with images of disease and perhaps death on every side, she could not but feel very desolate and miserable. If it seemed at this moment urgently necessary that she should go there, the matter would be different; but Wilkinson says that he considers her better. I wish, and she wishes, that something should be done by her to make a beginning, and set her mind a little at ease about her pursuit of art, and we both think that this more than anything would be likely to have a good effect on her health. It seems hard to me when I look at her sometimes, working or too ill to work, and think how many without one tithe of her genius or greatness of spirit have granted them abundant health and opportunity to labour through the little they can do or will do, while perhaps her soul is never to bloom nor her bright hair to fade, but after hardly escaping from degradation and corruption, all she might have been must sink out again unprofitably in that dark house where she was born. How truly she may say, " No man cared for my soul." I do not mean to make myself an exception, for how long I have known her, and not thought of this till so late—-perhaps too late. But it is no use writing more about this subject; and I fear, too, my writing at all about it must prevent your easily believing it to be, as it is, by far the nearest thing to my heart.

I will write you something of my own doings soon, I hope; at present I could only speak of discomfitures. About the publication of the ballads, or indeed of your songs either, it has occurred to me we might reckon Macmillan as one possible string to the bow. Smith ought to be bowstrung himself, or hamstrung, or something, for fighting shy of so much honour. By the bye, I turned up the other day, at my rooms, that copy of Routledge's poets which you brought as a specimen. Ought I to send it back? Good-morning.[1]

Your D. G. ROSSETTI.

P.S.—I hav'n't seen the Howitts very lately, but A. M. [Anna Mary] is very busy, I know. I shall get there soon. She has the *Folio*, which is beginning to circulate.

P.P.S.—Write soon and I'll answer soon.

[1] He had at first written " good-night."

Charles Bagot Cayley, translator of Dante and Petrarch, sat for the fifth head on the left (omitting Judas) in Madox Brown's picture of *Christ washing Peter's Feet*. Mr. W. M. Rossetti describes him as "the most modest, retiring, and shyly taciturn man of noticeable talent whom it has ever been my fortune to meet." He was for some years in the Patent Office in Chancery Lane. Rossetti must have dined well if the distance thither from the Bell Savage seemed very long.

John Ferguson Maclennan is known by his work on *Primitive Marriage*.

Rossetti was obliged to wait seven years longer before he could find a publisher for his poems. John Sterling, writing to Emerson on December 28, 1841, mentions "the singular fact, I believe, quite unexampled in England for three hundred years, that there is no man living among us—literally, I believe, not one—under the age of fifty, whose verses will pay the expense of publication." Browning, when Sterling wrote, was twenty-nine years old, Tennyson thirty-two, and Henry Taylor forty-two.

The following is Tennyson's sonnet so humorously parodied by Rossetti.

THE KRAKEN.

Below the thunders of the upper deep ;
Far, far beneath in the abysmal sea,
His ancient, dreamless, uninvaded sleep

> The Kraken sleepeth : faintest sunlights flee
> About his shadowy sides : above him swell
> Huge sponges of millennial growth and height :
> And far away into the sickly light,
> From many a wondrous grot and secret cell
> Unnumber'd and enormous polypi
> Winnow with giant arms the slumbering green.
> There hath he lain for ages and will lie
> Battening upon huge seaworms in his sleep,
> Until the latter fire shall heat the deep ;
> Then once by man and angels to be seen,
> In roaring he shall rise and on the surface die.

The sonnet which Rossetti "made two days ago " he gave himself time to forget again and again, for it was not published till 1881. Under the title of *Lost on Both Sides* it forms Sonnet XCI, of *Ballads and Sonnets*, in the following version :

> As when two men have loved a woman well,
>   Each hating each, through Love's and Death's deceit ;
>   Since not for either this stark marriage-sheet
> And the long pauses of this wedding-bell ;
> Yet o'er her grave the night and day dispel
>   At last their feud forlorn, with cold and heat ;
>   Nor other than dear friends to death may fleet
> The two lives left that most of her can tell :
> So separate hopes, which in a soul had wooed
>   The one same Peace, strove with each other long,
>   And Peace before their faces perished since :
> So through that soul, in restless brotherhood,
>   They roam together now, and wind among
>   Its by-streets, knocking at the dusty inns.

Rossetti wrote to W. B. Scott on a Tuesday in 1852 :—" I saw Woolner on board the vessel on Thursday. He is accompanied by Bernhard Smith and Bateman, and all of them plentifully stocked with corduroys, sou'-westers, jerseys, firearms, and belts full of little bags to hold the expected nuggets. Hunt, William, and myself, deposited them in their four months' home with a due mixture of solemnity and joviality. All his friends congratulate him on the move, with the sole exception of Carlyle, who seems to espy in it some savour of the mammon of unrighteousness. Tennyson was especially encouraging. The great Alfred even declares that were it not for Mrs. T., he should go himself. His expectations seem, however, to be rather poetical, as he gravely asked Woolner 'if he expected to come back with £10,000 a year.'" Later on Rossetti wrote :—"After seven months' digging they gave it up as a losing game ; having made £50 worth of gold apiece, and spent each about £90." Woolner soon found work as a sculptor at Melbourne, where he did several medallions at £25 each. On his coming back to England he wrote to W. B. Scott on October 23, 1854 :—" I should not have returned so soon, had I not returned to look after a statue of Mr. Wentworth, to be put up to his glory in Sydney. I am not sure of getting it now, after coming all this way. I saw Carlyle the other evening, who congratulated me on *not* being successful in my goldseeking. In this, as in everything, how different are his opinions from the world's !" In May, 1855, Woolner wrote :—" Concerning Wentworth's statue, which brought me home, it has turned out a failure. Wentworth has resolved on founding a fellowship at the Sydney University with the money instead. This is at least fifteen hundred out of my pocket, coming back to England when I did. It was the only chance I ever had of making money."

A subscription of £2,000 had been raised for a statue to William Charles Wentworth, the foremost statesman of his time in New South Wales. His bust by Woolner was exhibited in the Royal Academy in 1856.

Mr. W. M. Rossetti wrote to W. Allingham on March 21, 1851 :—" Woolner has a monument to do for Wordsworth's tomb." Mr. Rossetti tells me " that the group represented the poet seated in the centre ; on one side of him a man controlling a refractory boy ; on the other side, as a representation of the transition from the worship of nature to the worship of God, a girl holding a flower with a woman by her side directing her thoughts from it to the heaven above : Carlyle and Tennyson thought highly of it." The disappointment which followed on the rejection of the design had much to do in sending Woolner to Australia. In the words of Madox Brown, " He went to the gold-diggings hoping to amass millions to carry on his art."

He was elected an Associate of the Royal Academy in 1871, and a full Academician in 1874. He died, a wealthy man, on October 7, 1892 ; part of his fortune he had made by judicious purchases of pictures.

Lear was Edward Lear, the author of *The Book of Nonsense.*

Thomas Seddon wrote from Egypt (no date given) :—" Old Hunt came to join me yesterday, for I have spent the principal part of the last two months in a tomb, just at the back of the Sphinx, away from all the petty evening bustle of an hotel. We began in a tent, but a week's experience showed that the tomb possessed in comfort what it lost in picturesqueness. It is a spacious apartment, 25 feet by 14 feet, and about 6 feet high. My end is matted, and I recline, dine, and sleep on a sumptuous divan consisting of a pair of iron trestles with two soft boards laid across them. Poor Hunt is half-bothered out of his life here in painting figures ; but, between ourselves, he is rather *exigeant* in expecting Arabs and Turks in this climate to sit still (standing) for six or eight hours. Don't tell any one this, not even Rossetti."

Dr. Waagen's letter in the *Times* of July 13, 1854, thus ends :—" The smallness of the head in proportion with the figure is probably attributable to that ambition to imitate the early masters, even in their defects. . . . For the green shadows in the hand, though the picture is otherwise most carefully painted, the painter himself must be held responsible, as this is a defect which cannot be laid to the account of those early masters whom he may have studied." The "blasphemy" in the *Athenæum* was probably Frank Stone's.

Mrs. Combe told my wife that many years ago she visited the studio of ——, a Royal Academician. He said to the lady who had taken her there : "Would you believe it?   Holman Hunt has found some fool to buy his *Light of the World.*"   She replied, " Yes, I do believe it, for my friend here is the wife of the man who bought it." —— tried to wriggle out of it by pretending really to admire the picture.

Mr. Hunt, writing of the neglect each new picture met with, says :—" So constant was such experience that I was obliged to avoid taking up a new idea, knowing that I should be starved while the world was finding out the shallowness of the critic's strictures.   I could only pay my way by doing replicas of pictures which had run the gauntlet of abuse, and at last had won favour."

" Bacon was buried privately in St. Michael's Church near St. Alban's.   The spot that contains his remains lay obscure and undistinguished till the gratitude of a private man, formerly his servant, erected a monument to his name and memory."   It was, of course, the Abbey, not the Cathedral, which Rossetti visited.

Satire and Satirists was by Hannay.

For an account of Collins see note on Letter XX.

For Allingham's *Day and Night Songs* Rossetti and Millais each did a single illustration, Arthur Hughes doing eight.

" Smith who ought to have been bowstrung " has lived to do letters a noble, if ill-requited service, by the publication of the great *Dictionary of National Biography.*

The *Folio* was to contain the drawings of a newly

formed sketching-club, of which Mr. Hughes gives me the following account :—" Millais, who was the only man among us who had any money, provided a nice green portfolio with a lock, in which to keep the drawings. Each member of the club was to put into it every month one drawing in black and white, the case going the round. Millais did his, and one or two others did theirs. Then the *Folio* came to Rossetti, where it stuck for ever. It never reached me. According to his wont, he had at first been most enthusiastic over the scheme, and had so infected Millais with his enthusiasm that he at once ordered the case."

XI.

BLACKFRIARS,

Tuesday, August, '54.

DEAR ALLINGHAM,

I have got out my work this morning, but it looks so hopelessly beastly, and I feel so hopelessly beastly, that I must try to revive myself before beginning, by some exercise that goes quicker than the Fine Arts. So I'll e'en begin my answer to your last, wishing heartily that instead of writing to you I could have you here this glorious morning, that I might take a run with you somewhere and try to feel a little lively.

Two or three fellows were here last night, and among them Cayley, to whom I notified the call for my MSS. translations. I'll get them either to-day or to-morrow, and send them to you—I suppose by post, as I know of no other way. You will receive only those which have been copied by William, as my own first drafts are in a hopeless limbo of scrawl. W. has put no names of authors to them, on account of the necessity of classing them, when all copied, and only putting the name to the first production of each poet.

Of the two ballads you sent me, I prefer the one I knew already, and which is one of the very few really fine things of the kind written in our day. The other has many beauties, though—indeed, is all beautiful, except, I think, the last couplet, which seems a trifle homely, a little in the broadsheet-song style. The subject you propose for my wood-cut from it is a first-rate one, and I have already made some scratches for its arrangement. I have got one of the blocks from Hughes, and hope soon to tell you it is done. What a pity they will not let the blocks be a little larger! Is not the *Maids of Elfen-Mere* founded on some Northern legend or other? I seem to have read something about it in Keightley or somewhere.

Tell me whether I shall send you back the copy of it you sent, and the one of *St. Margaret's Eve.*

I don't bully the last lines of your ballad, by the bye, because you didn't like the last lines of my sonnet, which are certainly foggy. Would they be better thus ?—

> So in that soul,—a mindful brotherhood,—
>   (When silence may not be), they wind among
>   Its bye-streets, knocking at the dusty inns.

Or I should like better—

>   —they fare along
>   Its high street, knocking, etc.,

but fear the rhyme "long" and "along" is hardly admissible. What say you? Or can you propose any other improvement?

I've referred to my notebook for the above alteration, and therein are various sonnets and beginnings of sonnets written at crisises (? !) of happy inspiration. Here's one which I remember writing in great glory on the top of a hill which I reached one after-sunset in Warwickshire last year. I'm afraid, though, it isn't much good.

> This feast-day of the sun, his altar there
> In the broad west has blazed for vesper-song ;
> And I have loitered in the vale too long,
> And gaze now, a belated worshipper.
> Yet may I not forget that I was 'ware,
> So journeying, of his face at intervals,—
> Where the whole land to its horizon falls,
> Some fiery bush with corruscating [*sic*] hair.
> And now that I have climbed and tread this height,
> I may lie down where all the slope is shade,

> And cover up my face, and have till night
> With silence, darkness ; or may here be stayed,
> And see the gold air and the silver fade,
> And the last bird fly into the last light.

It strikes me, in copying, what a good thing I did not adopt the first alternative, or I mightn't be here to copy. Here's a rather better sonnet, I hope, written only two or three days ago. I believe the affection in the last half was rather "looked up," at the time of writing, to suit the parallel in the first. Do you not always like your last thing the best for a little while?

> Have you not noted, in some family
>   Where two remain from the first marriage bed,
>   How still they own their fragrant bond, though fed
> And nurst upon an unknown breast and knee ?
> That to their father's children they shall be
>   In act and thought of one good will ; but each
>   Shall for the other have in silence speech,
> And in one word, complete community ?
> Even so, when first I saw you, seemed it, love,
>   That among souls allied to mine was yet
> One nearer kindred than I wotted of.
>   O born with me somewhere that men forget,
>   And though in years of sight and sound unmet,
> Known for my life's own sister well enough !

What you say about my printing and your reviewing, &c., is very kind, and may be very true ; but the fact is, I think well of very little I have written, and am afraid of people agreeing with me, which I should find a bore. I believe my poetry and painting prevented each other from doing much good for a long while, and now I think I could do better in either, but can't write, for then I sha'n't paint. However, one day I hope at least to finish the few rhymes I have by me that I care for at all, and then there they'll be, at any rate. Your plan of a joint volume among us of poems and pictures is a capital one—and how many capital plans we have !

I've got the *Folio* here. It contains a design by Millais, of the *Recall of the Romans from Britain ;* one by Stephens, of *Death and the Rioters ;* one by Barbara S.—a glen scene ; and one by A. M. H., called the *Castaways*, which is a rather strong-minded subject, involving a dejected female, mud with lilies lying in it, a dust-heap, and other details. Of course, seriously, Miss H. is quite right in painting it, if she chooses, and she is doing so. I daresay it will be a good picture. William, Christina, and I were there lately. The Howitts asked me for your address, as they wanted to write to you. I don't know what design I shall put into the *Folio*. I'm doing one of Hamlet and Ophelia, which I meant for it—deeply symbolical and far-sighted, of course—but I fear I shall not get it done in time to start the *Folio* again soon, so may put in a design I have made of *Found.*

I'm finishing this late in the day (N.B. I've done no good and had better have cut work for the day), and must go out to that meal which combines the sweets of an assignation. I enclose a copy of an extract about Woolner, in case you can make use of it. I'll send you one of Hunt's letters with the MSS.

The other day, looking over papers, I turned up those sheets of Sutton's poetry, about which I remember a slight shrug of shoulders and contraction of eyebrows on your part, under the idea that the Fleet Ditch had engulfed them. I'll enclose them too.

What do you think of MacCrac having been *again* in town? I fear he is taking to wild habits. The epithet *one-eyed*, in his sonnet, had better stand *downy*, as the other is certainly ambiguous. By the bye, that is a kind accompaniment to his visit and my most cordial reception, isn't it?

I'll keep an eye on all whom I know who have contracted the bad habit of picture-buying, with a view to their ultimately finding themselves possessed of a Millais or a Boyce, as per instructions.

Write soon, and believe me,

Yours affectionately,

D. G. ROSSETTI.

P.S.—I hear this Wentworth (the " model " of Woolner's statue) is now in London ; and I dare say anything in the papers would meet his eye and do good. Millais and I have done all that could be done about the affair.

NOTES ON XI.

In the following account by Mr. Holman Hunt we see how Rossetti in a fit of impatience would throw down the brush :—" The last time Rossetti and I worked together was at Sevenoaks. He set himself to paint, near to my place of work, a boscage for a background. I went sometimes to see him at work, but I found him nearly always as if engaged in a mortal quarrel with some leaf which had perversely shaken itself off its branch just as he had begun to paint it, until he would have no more of such conduct, and would go back to his lodgings to write, and to try designs."

Rossetti's translations of the *Early Italian Poets*, which are frequently mentioned in these letters, were not published till 1861.

The "too homely" couplet in Allingham's *Maids of Elfen-Mere* is as follows :—

> " The pastor's son did pine and die :
> Because true love should never lie."

It was this ballad which Rossetti illustrated.

Of the first of the two new sonnets (*The Hill Summit*, Sonnet LXX. of *Ballads and Sonnets*), the first six lines were not changed. The last eight were modified as follows :—

> " Transfigured where the fringed horizon falls,—
> A fiery bush with coruscating hair.
> And now that I have climbed and won this height,

> I must tread downward through the sloping shade,
> And travel the bewildered tracks till night.
> Yet for this hour I still may here be stayed
> And see the gold air and the silver fade,
> And the last bird fly into the last light."

In the second sonnet (No. XV.) there are some slight changes.

The belief that Rossetti's poetry hindered his progress in painting led his father, writes Mr. W. M. Rossetti, "to reprehend him sharply, and even severely; and to reprehension he was at all times more than sufficiently stubborn. He grieved over the matter of our father's displeasure to his dying day."

Of Mr. Frederic George Stephens, one of the P.R.B., Millais, as Mr. Hughes informs me, "painted a perfect portrait as *Ferdinand lured by Ariel.*"

A. M. H. was Anna Mary Howitt. Of her Rossetti wrote to his sister a few months earlier: "Anna Mary has painted a sunlight picture of Margaret (Faust) in a congenial wailing state."

"The meal which combined the sweets of an assignation" was no doubt to be taken at "the Belle *pas* Sauvage" of Letters VII. and IX.

"Sutton was (if I remember right)," Mr. W. M. Rossetti tells me, "a man in a humble position of life, who professed to be descended from George Herbert. The Fleet Ditch ran under my brother's windows overlooking Blackfriars Bridge. There was a funny anecdote (true) about his throwing away into the ditch some book he scorned; he did this two or three times over, and each time it was brought back by a 'mud-lark.' Perhaps the book was this of Sutton's."

Patmore, writing to Allingham on August 15, 1849, says:—"I long to hear something of my admired, though unseen friend, Mr. Sutton." Many years ago a friend of mine told me that a stranger wished to hire from him an arch under one of the London railways, in which he meant to conduct a religious service every Sunday. "Of what sect?" asked my friend. "Of the Suttonians." "Who are the Suttonians?" "The followers of Sutton." "Who is Sutton?" "I am Sutton." Perhaps this holy man was Rossetti's Sutton.

In the last paragraph of this letter is seen an instance of that zeal of Rossetti's which never failed when there was a chance of helping a friend. The following record by my wife of a talk she had with an old friend of ours and his illustrates this, and explains, though it does not justify, one side of the great painter's character:—

"I said that these Rossetti letters had given us so much higher an opinion of the man than we had ever had before that we all the more regretted the want of honesty he had about the execution of commissions. He looked very sad, and, I could see, felt the subject painfully. 'Yes,' he said, 'it was much to be regretted; but, after all, I don't think W. B. Scott need have said what he did.

He was not the man to judge fairly Here was Scott, a typical Scotchman, caring for money and knowing its worth, and at the same time possessed of all a Scotchman's integrity as regards money matters ; and here was Rossetti, an Italian all over, caring for money, too, but lavish and generous, wanting it to give away as much as for himself. He was *awfully* generous, and he was a sort of Robin Hood in art ; he thought the rich ought to be made to pay for the good of the poor artists, and he would get all the money he could out of them ; but he would do this as much for others as for himself. Oh, he would work night and day to help a poor friend ; he would give a rich man, who he thought ought to buy a friend's picture, no peace, till the rich man bought it only to get rid of his importunity. And then how generous he was in his judgment of a friend's work !' Here he paused, and I could see his mind wandering back to the old days, fondly dwelling on the various acts of kindness he had himself received from Rossetti. I could say no more of shortcomings."

To his zeal for his friends others have borne like testimony. Madox Brown wrote of him in 1856 :—"No one ever perhaps showed such a vehement disposition to proclaim any real merit if he thinks he discovers it in an unknown or rising artist. I could narrate a hundred instances of the most noble and disinterested conduct towards his art-rivals, which places him far above [others] in his greatness of soul, and yet he will, on the most trivial occasion, hate and backbite any one who gives him offence."

Mr. Skelton says in *The Table-Talk of Shirley* :—
" I have preserved a number of Rossetti's letters, and there is barely one, I think, which is not mainly devoted to warm commendation of obscure poets and painters,—obscure at the time of writing, but of whom more than one has since become famous."

XII.

[*Endorsed,* '54.]

DEAR A.,

Here are all the translations copied as yet —a large dose, though there are many more behind, but very likely you'll find these quite enough. Please acknowledge their receipt at once, as I feel rather anxious about their safe carriage.

I send the only two letters I have of Hunt's. One is hardly worth sending, as it is before he reached his journey's end. The second is a very old one : perhaps my not having any since may be owing to the simple and shameful fact of my not having answered it yet, which I'm going to do.

Your D. G. R.

I've numbered the MSS. to prevent their

getting out of order. I hav'n't mustered courage or [*letter imperfect*] to look up my original scrawls, but if I can find anything I'll send it one day.

NOTE ON XII.

These translations were published in 1861 under the title of *The Early Italian Poets.* " Self reliant though my brother was when he made the translations," writes Mr. W. M. Rossetti, "and still more so when he was preparing to publish them, he was nevertheless extremely ready to consult well-qualified friends as to this book. In this way he showed his MS. to Mr. Allingham, Mr. Ruskin, Mr. Patmore, Count Aurelio Saffi, and no doubt to Mr. Swinburne and some others as well."

XIII.

Sept. 19 [1854].

DEAR ALLINGHAM,

I've just got your letter this morning. About the woodcut, I fancy the poem and extracts you send to-day are hardly so much in my "line" for illustration as the two others you sent before. The *Maids of Elfin Mere* will be the one, I dare say, after all. This chiefly because the Nursery Rhyme on which *S. M's. Eve*

[*Saint Margaret's Eve*] is founded is included and illustrated in *Child's Play*, by the Hon. Mrs. Boyle, and is there very well done.

I made a sketch for the *Maids* the first day you sent it—*i.e.*, for the arrangement, and think it would come nice. At any rate of that or of one of the others I *hope* you will soon hear that a block is drawn, and Hughes has sent me one.

Hughes was here the other evening, and showed me several sketches and wood-blocks he has drawn,—all of them excellent in many ways; but the blocks I think, especially the one of the man and girl at a stile, rather wanting in force for the engraver. He agreed with me, and I believe will do something to amend this. He has made a few very nice little sketches for cuts in the text, if such should prove admissible. One or two for the *Fairies* are remarkably original. I should really, I believe, have got mine in hand before this, but various troublesome anxieties have interfered with that and other work, among the rest with my duty to the *Folio*, which is still by me. I sha'n't put in my modern design, and must finish one of two or three I have going on, instead. I am doing one, which I think will be *the* one, of *Hamlet and Ophelia*, so treated as I think to embody and symbolise the play without obtrusiveness or interference with the subject *as* a subject.

By the bye Hughes showed me a little poem about *What it is they say and do*, which I think, if treated carefully, would illustrate very well. It was one of my favorites in your old vol.—but I think on reflexion [*sic.*] would not illustrate except in the text. Are you not going to include the *Young Man and Death* (if that is the title) one of your very best? There is among those translations of mine a longish dialogue with Death by Guido Cavalcanti, which always reminds me of that poem—*i.e.* the original.

I've been very unwell this morning, but have taken some physic and am much better. This must account for the flatness of my writing, for it *is* flat. I fear you must get the *Athenæum* rather late. When I began to have it sent on to you, I found, what I knew not, that they were in the habit of sending it to an uncle of mine at Gloucester. I gave you the priority, but it seems he " appealed " (though he does not care a dump about it), and we thought it better not to hurt his feelings. This will account if it reaches you now later than at first. I'll mention to them at Albany St. about the label. No doubt you saw the review of Hannay's excellent book on *Satire;* it will put him on a first-rate footing with that fool Dixon, and be of use no doubt. The book has proved a hit. I think, if you liked, I could send you it to read—a copy (*i.e.*) belonging to the *Spectator*. Hannay has also brought out a little book with Routledge called *Sand and Shells* and is writing a novel called *Hilton of the Lotus*, to be published in the *Home Circle*, and which pays very well. He has just come back to settle in London, and I spent last Wednesday evening with him. William has been back in London a day or two, after walking through a great part of Devon and Cornwall with Paul, and enjoying it vastly. I do not know whether he has yet left again *en route* for Belgium, where he is to end his holidays.

I wanted to send you a letter Stephens had from Hunt, but it seems there is some mystic matter in it, so he has copied what I enclose for you. It is the latest news, I believe. The *Chief of Zanquebar* is a lark, but I confess I begrudge him that whole sheet of note paper. The *Times* on Massey is loathsome indeed. Really some one ought to write to them about that prig from Poe, which has roused Hannay's bile. I've been reading a *Spectator* copy of *Firmilian* in its complete state—on second thoughts I'll post it now for you instead of describing it. Please return it soon. I've also read some of the *Stones of Venice* having received all Ruskin's books from him, really a splendid present, including even the huge plates of Venetian architecture. I've heard again from him at Chamounix. I've been greatly interested in *Wuthering Heights*, the first novel I've read for an age, and the best (as regards power and sound style) for two ages, except *Sidonia*. But it is a fiend of a book — an incredible monster, combining all the stronger female tendencies from Mrs. Browning to Mrs. Brownrigg. The action is laid in hell,—only it seems places and people have English names there. Did you ever read it?

I think you're quite right about leaving out a few of my translations from the volume, and should like to know *which* you think. I had thought so myself, but shall copy out all I have done before determining. I am very glad you like them so much, and will send more when copied.

My plan as to their form is, I think, a preface for the first part, containing those previous to Dante, and a connecting essay (but not bulky) for the second part, containing Dante and his contemporaries, as many of them are in the form of correspondence, etc., very interesting, and re-quire some annotation. I think you have few or none of this class. I shall include the *Vita*

Nuova, I am almost sure, and then the vol. will be a thick one. I think, if it were possible to bring some or all out first, as you say, in a good magazine, the plan might be a very good one. Indeed, anything that *paid* would be very useful just now, as I do not *forget* my debts. I've a longish story more than half done, which might likely be even more marketable in this way. It is not so intensely metaphysical as that in the *Germ*. If I possibly can manage to copy what I've done of it, I'd like to send it you. By the bye, in my last long letter (a *long* letter, Allingham) I put two sonnets which I'm afraid you didn't like. Pray tell me, too, about the alteration I there proposed in the last lines of one, which you objected to.

I fear this letter has as many *I's* as Argus: argal it is snobbish.

Tenez vous bien for the present and good bye.

Yours sincerely,

D. G. ROSSETTI.

NOTES ON XIII.

Rossetti, writing to W. B. Scott in the spring of this year, mentions a sketching-club which Millais was trying to found among the P. R. B. and their close allies, with the addition of the Marchioness of Waterford and the Honourable Mrs. Boyle, known as E. V. B. "The two ladies," wrote Rossetti, "are great in design." *Child's Play, Seventeen Drawings*, by E. V. B., was published by Addey & Co., Old Bond Street (no date given).

The sketches were for Allingham's *Day and Night Songs.* The *Fairies* is the charming nursery song, *Up the Airy Mountain*, known to thousands and thousands of children. Mr. Hughes's woodcut is the frontispiece of the volume.

Mr. W. M. Rossetti says that in 1859 "Mr. Plint bought a pen-and-ink drawing—a *Hamlet* (*Hamlet and Ophelia* I suppose) for £42." About the same time, or perhaps a little later, I saw a pen-and-ink *Hamlet and Ophelia* in Colonel Gillum's collection.

The following is Allingham's "little poem which would illustrate very well":—

WOULD I KNEW.

" Plays a child in a garden fair
   Where the demigods are walking;
Playing unsuspected there
 As a bird within the air,
   Listens to their wondrous talking:
 ' Would I knew—would I knew
 What it is they say and do !'

" Stands a youth at city-gate,
   Sees the knights go forth together,
Parleying superb, elate,
Pair by pair in princely state,
   Lance and shield and haughty feather:
 'Would I knew—would I knew
 What it is they say and do !'

> " Bends a man with trembling knees
>   By a gulf of cloudy border ;
> Deaf, he hears no voice from these
> Wingèd shades he dimly sees
>   Passing by in solemn order :
> ' Would I knew—O would I knew
> What it is they say and do ! ' "

The title of the *Young Man and Death* is *Death Deposed*. It is to be found on page 78 of *Thought and Word*.

Of Rossetti's uncle in Gloucester, Henry F. Polydore, a portrait by his nephew is given in Rossetti's *Letters and Memoir*, vol. ii. p. 181.

"That fool Dixon" was William Hepworth Dixon, the editor of the *Athenæum*.

Sands and Shells were sketches of "modern sea-life seen through the glasses of fiction." The *Home Circle* came to an end with this year. If Hannay's novel was finished it was not published, at least, under the title given by Rossetti.

Paul was Benjamin Horatio Paul, a scientific chemist.

The Chief of Zanquebar was mentioned, I had conjectured, in Mr. Holman Hunt's letter ; but he cannot explain the allusion.

The *Times*, reviewing Gerald Massey's *Poems* on August 24, 1854, quoted the following verse :—

> " Ah ! 'tis like a tale of olden
>   Time, long, long ago !
> When the world was in its golden
>   Prime, and love was lord below."

This, probably recalled to Rossetti, the second verse in Poe's *Haunted Palace* :—

> " Banners yellow, glorious, golden,
> On its roof did float and flow,
> (This—all this—was in the olden
> Time long ago.)

"There is," wrote Rossetti on May 11, 1854, "a very rich skit on A. Smith, *Balder*, &c., in *Blackwood*, professing to be a review of *Firmilian, a Tragedy* by Percy Jones." Sir Theodore Martin in his *Life of W. E. Aytoun* in the *Dictionary of National Biography*, says :—" *Firmilian* was written [by Aytoun] in ridicule of the extravagant themes and style of Bailey, Dobell, and A. Smith. It was, however, so full of imagination in fine rhythmical swing, that its object was mistaken, and what was meant for caricature was accepted as serious poetry."

Rossetti, writing about the books Ruskin gave him, says :—" He wished me to accept these as a gift, but it is such a costly one that I have told him I shall make him a small water-colour in exchange."

According to Mr. Clement Shorter, " Mr. Swinburne placed the authoress of *Wuthering Heights* [Emily Brontë] in the very forefront of English women of genius."

Sidonia the Sorceress is by William Meinhold. " For this work," writes Mr. W. M. Rossetti, " my brother had a positive passion ; he much preferred it to *The Amber Witch* of the same author."

Writing to his sister Christina, on December 3, 1875, about her new volume of poems, he says :— "The first of the two poems [on the Franco-Prussian war] seems to me just a little echoish of the Barrett-Browning style. . . . A real taint, to some extent, of modern vicious style, derived from the same source—what might be called a falsetto muscularity—always seemed to me much too prominent in the long piece called *The Lowest Room.*"

Mrs. Brownrigg is best illustrated by the following parody, in *The Anti-Jacobin,* of Southey's *Inscription for the Apartment in Chepstow Castle where Henry Marten, the Regicide, was imprisoned Thirty Years.*

INSCRIPTION

FOR THE DOOR OF THE CELL IN NEWGATE, WHERE MRS. BROWNRIGG, THE 'PRENTI-CIDE, WAS CONFINED PREVIOUS TO HER EXECUTION.

For one long term, or e'er her trial came,
Here Brownrigg linger'd.   Often have these cells
Echoed her blasphemies, as with shrill voice
She screamed for fresh Geneva.   Not to her
Did the blithe fields of Tothill, or thy street,
St. Giles, its fair varieties expand ;
Till at the last, in slow-drawn cart she went
To execution.   Dost thou ask her crime ?
She whipp'd two female 'prentices to death
And hid them in the coal-hole.   For her mind
Shaped strictest plans of discipline.   Sage schemes !

> Such as Lycurgus taught, when at the shrine
> Of the Orthian goddess he bade flog
> The little Spartans ; such as erst chastised
> Our Milton when at college.   For this act
> Did Brownrigg swing.   Harsh laws!   But time shall come
> When France shall reign, and laws be all repealed.

Rossetti's translation of the *Vita Nuova* was included in his *Early Italian Poets*, now named *Dante and his Circle*.

His debts, which he says he does not forget, troubled him through life.   Of his old father, the poor exile, even when his sight was failing and "a real tussle for the means of subsistence arose," his son William could say : "No butcher, nor baker, nor candlestick-maker ever had a claim upon us for a sixpence unpaid."   On April 24, 1876, Rossetti told his mother that in the last year he had made £3,725.   He added : " I believe this is somewhere about my average income, yet I am always hard up for £50."

" 'A longish story,' says Mr. W. M. Rossetti, must be the one which was first called *An Autopsychology*, and afterwards *St. Agnes of Intercession*, written towards 1850.   It is published (uncompleted) in his Collected Works."   It was to have been published in *The Germ*.   "Millais did an etching for it."

Of the "metaphysical" story, *Hand and Soul*, in the first number of *The Germ*, Rossetti writes :—
" I wrote it (with the exception of an opening page or two) all in one night, in December, 1849;

The Germ — If better than Seed

Several words expressing
Progress —

The Accelerator
The Precursor !!!
The Advent
The Harbinger .!!!
The Innovator

Modest titles

The point   Seriet Thoughts
The Atom   Earnest Thoughts
The Ant   Accummulator
The Lantern   The Aspirant.

The Adventurer . ✗

The Student   The Expansive
The Scholar   The United Arts
The Chalice   The Mirror of Nature
The Casket   The Anti Archeologist?
The Repository   The Circle
The Investigator   The Sphere
The Enterprise   The Prism

SUGGESTED TITLES FOR THE PRÆRAPHAELITE
MAGAZINE.

[To face page 65.

beginning, I suppose, about two A.M., and ending about seven."

" *The Germ*," writes Mr. W. M. Rossetti, " was projected as the organ of the P.R.B. for promulgating their views in art and in literature—especially poetic literature. The seven members of the Brotherhood were owners of the concern. The prime-mover was Dante Rossetti, who was at this date just as keen in literary as in pictorial interest and ambition. Next to him, Woolner was the most active spirit, and, for artistic purposes, Holman Hunt. I (at the mature age of twenty) was appointed editor. The title of the magazine was not my brother's invention. I recollect a conclave which was held one evening in his studio, then in Newman Street. A great number of titles were proposed, and jotted down on a fly-sheet which I still possess. Mr. W. C. Thomas, the painter, suggested *The Germ*." Mr. Rossetti has kindly lent me two fly-sheets on which the following titles were written down. The first ends with a note by Mr. Thomas.

" The Germ.   Qy. better than Seed.

Several words expressing Progress.

The Acclerator.
The Precursor ! ! !
The Advent.

The Harbinger!!!
The Innovator.

Modest Titles.

The print.
The Atom.
The Ant.
The lantern.
The Adventurer.
The Student.
The Scholar.
The Chalice.
The Casket.
The Repertory.
The Investigator.
The Enterprise.
The Lustre.
The Illuminator.
The Appeal.
The Die.
The Mould.
The principle.

First thoughts.
Earnest thoughts.
Accumulator.
The Aspirant.

———

The Expansive.
The United Arts.
The Mirror of Nature.
The Anti-Archeologist.
The Circle.
The Sphere.
The prism.

"As your brother Gabriel was speaking of christening the journal, I've sent you all that I can think of, which may perhaps suggest something to you or yours which may be much better than anything I've thought of.

"It is an important matter. There is something in a name.

"Yours W. C. T.

"The number of Notes of Admiration represent my notion of the value of each. Five being the highest value. W. C. T.

The Sower!!!!!
The progressist!!!!
The Seed!!!!!
Aspects of Nature!!!!
The Guide to Nature!!
The prospective!!　　The Messenger.
The View.　　The Chariot.
The Alert.　　The Wheel.
The Opinion.　　The Spur.
The Meditator!!!　　The Goad.
The Reflector.　　The Bud.
The Effort.　　The Acorn.
The Attempt.
Aspirations towards Truth!!!
The Truthseeker!!!
The Dawn.
The Well.
The Spring.
The fountain.
The Dawn.
　　"The first four names are the best."

The Germ changed its name after the second number. "For numbers three and four," writes Mr. W. M. Rossetti, "which were brought out at the risk of our friendly printing-firm, a new title,

Art and Poetry, was invented by a member of the firm, Mr. Alexander Tupper."

Patmore wrote to Allingham on January 5, 1850 : —" A few artists—young, and for the most part illustrious, though as yet obscure—(Hunt, Millais, G. Rosetti [*sic.*], &c.), have set a - going a small magazine upon a sound system. The first number has appeared, and it is full of good poetry, and noticeable criticism, and has an exquisite etching by Hunt. I think you would like to form one of the little corporation, subscribing (one shilling per month) and contributing (gratis). The title is *The Germ*. I will send you a number to judge of. The little poem called *The Seasons* is mine."

Holman Hunt, writing of his *Rienzi*, says :—" I asked £100 for it, and had great need of the money, for my store was well-nigh exhausted. With the little remaining, however, I began *The Christian Missionary* picture, and became part-proprietor and co-operator as illustrator of *The Germ*, which was started soon after this without stock of either matter or capital—of nothing but faith, in short. As weeks and months went by, the indignation of our opponents became fiercer, and made itself heard through the Press. By the end of July I had well-nigh come to my last penny, some work that I had been commissioned to do, and on which I had spent time and money, coming to nothing from the change of feeling about our school. The unpunctuality of so important a contributor as Rossetti made it impossible to go on,

No. 1. *(Price One Shilling.)*   JANUARY, 1850.

With an Etching by W. HOLMAN HUNT.

The Germ:

Thoughts towards Nature

In Poetry, Literature, and Art.

When whoso merely hath a little thought
    Will plainly think the thought which is in him,—
    Not imaging another's bright or dim,
Not mangling with new words what others taught;
When whoso speaks, from having either sought
    Or only found,—will speak, not just to skim
    A shallow surface with words made and trim,
But in that very speech the matter brought:
Be not too keen to cry—"So this is all!—
    A thing I might myself have thought as well,
But would not say it, for it was not worth!"
    Ask: "Is this truth?" For is it still to tell
That, be the theme a point or the whole earth,
Truth is a circle, perfect, great or small?

London:

AYLOTT & JONES, 8, PATERNOSTER ROW.

G. F. Tupper, Printer, Clement's Lane, Lombard Street.

[*To face page* 68.

although Millais then had his plate ready to illustrate a mystic story by him. Of course the want of capital also told, and the poor *Germ* died, but not without making itself heard."

"After balancing receipts and expenditure," writes Mr. W. M. Rossetti, "we had to meet a printer's bill of £33 odd. This seems now a very moderate burden ; but it was none the less a troublesome one to all or most of us at that period. For many years past it has been a literary curiosity, fetching high fancy prices." For the four numbers so much as £9 has been given. Mr. Hughes tells me that one day when he was working among the students at the Royal Academy, Munro brought in the first number. It was handed round, and on all sides jeered at. When it came to him, he was greatly struck with it, above all with Mr. W. M. Rossetti's sonnet on the title-page, which had a real influence on his life. His admiration of it made him known to Munro, and through h'm to Rossetti and the other Præraphaelites.

Mr. Ruskin in his *Lectures on Architecture and Painting* speaking of the P.R.B. in 1854, says :— "Their fellow-students hiss them when they enter the room."

XIV.

Sunday, 15 *October* [1854].

DEAR ALLINGHAM,

What do you think? Woolner is back. Rather broader and stouter, and certainly looking healthier, but unaltered otherwise. [*Letter imperfect*] manner, which I expected perhaps to find a little changed and sobered, but it is just the same. William and I have spent last night and this morning with him, and talked of all things and all friends, of yourself more than once, to whom he sends friendly greetings.

It is jolly to have him again among us, and I hope with good prospect of success before him. As far as he can judge hitherto, he has a right to think himself almost sure of the statue commission of which I wrote to you, and if so he will be set up for life, there can hardly be a doubt. He is going to find a studio [*letter imperfect*], and there I trust we may all meet and enjoy ourselves when you are next in London. Hunt may be back too perhaps, and the old circle meet again—poor Deverell excepted.

Now to speak of your volume. I have drawn the *Maids of E.M.* [*Elfin Mere*] once on the wood, and find I have committed a stupid mistake in not drawing the actions reversed, so that, when printed, the figures will be left-handed. I am therefore going to trace and draw it again on another block, which I trust will soon be done, and in Routledge's hands. I shall like, if I can find time, to do a second drawing from some other of the poems.

My time has lately been engrossed by the background of my modern subject, which I have been painting out of doors at Chiswick—cold work these last days, but much finer weather hitherto than I dare to hope for again in all probability. It will be a disappointment to me if I am baulked, after all, and cannot get done before the unmanageable weather. I paint daily within earshot almost of Hogarth's grave—a good omen for one's modern picture! This work has left me no time at all for anything else lately. Ruskin is back again, and wrote to me, naming a day when he meant to call, but I was obliged to write I could not be at my rooms. He has written again since, saying he wants to consult with me about plans for "teaching the masons"; so you may soon expect to find every man shoulder his hod, "with upturned fervid face and hair put back." I am painting near the house of some old friends of ours at Chiswick, the family of Mr. Keightley, whom you have heard me name. They are Irish people, and of course I introduced the *Songs*.

Old K. was taken with the *Fairies*, and there is a very nice girl who especially delights in *Æolian Harp No.* 1, and dreamt your *Dream* right through the night after reading it.

I can't make out why the *Autumn Evening* forms a section by itself in your list. I shall try to call at Routledge's, and look at the MS., as I have no doubt of a pleasure in store from the new ones, though there do not seem to be many. Hughes showed me some pretty and very simple sketches he had made, and meant to propose to R. for titles and sections and heads of pages. He also showed me his picture of *Orlando*, which he has immensely improved this year ; in fact, made quite another thing of the background. I trust Routledge means to do you and us justice in the cutting of the blocks. I shall lecture him about it, and tell him that if they are to be badly done and I could know it beforehand, he should not have one from me on any consideration. I have really not been forgetting my blocks, but the background painting has been peremptory and impossible to defer.

Thanks for your kind suggestions and offers of mediation as to printing some of my Italian poems in a magazine. *Fraser's*, if attainable, would be the one I should prefer to any other. But I have had no time to think about this yet since reading

your letter, and must answer at more length next
time. When you send me back the MSS. you
have, I think there will be another batch ready
copied for you. I am very anxious indeed to see
your annotations, and doubt not to profit by them.
Thanks also for your criticism on the *Sonnet*.
The construction of those four lines is thus :

> " Yet may I not forget that I was ware,
> So journeying, of his face at intervals,
> Some fiery bush with coruscating [1] hair,
> Where the whole land to its horizon falls ! "

Only the metre forced me to transpose. It is
meant to refer to the effect one is nearly sure to
see in passing along a road at sunset, when the
sun glares in a radiant focus behind some low
bush or some hedge on the horizon of the
meadows. But it *is* obscure, I believe, though
if I were disposed to be stiff-necked, I might lug
up William, to whom I have just showed the
sonnet, and who understood the line in question
at once. But I'll try to alter it—if worth working
at. In the hateful mechanical brick-painting I
have been at I have had time to make verses,
and have finished a ballad—professedly modern-
antique, of which I remember once telling you
the story as we were walking about Mrs. Orme's
garden. I'll copy it for you and inclose it with_

[1] "? Has coruscating one or two r's."—Note by Rossetti.

this, asking your *severest* criticism. I doubt myself whether it at all succeeds in its attempt. However, I don't think it is finished yet, and if any feature should suggest itself to you as [*letter imperfect*] to the story or preferable, pray mention it. I have purposely taken an unimportant phrase here and there from the old things. I was doubting whether it would not be better to make the improper lord and lady slip into a new-made grave, while wading through the churchyard, and be drowned. This might make a good description and conclusion, and I fear the thing is at present almost too unpoetical in style. Tell me what you think—or whether the present ending seems the more or less hackneyed of the two.

I send you the last bit of Hunt received last night. Let me have it again, please, at once, as I must answer it soon for conscience' sake, as that projected letter he writes that he was expecting from me was never written, after all.

I think I remember your speaking to me of *Wuthering Heights*, long ago. I never read any of *Currer* Bell. Is she *half* as good? I see by the advertisements of Smith & Elder that W. B. Scott's Poems are out, and hope soon to get one from him. He and his family have happily escaped from any injury in that dreadful affair at Newcastle.

Write soon, and with a better pen than this, lest your letter should be a torment to write and read. I lay awake this morning [*letter imperfect*] with Woolner till 5 o'clock talking of old times, so sleepiness now must account for stupidity.

Yours always D. G. R.

[On the margin of the first page of the letter the following is written :] " Rossetti kindly gives me this border to myself, which I use to say, what you of course know, that I shall rejoice to meet and have a yarn and talk over the world's [*letter imperfect*] ours and our friends' prospects. I never thanked you for the sweet little poems you sent me 2¼ years ago at Plymouth.

" Your, Dear Allingham,

" THOS. WOOLNER."

NOTES ON XIV.

Rossetti, writing in the autumn of 1853, says :— " Woolner has sent an Australian newspaper. It says that ' Mr. Woolner is a gentleman of very affable and agreeable manners,' which is rather rich." On this Mr. W. M. Rossetti remarks that " Woolner was much more laudable for sturdy independence and resolute decision than for anything to be classed under the term ' affable.' "

" For sculpture," writes Mr. Holman Hunt, " Rossetti in private expressed little regard ; he professed admiration for the minds of many men engaged in it, but he could scarcely understand their devotion to work which seemed in modern hands so cold and meaningless, and which was so limited in its power of illustration."

"Poor Deverell" had died a few months earlier. "He was," Mr. Arthur Hughes tells me, "a manly young fellow, with a feminine beauty added to his manliness; exquisite manners and a most affectionate disposition. He died early, after painting two or three pictures. Had he lived he would have been a poetic painter, but not a strong one. Millais, hard-working and ambitious though he was, used to sit hour after hour by his bedside reading to him." I have seen him described by one of the artist set in a letter to Allingham as "little Deverell, with his soft, effeminate, alluring face." W. B. Scott wrote of him as "a youth, like the rest of them, of great but impatient ability, and of so lovely yet manly a character of face, with its finely-formed nose, dark eyes and eyebrows, and young silky moustache, that it was said ladies had gone hurriedly round by side streets to catch another sight of him." He sat for the page in Madox Brown's *Chaucer at the Court of Edward III*. At the sale this summer at Christie's of Mr. Leathart's collection his picture of *A Lady with a Birdcage* fetched only six guineas.

"To the best of my recollection," writes Mr. W. M. Rossetti, "the very first woodcut my brother actually produced was *The Maids of Elfin Mere*."

This inexperience would account for his "stupid mistake."

Rossetti's "modern subject" is the picture called *Found*. "It represents a rustic lover, a drover [a farmer?], who finds his old sweatheart at a low depth of degradation, both from vice and penury, in the streets of London. He endeavours to lift her as she crouches on the pavement." Madox Brown sat for the head of the man. It was the brick wall in this picture that was painted at Chiswick. The calf and cart, as the next letter shows, were painted at Finchley. "This picture," writes Mr. W. M. Rossetti, "was a source of lifelong vexation to my brother and to the gentlemen—some three or four in succession—who commissioned him to finish it. It was nearly completed, but not quite, towards the close of his life." In 1859 a commission was given him for the picture at three hundred and twenty guineas. On February 4, 1881, he wrote:—*Found* progresses rapidly." "There is no knowing (he once said) in such a lottery as painting, where all things have a chance against one—weather, stomach, temper, model, paint, patience, self-esteem, self-abhorrence, and the devil into the bargain."

The epitaph on Hogarth's grave was composed by Garrick, "working upon" some lines furnished to him by Johnson.

Ruskin's "plans for ' teaching the masons,' " are explained in the next letter.

That "upturned fervid face and hair put back" is from *Sordello*, ed., 1885, p. 214.

Mr. Keightley was "the historian and author of *The Fairy Mythology,* a book," writes Mr. W. M. Rossetti, "which formed one of the leading delights of our childhood."

The *Dream* which the girl "dreamt right through" is as follows :—

> " I heard the dogs howl in the moonlight night,
> And I went to the window to see the sight ;
> All the dead that ever I knew
> Going one by one and two by two.
>
> On they pass'd and on they pass'd ;
> Townsfellows all from first to last ;
> Born in the moonlight of the lane,
> And quench'd in the heavy shadow again.
>
> Schoolmates, marching as when we play'd
> At soldiers once—but now more staid ;
> Those were the strangest sights to me
> Who were drown'd, I knew, in the awful sea.
>
> Straight and handsome folk ; bent and weak too ;
> And some that I loved, and gasp'd to speak to ;
> Some but a day in their churchyard bed ;
> And some that I had not known were dead.
>
> A long, long crowd—where each seem'd lonely,
> And yet of them all there was one, one only,
> That rais'd a head, or look'd my way ;
> And she seem'd to linger, but might not stay.
>
> How long since I saw that fair pale face !
> Ah, mother dear, might I only place
> My head on thy breast, a moment to rest,
> While thy hand on my tearful cheek were prest !

> On, on, a moving bridge they made
> Across the moon-stream, from shade to shade,
> Young and old, women and men ;
> Many long-forgot, but remember'd then.

> And first there came a bitter laughter ;
> And a sound of tears a moment after ;
> And then a music so lofty and gay,
> That every morning, day by day,
> I strive to recall it if I may."

An Autumn Evening, as it is printed, does not " form a section by itself" any more than any other poem in the collection.

Mr. Arthur Hughes's *Orlando* is mentioned again in Letter XX.

Into *Fraser's Magazine* Rossetti was not likely to find admittance. *The Table Talk of Shirley* shows how hostile John Parker, the editor, was to the new school of poetry. Some six years later Rossetti tried, through Ruskin, to get some of his poems published in *The Cornhill Magazine*, but nothing came of it.

Mr. W. M. Rossetti has done much to smooth the reader's course through his brother's sonnets in his *Prose Paraphrase* of the *House of Life* in his work entitled *Dante Gabriel Rossetti as Designer and Writer.* " Not long ago," he writes, " one of his most intimate friends put it to me pointedly in the phrase, ' They cannot be understood.' I should like them to be understood ; and, as I appear to myself to understand the great majority of their bulk and contents, I have thought it not inconsistent with respect to my brother's memory, and with a desire to extend the right estimate of his writing, that I should take it upon me to expound their meaning."

The ballad which Rossetti had finished was *Stratton Water*. Fifteen years later he added a few stanzas.

He wrote to his sister on November 8, 1853 :— "Last night Miss Barbara Smith invited us all to lunch with her on Sunday ; and perhaps I shall go, as she is quite a *jolly fellow*---which was Thackeray's definition of Mrs. Orme." On this Mr. W. M. Rossetti remarks, " Mrs. Orme, whom Thackeray called ' a jolly fellow,' was the sister-in-law of Mr. Coventry Patmore. Hers was a rich abundant nature, only partially indicated in Thackeray's phrase, for her whole type of character was most essentially that of a woman and not a man ; among many kind friends of my youth she was nearly the kindest of all."

For so young a man, Rossetti had been strangely careless of the talk of the day. He had never read any of Charlotte Brontë's stories, and yet he was but nineteen years old when *Jane Eyre* was published. I well remember, boy though I was at the time, the stir it made. I remember, too, the affectation of a prude who, in my father's house, when a man came into the parlour, hid the book away under the sofa cushion, as unfit for a spinster's reading.

W. B. Scott's new volume of *Poems* is mentioned in the next letter. He was head of the Newcastle School of Design. On October 6th of this year there had been "a great destruction of life and property in that town and Gateshead, by the explosion of vast stores of combustibles."

XV.

FINCHLEY, *November*, 1854.

MY DEAR ALLINGHAM,

Your last letter has been carried carefully in my pocket all this time, with the view of its being answered, as it ought to have been long ere now. To-night I search my pockets for it at last for that immediate purpose, and of course it has somehow flown. I hope I shall not have forgotten anything that ought to be spoken of in this. One thing I must not forget is to say how very busy and bothered I have been, and to beg that may plead my excuse for delay, not only with the letter, but with the more important wood-block, which is not yet sent in. It would have been so before now, but that staying out here, I am prevented from working on it from nature except by flying visits to London on Sundays, and I am loth to finish it without nature. The delay in this has kept me from writing, as I wanted to say it was done, as I trust it now will be very soon. I shall like, if at all practicable, to do another, but meanwhile Hughes is drawing the last block to prevent disappointment, and my second, if done, must take its chance with the publishers as an additional illustration. I hope, above all, they mean to have the drawings well cut. For my part I should like to tell them that they had better in my own case give the price of the *drawing* as an extra bonus to the *engraver*, and that then they must let me see a proof as soon as cut—the thing to be cancelled altogether if not approved of by me. I expect this might partly impress upon them that some care was necessary, and that there was a reputation of some sort in some quarters that I had to take care of.

Do you see any objection to my following this plan? I feel it both pleasure and credit to be associated at all with your volume, and should not like to cut too sorry a figure there, as it is a book which every one will be sure to see.

I have had a hasty look (such as my leisure lately has left possible) through your MS., much of which is as exquisite as can be or ever has been —pure beauty and delight. The *Queen of the Forest*, Hughes tells me, is to be withdrawn, as capable of fuller treatment. I am quite of your mind about it, and chiefly because it is already so peculiarly lovely as to be worthy of any elaboration. The *Æolian Harp* in long lines is equal to any of that series, and I should have many things to say of many others, if the MS. were only by me. I must write of them when they are printed, and I hope talk of them too with you by that time. You mention having sent a copy of *Day and Night Songs* to Ruskin: did you remember that I had already given him one? I trust he and you will meet when next in London. He has been back about a month or so, looking very well and in excellent spirits. Perhaps you know that he has joined Maurice's scheme for a *Working Men's College*, which has now begun to be put in operation at 31, Red Lion Square. Ruskin has most liberally undertaken a drawing-class, which he attends every Thursday evening, and he and I had a long confab about plans for teaching. He is most enthusiastic about it, and has so infected me that I think of offering an evening weekly for the same purpose, when I am settled in town again. At present I am hard at work out here on my picture, painting the calf and cart. It has been fine clear weather, though cold, till now, but these two days the rain has set in (for good, I fear), and driven me to my wits' end, as even were I inclined to paint notwith-standing, the calf would be like a hearth-rug after half an hour's rain; but I suppose I must turn out to-morrow and try. A very disagreeable part of the business is that I am being obliged to a farmer whom I cannot pay for his trouble in providing calf and all, as he insists on being good natured. As for the calf, he kicks and fights all the time he remains tied up, which is 5 or 6 hours daily, and the view of life induced at his early age by experience in art appears to be so melancholy that he punctually attempts suicide by hanging himself at $3\frac{1}{2}$ daily P.M. At these times I have to cut him down, and then shake him up and lick him like blazes. There *is* a pleasure in it, my dear fellow : the Smithfield drovers are a kind of opium-eaters at it, but a moderate practitioner might perhaps sustain an argument. I hope soon to be back at my rooms, as I have been quite long enough at my *rhumes*. (The above joke did service for MacCrac's benefit last night.)

Before I came here I had been painting ever so long on a brick wall at Chiswick which is in my foreground. By the bye, that boating sketch of yours is really good in its way, and would bear showing to Ruskin as an original Turner—and perhaps selling to Windus afterwards.

Many thanks for your minute criticism on my ballad, which was just of the kind I wanted. Not, of course, that a British poet is going to knock under on all points ;—accordingly, I take care to disagree from you in various respects—as regards abruptnesses, improbabilities, prosaicisms, coarsenesses, and other *esses* and *isms*, not more prominent, I think, in my production than in its models. As to dialect there is much to be said, but I doubt much whether, as you say, mine is more Scotticised than many or even the majority of genuine old ballads. If the letter and poem were here, I might perhaps bore you with counter-analysis. But in very many respects I shall benefit greatly by your criticisms, if ever I think the ballad worth working on again, without which it would certainly not be worth printing.

I have read Patmore's poem which he sent me, and about which I might say a good deal of all kinds, if I felt up to it to-night ; but I don't. He was going to publish (and had actually printed the title) with the pseudonym of C. K. Dighton ; but was induced at the last moment to cancel the title, as well as a marvellous note at the end, accounting for some part of the poem being taken out of his former book by some story of a butterman and a piece of waste paper, or something of that sort! (I see my description is as lucid as the note.)

Did you see a paragraph in the *Ill. Lond. News* headed Americans at Florence, and giving a longish account of a backwoods poem called *The New Pastoral*, to be immediately published by Read?

Have you seen anything of W. B. Scott's volume?
I may be able to send it you sooner or later, if you
like. The title-page has a vignette with the words
Poems by a Painter printed very gothically indeed.
A copy being sent to old Carlyle, he did not read
any of the poems, but read the title "Poems by
a Printer." He wrote off at once to the imaginary
printer to tell him to stick to his types and give up
his metaphors. Woolner saw the book lying at
Carlyle's, heard the story, and told him of his
mistake, at which he had the decency to seem
a little annoyed, as he knows Scott, and esteems
him and his family. Now that we are allied with
Turkey, we might think seriously of the bastinado
for that old man, on such occasions as the above.

This is the last of Brown's note-paper (I am
staying with him here), so I must leave some other
thing till next time, especially as it is fearfully late.
Miss Siddal is moderately well and making
designs, etc.

Yours affectionately,

D. G. ROSSETTI.

P.S.—Hughes asked me for Millais' address from
[? for] you. The surest way I know of reaching
him is to address to him at M. Halliday, Esq.,
3, Robert St., Adelphi.

Notes on XV.

The manuscript poems through which Rossetti had a hasty look form the second series of *Day and Night Songs*. *The Queen of the Forest* was published in *Flower Pieces*, a volume which bears the following inscription: "To Dante Gabriel Rossetti, whose early friendship brightened many days of my life, and whom I never can forget. W. A."

In *Preterita* (volume iii.) Ruskin thus traces "the story of his relations with the Working Men's College: —'I knew of its masters only the Principal, F. D. Maurice, and my own friend Rossetti. It is to be remembered of Rossetti with loving honour, that he was the only one of our modern painters who taught disciples for love of them. He was really not an Englishman, but a great Italian tormented in the Inferno of London; doing the best he could, and teaching the best he could; but the ' could ' shortened by the strength of his animal passions, without any trained control, or guiding faith.

" I loved Frederick Maurice, as every one did who came near him; and have no doubt he did all that was in him to do of good in his day. Which could by no means be said of Rossetti and me. . . . Maurice, in all his addresses to us, dwelt mainly on the simple function of a college as a collection or collation of friendly persons—not in the least as a place in which such and such things were to be taught and others denied ; such and such conduct vowed, and other such and such abjured.

"So the college went on—collecting, carpentering, sketching, Bible criticising, etc., virtually with no head ; but only a clasp to the strap of its waist, and as many heads as it had students. The leaven of its affectionate temper has gone far ; but how far also the leaven of its pride, and defiance of everything above it, nobody quite knows. . . . And finally, in this case, and many more, I have very clearly ascertained that the only proper school for workmen is of the work their fathers bred them to, under masters able to do better than any of their men, and with common principles of honesty and the fear of God to guide the firm.'"

Rossetti wrote to W. B. Scott about this time :— "You think I have turned humanitarian perhaps, but you should see my class for the model ! None of your *Freehand Drawing-Books* used ! The British mind is brought to bear on the British *mug* at once, and with results that would astonish you." Of his method of teaching I have received the following account from a drawing-master who was one of the students of the college :—

" I was not exactly a pupil of Rossetti's, although I was of Ruskin's. The classes were on the same floor, and there was constant communication between them. We saw the work done, and discussed the methods and incidents. Rossetti began at once with colour, not with light and shade. At a time when this was heresy, when even Mr. Ruskin objected, Rossetti gave his students colour, and full colour, to begin with. Most of them could draw a little; but even that would not have stopped him. Draw or not, he gave them colour. A teacher is supposed to analyze his subject, and prepare for its difficulties by giving beforehand its elements in a simple form, one at a time. Rossetti put a bird or a boy before his class, and said, ' Do it'; and the spirit of the teacher was of more value than any system. I look back to those times with great pleasure; they have helped me much. Only about a month since a new syllabus for drawing for elementary schools was issued by the Government, in which children are allowed to use colour as soon as they begin. Here to-day we have, forty years afterwards, Rossetti's principle acknowledged by the Government. That it did not come direct from Rossetti, but by another and independent course, is some evidence in its favour.

"Again, Rossetti often brought the works he was engaged on, in their incomplete state, for us to see. I remember some of them, and here again he helped me years afterwards; but he did not generally get the class to do what he was doing himself. I think he should have required imaginative work from all the class,— pictures from their own imagination of scenes from poetry, story, and myths."

On March 19, 1858, Madox Brown recorded in his diary :—" At night went with Gabriel to the

Working Men's College.   There was a public meeting, and we heard Professor Maurice and Ruskin spouting.   Ruskin was as eloquent as ever, and as wildly popular with the men.   He flattered Rossetti hugely, and spoke of Munro in conjunction with Baron Marochetti, as the two noble sculptors of England whom all the aristocracy patronised." Towards November, 1858, Madox Brown took over Rossetti's class.

The following account has been given me of Rossetti's residence at Finchley while he was working at *Found.*   He had for some time been painting in Madox Brown's studio in town, when his friend took a small cottage at Finchley for himself, wife, and baby.   Besides the kitchen it had but two rooms, a parlour and a bedroom. Rossetti wanted to paint a white calf.   Brown, thinking that he would take only a day or two over such a piece of work, asked him to visit him.   There was, he said, a farmyard on the other side of the road, where there were several calves ; as for a bed, he could have a mattress on the floor of the parlour.   Rossetti, who had never painted a calf before, found greater diffi- culties in the subject than either he or his friend expected.   Moreover, his ideas of the picture grew. Long before the sketch was finished the calf had grown too big, and another had to be provided. The visit was prolonged, to the great discomfort of the little family.   Brown, who was most good- natured, took it all good-humouredly, though he would now and then complain to a friend that Gabriel would sit up half the night talking poetry, and lie half the day in bed in their one sitting-room, excluding Mrs. Brown and the baby.

Before Rossetti went to Chiswick to paint the brick wall he wrote to his mother :—" Have you or Christina any recollection of an eligible and accessible brick wall ? I should want to get up and paint it early in the mornings, as the light ought to be that of dawn. It should be not too countrified (yet beautiful in colour), as it is to represent a city wall. A certain modicum of moss would therefore be admissible, but no prodigality of grass, weeds, ivy, etc."

Windus, who was to buy Allingham's sketch, was a retired man of business, who lived in the village in which I spent my early days. He had inherited a fortune, it was said, from an uncle after whom he was named, the proprietor of a cordial by which many fretful infants had been soothed into the next world. He had a fine collection of the early Præraphaelite pictures. Whether he had any real knowledge of painting I do not know. I have rarely seen any one who, to judge by external appearances, was farther removed from poetry or art. The following anecdote I have from my wife :—" I one day took some friends from the country to see Mr. Windus's collection of paintings in his very pretty old-fashioned house on Tottenham Green. He was one of the earliest buyers of the P. R. B. work, and in one of the quaint

panelled drawing-rooms Holman Hunt's *Scapegoat*
hung over the fireplace, with one of Turner's
drawings in his latest style on each side of it, and
Millais's *Vale of Rest* on the opposite wall.   Four
rooms were thickly hung with pictures, and we
found enough to keep us interested for some time.
Before leaving, ' Let us go back into the first room,'
I said, 'and have one more look at the *Scapegoat*.'
We did so, and then I gazed for some time at the
Turner drawings, trying very hard to make out
what they were about, and feeling that I was very
dull of comprehension. ' It's of no use!' I exclaimed at last : ' I cannot see what it means !
Those lovely shades of orange and blue and grey
are beautiful, but I cannot for the life of me tell
what they are meant to represent.' ' That only
shows that you know nothing at all about it ! '
said a squeaky little voice over my shoulder ; and
looking round, I saw that the owner of the
pictures had come in, unperceived, and had overheard my remark."

Rossetti, in spite of his parentage (of his grand-
parents, three were Italian, and only one was
English), speaks of himself in this letter as "a
British poet."   "He liked England and the
English," writes his brother, "better than any
other country and nation.   He was in many
respects an Englishman in grain, and even a
prejudiced Englishman.   He was quite as ready
as other Britons to reckon to the discredit of
Frenchmen, and generally of foreigners, a certain

shallow and frothy demonstrativeness ; *too* ready.
I always thought."

Patmore's poem was *The Angel in the House.*
He wrote to Allingham in October, 1854 :—"You
will receive in a day or two a copy of a Poem by
'C. K. Dighton,' under which name I wish, if
possible, to pass for the present—chiefly because
the weight of the *Times* attack on my father's
book has fallen on me—even *Punch* abusing me
by my full name on account of it. Only two or
three of the P. R. B. coterie are in the secret."
His full name was Coventry Kearsey Dighton
Patmore. In the *Times* of August 19, 1854,
there was a very long and unfavourable review
of *My Friends and Acquaintance, being memorials,
mind portraits, and personal recollections of deceased
celebrities of the nineteenth century.* By T. G.
Patmore. There is, I believe, no mention of
Coventry Patmore in *Punch.*

Thomas Buchanan Read was an American poet,
and a painter by profession as well, author of
Rural Poems, Lays, and Ballads. He died in
1872. "He was a curiously small man in stature,
and had a pleasant little wife on exactly a corres-
ponding scale." He had suffered with Rossetti
under the unjust law of distraint. Mr. W. M.
Rossetti wrote to Allingham on August 10, 1850:—
"As for Read, he left on Friday week in something
of a hurry and confusion, owing to an execution
for rent put into Gabriel's lodgings on the fugitive
landlord's account ; whereby Read's trunk, etc.

were, *inter alia*, laid under embargo; indeed, he has been compelled to leave them behind." Rossetti's landlord was a dancing-master, "who failed to pay his rent. According to the oppressive system of those days, the goods of his sub-tenant were seized to make good the default. Dante and I," continues his brother, "carried away a considerable number of books. The bulk of his small belongings was confiscated, and appeared to his eyes no more."

According to Mrs. Howitt, Rossetti had come across some lyrics in the *Philadelphia Courier*, written from Hazeldell on the Schuylkill. "I was so delighted with them," he one day said to Allingham, "that I sent to Philadelphia for all the papers containing the poems from Hazeldell, cut them out and pasted them in a book." Allingham asked Read, whom he had met at the Howitts, whether he knew the unknown poet's name. As he spoke of Rossetti's admiration of the lyrics, "Read's face became crimson and his entire form agitated. 'I am the writer of those poems,' he replied with tears in his eyes." He had at first seemed to the Howitts "a timid nonentity, but we found him," Mrs. Howitt continues, "a very generous, grateful young man, possessing much original power and fine discrimination of art. At the close of 1870 we met him once more in Rome, where he was then residing with his gentle and wealthy wife (his second wife), and dispensing hospitality with a most lavish hand."

Carlyle's blunder about W. B. Scott's book was the stranger as the title-page is as clear as a title-page can be. He could have looked only at the frontispiece. When he found out his mistake he wrote to Scott:—" It is too certain I have committed an absurd mistake, which indeed I discerned two weeks ago with emotion compounded of astonishment, remorse, and the tendency to laugh and cry both at once! The truth is I am pestered with incipient volumes of verses from young lads that feel something stirring in them; on the frontispiece of your little volume I read *Printer* (not Painter), as I should have done . . . Fancying, therefore, it was an ingenious printer lad in your coaly town, who was rashly devoting his extra gifts, evidently rather valuable ones, to the trade of verse-making, I wrote and admonished (hastily reading five or six stanzas here and there) in the singular manner you experienced."

XVI.

BLACKFRIARS BRIDGE.

Tuesday Evening, 23 January, 1855.

DEAR ALLINGHAM,

I am sure you have attributed my silence for so long to its real motive—the wish to tell you, when I *did* write, that *the* block was finished at last. It is finished now. I shall keep it by me to-morrow for anything that may suggest itself, and give it next day to R[outledge] & Co., by whom I expect it to be walked round and looked at as a real curiosity found at length. I find Boyce knows the engraver, Dalziel, who, I believe is to do all the blocks, and he (Boyce) will plead their cause with him.

I suppose no doubt the book is to be issued as speedily now as possible, when Millais has done his sketch, which was undone two nights ago, but I urged him with some indignant morality, and I have no doubt it will soon turn up. I hope my own drawing is not so bad as it looks to me now it is finished, but in any case I am sure it will *not bear* being made worse in the cutting. In this *second edition* of it I have tried to draw all the shadow in exact lines, to which, if the engraver will only adhere, I fancy it may have a chance, but hardly otherwise, as there is a good deal of strong shade—dangerous especially to the faces, but I could find no other way.

If the delay in publishing should, owing to Millais or anything else, prove long enough, I should like much, and will try to find leisure for another block, but probably this "may not be." I have made one or two enquiries after the original of that ballad by Heine, and looked right through a pretty extensive collection of his poems in one volume, but without success. I hope for another chance of finding it in a few days through a German friend, who, I fancy, must know Heine's works well. I trust somehow still to write to you about it.

The other day Moxon called on me, wanting me to do some of the blocks for the new Tennyson. The artists already engaged are Millais, Hunt, Landseer, Stanfield, Maclise, Creswick, Mulready, and Horsley. The right names would have been Millais, Hunt, Madox Brown, Hughes, a certain lady, and myself. No OTHERS. What do you think? Stanfield is to do, *Break, break*, because there is the sea in it, and *Ulysses*, too, because there are ships. Landseer has *Lady Godiva*—and all in that way. Each artist, it seems, is to do about half-a-dozen, but I hardly expect to manage so many, as I find the work of drawing on wood particularly trying to the eyes. I have not begun even designing for them yet, but fancy I shall try the *Vision of Sin* and *Palace of Art*, etc.,—those where one can allegorize on one's own hook on the subject of the poem, without killing for oneself and every one a distinct idea of the poet's. This, I fancy, is *always* the upshot of illustrated editions,— Tennyson, Allingham, or any one,—unless where the poetry is so absolutely narrative as in the old ballads, for instance. Are we to try the experiment ever in their regard? There are one or two or more of Tennyson's in narrative,—but generally the worst, I think,—*Lady Clare*, *Lord of Burleigh*, to wit.

News must have grown so old since I wrote to you that most likely I shall forget the most of it. For myself, I got nearly finished (and shall make it do for quite, I think) with my calf and cart at Finchley, when I was laid up all of a sudden for some little time, through the wind blowing my picture down on my leg, which caused it to gather and create a nuisance. Since I got over this I have been water-colouring again, somewhat against the grain, and have not yet got my picture to London. I began my class last night at the Working Men's College: it is for the figure, quite a separate thing from Ruskin's, who teaches foliage. I have set one of them as a model to the rest, till they can find themselves another model. I intend them to draw only from nature, and some of them—two or three—show unmistakable aptitude— almost all more than one could ever have looked for. Ruskin's class has progressed astonishingly, and I must try to keep pace with him. The class proceeds quite on a family footing, and I feel sure, will prove amusing.

You will be sorry to hear that Miss Howitt has been seriously ill since her father's return, and is still quite an invalide [*sic*]. I have made an engagement to go and see them next week, having been absent from their circle a longer time than I meant. I am sure, if you ever have time to write to any of them, they will be really pleased to hear from you.

Barbara Smith has been suddenly declared very ill—her lungs, I believe, are affected—and is gone to Rome—whence the news of her only just now begins to be rather better it seems. I wish there were any Rome for my good pupil, whose life might matter a little. She bears the cold weather, however, on the whole, better than I looked for, and of course progresses always as an artist. She is now doing two lovely water-colours (from *We are Seven*, and *La Belle Dame sans merci*)—having found herself always thrown back for lack of health and wealth in the attempts she had made to begin a picture.

The drawings will, I hope, soon be finished, and then I shall see what can be done with them—through Ruskin especially I hope.

I have only one of your letters at hand, and hope I am omitting no answer required in the other. I remember, for one thing, you asked me how I liked *The Angel in the House*. Of course it is very good indeed, yet will one ever want to read it again? The best passages I can recollect now are the one about "coming where women are," for the simile of the frozen ship—and the part concerning the "brute of a husband." From what I hear, I should judge that, in spite of idiots in the *Athenæum* and elsewhere, the book will be of use to its author's reputation—a resolute poet, whom I saw a little while back, and who means to make his book bigger than the *Divina Commedia*, he tells me. He and his are removed to Hampstead for the present, as perhaps you know.

Woolner's chance for that commission seems to be up, I fear. He has been once more shabbily treated by a committee, and is quite at a loss what to be at; but I think, at any rate, he will produce one or two small groups here before returning to Australia. Millais has taken a studio at the corner of Langham Place, where a man has just run up some buildings especially for artists, and splendid affairs. He is painting his picture of a fireman rescuing some children, of which I think I spoke to you. Hunt will be back, I believe, before long. Seddon, who went with him, has returned, and has done some notable things for fidelity and completeness—the truest views of the country in some respects, I dare say, that have been done. Boyce has been to Venice again and is back.

Poor North! There was a long account of

that doleful affair in the *Daily News*. He appears to have been going on in his usual style up to the very last, with a new comic paper in prospect, . an advertisement of which in MS. was just written and lying on his table. It (the advertisement) concluded comically enough by saying :—" Agents wanted in New Zealand, Australia, Polynesia, &c. N.B.—No cannibals need apply."

Pray don't hurry about the Italian MSS., if hurying is to prevent my having your fullest marginal attention to them, which I really feel anxious to see, and shall send another batch as soon as possible, being bent on publishing them at an early day with an *acharnement* almost Patmorian, though lately I have had no time to give to them. I have often turned in my mind your kind proposal about magazine publication for them, but cannot fully settle what I think about it till I have shown them to Ruskin, and tried what chance there might be of getting Smith and Elder to shell out something for them in a lump, which arrangement, if possible, I should prefer to any other, especially as it would spur me on to a speedy completion of the book.

By the bye Ruskin has procured a situation at Smith and Elder's for the youngest male Deverell —similar, I suppose, to what E. Blanchard had at Chapman's. You know Blanchard has given this up, and thrown himself on literature and a discerning public! He sub-edits the *Leader*, and called on me the other day with a request involving you also, viz., that either or both of us would contribute poetry to that " organ." Finding there was no tin in the case I declined, but as he asked me still to ask you, promised to do so, which duty I now perform, though I told him he had no chance with you. Did you see Hannay's pill for M. F. Tupper in the *Athenæum?* And by the bye, I am asked by William to request from you the re-postage of *Athenæums* when quite done with, as he requires them sometimes for reference to artistic matters as to dates, &c.

I am awfully sleepy and stupid, or should try to say something about the only book I have read for a long while back—Crabbe, whose poems were known to me long ago, but not at all familiarly till now. I fancy one might read him much oftener and much later than Wordsworth—than almost any one.

I must try and fill this paper. So I substitute one of my "clever" moments for the present helpless one, and copy you my last sonnet :—

> " The gloom which breathes upon me with these airs
>   Is like the drops that strike the traveller's brow
>   Who knows not, darkling, if they menace now
>   Fresh storms, or be old rain the covert bears.
>   Ah ! bodes this hour its harvest of new tares ?

> Or keeps remembrance of that day whose plough
>   Sowed hunger since,—that night at last when thou,
> O prayer found vain ! didst fall from out my prayers ?
> How prickly were the griefs which yet how smooth,
>   On cobwebbed hedgerows of this journey shed,
> Lie here and there till night and sleep may soothe !
>   Even as the thistledown from pathsides dead
> Gleaned by a girl in autumns of her youth,
>   Which, one new year, makes soft her marriage bed."

Does it smack, though, of Tupper at all?—it seems to, in copying. The last simile I heard as a fact common in some parts of the country.

I wish I could see you again ; I really do. When is it to happen ? Let us write again regularly, now that we feel réhabilité about the block.

Yours D. G. R.

NOTES ON XVI.

Mr. W. M. Rossetti describes George Price Boyce, the water-colour painter, as " my brother's old and constant friend."

The " certain lady " referred to in connection with the new Tennyson was, of course, Miss Siddal. About the time the new volume appeared, many of the Præraphaelite artists were staying in Oxford. I well remember how they scorned the illustrations of some of those men whom Rossetti would have excluded. One of them even encouraged me to scribble over the feeblest of the pictures in my copy of the work, promising to supply their places with designs of his own. I left the volume with him for many weeks, but nothing came of it. My book is still disfigured, and his promise is still unkept.

How much Rossetti "allegorized on his own hook" in illustrating Tennyson is shown by his brother, who writes:—"It must be said that himself only, and not Tennyson, was his guide. He drew just what he chose, taking from his author's text nothing more than a hint and an opportunity. The illustration of St. Cecilia puzzled Tennyson not a little, and he had to give up the problem of what it had to do with his verses." In an autograph letter of Rossetti's, in my collection, he says, " T. loathes mine [my designs]."

Allingham wrote to W. M. Rossetti on August 17, 1857:—"I spent one day with Clough near Ambleside, and two or three with Tennyson at Coniston, who is cheerful. His chief affliction now is the bad poetry which keeps showering on his head very fast. He ought to put up the umbrella of utter neglect, and talks of doing so. He praised the P. R. B. designs to his poems in a general way, but cares nothing about the whole affair." This mention of Coniston reminds me how, in my boyhood, I one day heard the curate of that village tell some brother clergymen that he could not think of knowing Mr. Tennyson, as the poet never went to church.

The first of the two passages in *The Angel in the House*, which Rossetti praised is the following:—

" Whene'er I come where ladies are,
    How sad soever I was before,
Though like a ship frost-bound and far
    Withheld in ice from the ocean's roar,
Third-wintered in that dreadful dock
    With stiffen'd cordage, sails decay'd,
A crew that care for calm and shock
    Alike, too dull to be dismay'd,
Yet if I come where ladies are,
    How sad soever I was before,
Then is my sadness banish'd far,
    And I am like that ship no more ;
Or like that ship if the ice-field splits,
    Burst by the sudden Polar spring,
And all thank God with their warming wits,
    And kiss each other, and dance and sing,
And hoist fresh sails, that make the breeze
    Blow them along the liquid sea,
Out of the North, where life did freeze,
    Into the haven where they would be."

How "resolute a poet" Patmore was is shown
by the following passage in a letter he wrote to
Allingham more than four years earlier :—" I am
working hard at my Poem, and average six lines
or so a day, which will bring the affair about in
six years or so ! "

Hawthorne, who met him on the last day of
1857, recorded in his note-book :—" *The Angel in
the House* is a most beautiful and original poem ;
but I doubt whether the generality of English
people are capable of appreciating it. I told Mr.
Patmore that I thought his popularity in America
would be greater than at home, and he said that it
was already so ; and he appeared to estimate highly

his American fame, and also our general gift of quicker and more subtle recognition of genius than the English public."

The Committee was that mentioned in Letter X., which was to report on Woolner's "competency" to make a statue of W. C. Wentworth.

Of Thomas Seddon some account will be found in notes on Letters XXXIII. and XXXIV.

"Poor North" was William North, whom Mr. W. M. Rossetti describes as "an eccentric literary man, not without a spice of genius, of whom we then [about 1849] saw a goodish deal—author of *Anti-Coningsby* and *The Infinite Republic.* He emigrated to the United States, and in 1854 committed suicide."

The literary editor of the *Leader* was G. H. Lewes. It is recorded in the *Life of Anne Gilchrist* that Carlyle one day speaking to him about that journal, "asked, 'When will those papers on Positivism come to an end?' 'I can assure you they are making a great impression at Oxford,' says Lewes. 'Ah! I never look at them, it's so much blank paper to me. I looked into Comte once; found him to be one of those men who go up in a balloon and take a lighted candle to look at the stars.'" The papers on Comte were by Lewes.

Of Hannay's review of the eighteenth edition of *Proverbial Philosophy* in the *Athenæum* for December 30, 1854, the following is a specimen :—
"Probably Mr. Tupper's most distinguished talent

is a certain judicious knowingness, which enables him to turn his labours to good pecuniary account. So at least it would appear from an advertisement at the end of this 'eighteenth edition,' where a French version of it is 'highly recommended for schools in conjunction with the English edition!' Mr. Tupper, in the frenzies of his inspiration, has still, it seems, an eye to the oven, and mounts the tripod to heave in coals at the kitchen window."

Of Crabbe I only find one mention in *D. G. Rossetti's Family Letters*. Writing on October 8, 1849, to Mr. W. M. Rossetti, who had written a poem entitled *Mrs. Holmes Grey*, he says :—"Its story is more like Crabbe than any other poet I know of ; not lacking no small share of his harsh reality—less healthy and at times more poetical." It was, I suppose, Crabbe's "harsh reality" which so attracted Rossetti.

Rossetti's "last sonnet," under the title of *A Dark Day*, is No. LXVIII. in *Ballads and Sonnets*. The only important alterations are in the tenth and eleventh lines, which now stand :—

> " Along the hedgerows of this journey shed,
>   Lie by Time's grace till night and sleep may soothe."

XVII.

Saturday, March 18, 1855.

Dear Allingham,

I am going to write a most vexatious letter—however, the news cannot be more so to you than to me, and its extreme disagreeableness has prevented my writing it before. That wood-block! Dalziel has made such an incredible mull of it in the cutting that it cannot possibly appear. The fault, however, is no doubt in great measure mine—not of deficient care, for I took the very greatest, but of over-elaboration of parts, perplexing them for the engraver. However, some of the fault is his too, as he has not always followed my lines, but a rather stupid preconceived notion of his about intended " severity " in the design, which has resulted in an engraving as hard as a nail, and yet flabby and vapid to the last degree. In short, it is such a production as could give no idea of anything like care or skill on the part of the designer—of anything but the most conceited attempt of a beginner to be grand and "severe." Before I sent in my drawing, however, to the engraver, I consulted a friend—Clayton, who has drawn much on wood—as to whether it were done in the right way for cutting, and he assured me it was not only adaptable but remarkably so: certainly I kept every line as distinct as I could ; and on this account Clayton was of opinion that it was very much more the thing for the purpose than the drawings made by Hughes, which, however, turns out a complete mistake, as Hughes's drawings, also cut by Dalziel, have come, with one exception, quite remarkably well. Three or four of them are most beautiful designs, and will be worthy of your book. Before sending in the block I took the precaution to write to Routledge that, if not approved by me when cut, it must not appear, and Dalziel himself called on me before cutting it, and understood this, so that I must trust they will act accordingly, as I have written to Dalziel since also. If you like, I will send you the proof of it which I have, though at cost of considerable humiliation to myself, as you cannot possibly imagine by looking at it, even after this letter, *how far* different it is from my drawing—Hughes, Boyce, Woolner, and Clayton, who saw it before the cutting would tell you this. I would enclose the proof now, but really don't like to, before you've been prepared for the horror of it.

All this is of course most vexatious for you and for me, especially after the delay which was made for the sake of this abortive attempt. *Mais que faire?* I have done my best and failed. As things have turned out, you could not wish it to be published more than I do, for it would disgrace your book as much as my capacities.

Let me try to devote the rest of this second sheet to more pleasant news—news which would compensate me for a hundred bothers, and will, I am sure, go far to put you in a good temper, even after I have gone so far to try it.

About a week ago, Ruskin saw and bought on the spot every scrap of designs hitherto produced by Miss Siddall. He declared that they were far better than mine, or almost than any one's, and seemed quite wild with delight at getting them. He asked me to name a price for them, after asking and hearing that they were for sale ; and I, of course, considering the immense advantage of their getting them into his hands, named a very low price, £25, which he declared to be too low *even* for a low price, and increased to £30. He is going to have them splendidly mounted and bound together in gold ; and no doubt this will be a real opening for her, as it is already a great assistance and encouragement. He has since written her a letter, which I enclose, and which, as you see, promises further usefulness. She is now doing the designs wanted. Pray, AFTER READING IT, ENCLOSE IT AND RETURN IT TO ME AT ONCE, as I want much to have it by me and show to one or two friends ; and accompany it with a word or two

A DESIGN BY MISS SIDDAL.

[To face page 111.

as I want to know that you are not quite disgusted with me on account of that unlucky job. Ruskin's praise is beginning to bear fruit already. I wrote about it to Woolner, who has been staying for a week or two with the Tennysons ; and they, hearing that several of Miss Siddal's designs were from Tennyson, and being told about Ruskin, etc., wish her exceedingly to join in the illustrated edition ; and Mrs. T. wrote immediately to Moxon about it, declaring that she had rather pay for Miss S.'s designs herself than not have them in the book. There is only one damper in this affair, and that is the lesson as to the difficulty of wood-drawing which I am still wincing under ; but she and I must adopt a simpler method, and then I hope for better luck. All this will, I know, give you real pleasure, so I write it at such length.

By the bye, Miss Siddal reminded me after the *sale of the design*, which was my doing and quite unexpected, that we owe *you* a compensation, as one of them, the two nigger girls playing to the lovers, belonged to you, which I had, I am ashamed to say, forgotten, but remembered when she named it. She means to do another and better one for you, from one of your own poems, and meanwhile apologises with me for the mistake.

Yours affectionately,

D. G. Rossetti.

Notes on XVII.

"My brother," says Mr. W. M. Rossetti, "was exceedingly (I think overmuch) dissatisfied with the wood-cutting of the design of *The Maids of Elfin-Mere*." In a letter written a few months later Rossetti said : "It used to be by me till it became the exclusive work of Dalziel, who cut it. I was resolved to cut it out, but Allingham would not, so I can only wish Dalziel had the credit as well as the authorship." Dalziel said to Mr. Hughes : "How is one to engrave a drawing that is partly in ink, partly in pencil, and partly in red chalk?" "He took," Mr. Hughes tells me, "a great deal of trouble; but Rossetti was as impatient as a genius usually is. He wanted to crowd more into a picture than it could hold."

Of J. R. Clayton I find mention in the following entry made by Madox Brown in his journal at the beginning of 1856 :—"The room was too full to talk, and Bill with a man named Clayton, jawed so nauseously about Ruskin and art, that I felt quite disgusted and said nothing." It was probably not so much art as Ruskin which made the "jaw" so nauseous. His constant silence about Brown's pictures sank deep into the painter's soul.

Mr. W. M. Rossetti, writing of a period a few weeks later than the date of this letter, says :— "Mr. Ruskin committed one of those unnumbered acts of generosity by which he will be remembered hardly less long than by his vivid insight into many

things, and by his heroic prose. He wanted to
effect one of two plans for Miss Siddal's advantage :
either to purchase all her drawings one by one, as
they should be produced, or else to settle on her
an annual £150, he taking in exchange her various
works up to that value. . . . This latter plan was
carried into actual effect by May 3. It will easily
and rightly be supposed that Rossetti used to find
funds for Miss Siddal whenever required ; but his
means were both small and fitful." None of her
designs were included in the illustrated edition of
Tennyson.

XVIII.

Blackfriars Bridge,
  [*Postmark, March* 22, 1855].

Dear Allingham,

  I have been looking at the mangled
remains of my drawing again by the light of your
friendly letter, but really can only see it, in its
present state, as a conceited-looking failure, and as
to the execution, it is on a par with woodcut
"Executions" in general ; only in such cases the
"copy of verses" ought to be made to match.

My wish was, and is, to make you a small water-
colour, or pen and ink drawing, of the subject,
as I should feel pleasure in doing it, and in your
having it, in some shape ; and that, since we cannot

hang the engraver, the drawing, at any rate, should receive no quarter. By the bye, I have written to Dalziel, and though my letter was not indited, at a severe crisis of punning, it seems to have treated the subject in a manner to make him crusty, as he has never answered.

I showed the proof yesterday to Woolner, who saw the original drawing, and he was as shocked as myself. Nevertheless, I am not wholly unimpressed by your unprejudiced view of it, I confess. Moreover, it would be possible to improve it a good deal, I believe — not by adding shadows, which, though very advisable (as in the finger you mention) would not be practicable ; but by cutting out lines, by which means the human character might be partially substituted for the oyster and goldfish cast of features, and other desirable changes effected. On getting your letter I marked parts of the proof with white, and find something might probably be done. But first I should like to show the whitened proof to one or two friends, and take their opinion as to whether, even if the changes were properly made, the thing could possibly be allowed to come out. I write to you before doing this, as I do not wish to delay answering. I confess I was most sincerely of opinion that, as I said, you would have an equal horror with myself at its appearing in your poems. At any rate I cannot at present conceive of its being brought to any state in which my name could be put to it, much as I should like my name to appear in your book. But the water-colour substitute would be the best.

Perhaps before this reaches you I shall get from you Ruskin's letter to Miss S——, but if you have not posted it before, pray do so at once on receiving this, as I think I may want it. Ruskin's interest in her continues unabated, and he is most desirous of benefiting her in any way in his power, and of her becoming a frequent visitor at his house. Some thoroughly fine day she and I are to pay him our first visit together.

Now to answer your question about Dr. Polidori. The fact of his suicide does not, unfortunately, admit of a doubt, though the verdict on the inquest was one of natural death; but this was a partly pardonable insincerity, arising from pity for my grandfather's great grief, and from a schoolfellow of my uncle's happening to be, strangely enough, on the jury. This death happened in the year '21, and he was only in his 26th year. I believe that, though his poems and tales give an impression only of a cultivated mind, he showed more than common talents both for medicine, and afterwards for law, which pursuit he took to, in a restless mood, after his return from Italy. The "pecuniary difficulties" were only owing, I believe, to sudden losses and liabilities incurred at the gaming-table, whither, in his last feverish days, he had been drawn by some false friend, though such tastes had always, in a healthy state, been quite foreign to him. I have met accidentally, from time to time, persons who knew him, and he seems always to have excited admiration by his talents, and with those who knew him well affection and respect by his honourable nature; but I have no doubt that vanity was one of his failings, and should think he might have been in some degree of unsound mind. He was my mother's favourite brother, and I feel certain her love for him is a proof that his memory deserves some respect. In Medwin, in Moore, and in Leigh Hunt, and elsewhere, I have seen allusions to him which dwelt on nothing but his faults, and therefore I have filled this sheet on the subject, though, of course, as far as your proposed criticism goes, I am only telling you that the book tells truth in this particular.

Write soon, and believe me,

Yours affectionately,

D. G. ROSSETTI.

By the bye, I am delighted at your appreciation of Scott. I shrewdly suspect that the last time I heard you talk of him there " was nothing in him." [Allingham grates a little.] I think myself that *Maryanne*, with all its faults, is better worth writing than *The Angel in the House.* As exemplified in this poem, as well as in other respects, Scott is a man something of Browning's order, as regards his place among poets, though with less range and even much greater incompleteness, but also, on the other hand, quite without affectation ever to be found among his faults, and I think, too, with a more commonly appreciable sort of melody in his best moments.

NOTES ON XVIII.

The following passage in Mr. W. M. Rossetti's work, entitled *D. G. Rossetti as Designer and Writer*, illustrates the difficulty Dalziel had in working with him :—" My brother was, no doubt, a difficult man with whom to carry on work in co-operation : having his own ideas, from which he was not to be moved ; his own habits, from which he was not to be jogged ; his own notions of business, from which he was not to be diverted. Co-operators, I can easily think, railed at him, and yet they liked him too. He assumed the easy attitude of one born to dominate—to know his own place, and to set others in theirs. . . . He was a genial despot, good-naturedly hearty and unassuming in manner, and only tenacious upon the question at issue."

Mr. W. M. Rossetti quotes the following passage from an undated letter of Ruskin's to his brother, evidently written later than the one in the text :—

" I shall rejoice in Ida's success with her picture, as I shall in every opportunity of being useful either to you or her. The only feeling I have about the matter is of some shame at having allowed the arrangement between us to end as it did ; and the chief pleasure I could have about it now would be her simply accepting it as she would have accepted a glass of water when she was thirsty, and never thinking of it any more."

The opinion formed of her by the Ruskin family when she visited them is recorded in a note on Letter III.

John William Polidori, brother of Rossetti's mother, an Englishman by birth, took his degree at Edinburgh as doctor of medicine at the early age of nineteen. A year later, in 1816, he accompanied Lord Byron as his travelling-physician. In less than six months they parted company. Polidori returned to England. Abandoning medicine, he studied for the bar. He published two volumes of verse and two of prose. " In August, 1821, the end came in a melancholy way : he committed suicide with poison, having through losses in gambling, incurred a debt of honour which he had no present means of clearing off. The jury returned a verdict of ' Died by the visitation of God.' "

Moore, in his Life of Byron, describes " the strange sallies of this eccentric young man, whose vanity made him a constant butt to Lord Byron's sarcasm and merriment." Moore allows that " he seems to have possessed both talents and disposition which, had he lived, might have rendered him a useful member of his profession and of society." One day, after an altercation with Byron, thinking his dismissal inevitable, "retiring to his room, he had already drawn forth the poison from his medicine-chest, when Lord Byron tapped at the door, and entered with his hand held forth in sign of reconciliation. The sudden revulsion was too much for poor Polidori, who burst into tears. He afterwards declared that nothing could exceed the gentle kindness of Lord Byron in soothing his mind."

Byron, writing of him, said :—" I know no great harm of him ; but he had an alacrity of getting into scrapes, and was too young and heedless ; and having enough to attend to in my own concerns, and without time to become his tutor, I thought it much better to give him his *congé*."

What could have been expected of a clever young fellow who had been turned by a university into a doctor of medicine at the age of nineteen, and then had had entrusted to his care the health of the most famous poet of the age?

" Scott " is William Bell Scott. Rossetti wrote on July 1, 1853 :—" Scott and I have looked through his poems together, and have made some very advantageous amendments between us. *Rosabell*, especially, is quite another thing, and is now called *Mary Anne*."

Mr. Holman Hunt, describing Rossetti's " storehouse of treasures," says :—" If he read twice or thrice a long poem, it was literally at his tongue's end ; and he had a voice rarely equalled for simple recitations. *Sordello* and *Paracelsus* he would give by forty and fifty pages at a time. Then would come the pathetic strains of W. B. Scott's *Rosabell.*"

Mr. W. M. Rossetti has shown how groundless was Scott's assertion that the subject of *Found* was taken from *Mary Anne.*

It will be seen in Letter XXVIII. how highly Browning's genius was valued by Rossetti—far more highly than the comparison with W. B. Scott indicates. " Browning," he wrote in 1871, " seems likely to remain, with all his sins, the most original and varied mind, by long odds, which betakes itself to poetry in our time."

XIX.

Thursday [March 23, 1855].

DEAR ALLINGHAM,

Your repeated wish to - day about the wood-cut is conclusive to me, of course, if on reading my yesterday's letter you do not prefer having a drawing on paper, *which I wish you would.* Let me hear at once, and if you continue in favour of the cut, I will at once try and see Dalziel, and myself superintend, if he will stand it, such alterations as may be possible ; and on the degree of success with which he makes them I hope you will allow the appearance of my name to the drawing to depend. If he makes it look as I have made the proof look with white, it will be pretty tolerable comparatively, but I suppose that is not to be hoped.

I have only the proof in question, which, as I may need it for this purpose, I do not send you.

I write in haste and mid-work.

Yours affectionately,

D. G. R.

XX.

May 11, 1855.

Dear Allingham,

Thanks for the returned MSS., which I ought to have acknowledged before, but this is absolutely the first evening I have been able to find since then for letter-writing. Your remarks in the margin I value much, and am sure I shall adopt many of the suggestions, if ever that book come to aught. Indeed, I have a further large relay of them in course of copying, which may perhaps meet your eye, if you care for them, and would no doubt benefit under your hand. I take one out at long intervals and copy and yawn ;

but "is it not all in vain?" A man of many journeys must needs find his path crossed here and there by some old hobby, each time, grown seedier and sleepier, and sometimes he may say:— "Now will I saddle thee, for where our pastures lay, there they lie;" and, no doubt, so they do; but even one's hobby is not so soft to ride as to lay one's head on; and so they two snooze together. If either is ever woke up, it may be the hobby, which somebody saddles awry to fetch the sexton, to risk a cheap bell or so for him who is still asleep, and have him enough remembered to be forgotten.

This fine writing, you'll say, is wronging you of news. Yesterday I took the MSS. to Ruskin, who, on hearing that they came from you, said you were one to whom he owed and would yet pay a letter of thanks, which he was sorry remained so long unwritten; and therewith spoke again with great delight of your poems. He was not delighted, by the bye, with that design beyond designation which your readers are to suppose I did; and he even saw it to great advantage, as I had been over the proof with white, to get Dalziel to alter parts of it. I have since given it him to do so, and have seen it in part done. Well! I have supped full with horrors, served (out) in three courses, which, as Hood says, can't

be helped. I wish D—— only had his desert as
a finish.

Meanwhile, how is Millais' design which I have
not yet seen? I hope it is only as good as his
picture at the R.A.—the most wonderful thing he
has done, except perhaps the *Huguenot*. He
had an awful row with the hanging committee,
who had put it above the level of the eye ; but
J. E. M. yelled for several hours and threatened
to resign, till they put it right. Anthony's landscape of *Stratford-on-Avon*, a noble thing badly
hung—though, of course, not *so* badly. They
have been running wilder than ever this year in
insolence and dishonesty ; have actually turned out
a drawing by Hunt (his pictures have not reached
England ; I heard from him the other day, and
he is likely to be back in two or three months) ;
put the 4 best landscapes in the place — 3 by
Inchbold, 1 by some new Davis — quite out of
sight ; kicked out 2 pictures by one Arthur
Hughes — *Orlando*, and a most admirable little
full-length of a child in a flannel night-gown ; and
played "warious games of that sort." There is
a big picture of *Cimabue*, one of his works in
procession, by a new man, living abroad, named
Leighton—a huge thing, which the Queen has
bought, which every one talks of. The R.A.'s
have been gasping for years for some one to

back against Hunt and Millais, and here they
have him ; a fact which makes some people do
the picture injustice in return. It was *very* un-
interesting to me at first sight ; but on looking
more at it, I think there is great richness of
arrangement—a quality which, when *really* exist-
ing, as it does in the best old masters, and perhaps
hitherto in no living man—at any rate English—
ranks among the great qualities.

But I am not quite sure yet either of this or of
the faculty for colour, which I suspect exists very
strongly, but is certainly at present under a thick
veil of paint ; owing, I fancy, to too much continental study. One undoubted excellence it has—
facility without much neatness or ultra-cleverness
in the execution, which is greatly like that of Paul
Veronese ; and the colour may mature in future
works to the same resemblance, I fancy. There is
much feeling for beauty, too, in the women. As
for purely intellectual qualities, expression, intention, etc., there is little as yet of them ; but I think
that in art richness of arrangement is so nearly
allied to these that where it exists (in an earnest
man) they will probably supervene. However, the
choice of the subject, though interesting in a
certain way, leaves one quite in the dark as to
what faculty the man may have for representing
incident or passionate emotion. But I believe,

as far as this showing goes, that he possesses qualities which the mass of our artists aim at chiefly, and only seem to possess ; whether he have those of which neither they nor he give sign, I cannot yet tell ; but he is said to be only 24 years old. There is something very French in his work, at present, which is the most disagreeable thing about it ; but this I dare say would leave him if he came to England.

I suppose there is no chance of your having written an unrhymed elegy on Currer Bell, called *Haworth Churchyard*, in this *Fraser*, and signed " A." There is some *thorough* appreciation of poor *Wuthering Heights* in it, but then the same stanza raves of Byron, so you can't have done it ; not to add that it wouldn't be up to any known mark of yours, I think.

You heard, I suppose, that Mac Cracken was going finally to sell his pictures in a lump at Christie's, but perhaps I wrote to you since the event. The utmost offered for Hunt's was 220 gs., so he retains it still, having put a reserve of £300 on it. *My Annunciation*, 76 gs. ; water-colour Dante, 50. These are both sold : 1st to one Pearse, I hear ; 2nd, to Combe of Oxford. Collins' *St. Elizabeth* only had 31 gs. bid, so he keeps that too. None of the other pictures went well, but I think the Bernal humbug has been settling all other sales lately.   Hunt's father, who was at the sale, called on me with the above information, which I suppose is right.

What do you think? Collinson is back in London, and has 2 pictures in the R.A. The Jesuits have found him fittest for painting, and have restored him to an eager world. Woolner's Wentworth job is up, I fancy, altogether. However, lately, owing to Woolner's writing a cheeky answer to a very snobbish letter of old W.'s, that magnanimous crittur seems to have restored him his confidence; and if the statue is done (which seems very doubtful) I think Woolner may possibly do it. Your bust is in the R.A. and in rather a good place, and your lines also appear to Munro's *Lovers* in the catalogue, as well as to an admirable little picture by Hughes in the Patriotic Fund Exhibition. Munro's group of Ingram's children has been put by MacDowell in the place of honour in the Sculpture-room at the R.A.! and is likely to do him great good.

I would greatly like the walking tour you propose this summer, and better with you than any one—now in good sooth, la! But I don't know well yet what my abilities and advisabilities may be; will write you of my probable movements as soon as I know them.

Good-morning. I am just told very loudly

that it is 3 A.M.; and lo! it is horridly light. *Write soon, and I'll write soon.*

By the bye, this morning (12 May), through the first 2 hours of which I have slept over this letter, is the very morning on which I first woke up, or fell a-dreaming, or began to be, or was transported for life, or what is it?—27 years ago! It isn't your birthday, so *I* can wish *you* many happy returns of it.

Yours affectionately,

D. G. ROSSETTI.

NOTES ON XX.

The MSS. which Rossetti took to Ruskin were, as the next letter shows, the translations of the *Early Italian Poets* with Allingham's critical remarks on the margin.

Millais's design is entitled *The Fireside Story*. It illustrates the following stanza of *Frost in the Highlands*, in the second series of *Day and Night Songs* :—

> " At home are we by the merry fire,
> Ranged in a ring to our heart's desire.
> And who is to tell some wondrous tale,
> Almost to turn the warm cheeks pale,
> Set chin on hands, make grave eyes stare,
> Draw slowly nearer each stool and chair ? "

His picture in the Royal Academy was *The Rescue*. On November 8, 1853, Rossetti wrote to his sister Christina :—" Millais, I just hear, was last night elected Associate. 'So now the whole Round Table is dissolved.'" His "awful row with the hanging committee" is mentioned in the *Life of W. B. Scott*, to whom "Woolner writing in May, 1855, said that the Academy Committee hung Millais—even Millais, their crack student—in a bad place ; he being too attractive now ; but that celebrity made such an uproar the old fellows were glad to give in and place him better. Millais's amusement, when Woolner wrote, was to go about and rehearse the scene that took place at the Academy between him and the ancient magnates."

Seddon wrote on May 3, 1855:—"The Academy opens on Monday. The hangers were of the old school, and they have kicked out everything tainted with Præraphaelitism. My *Pyramids*, and a head in chalk of Hunt's ; and all our friends are stuck out of sight or rejected. Millais's picture was put where it could not be seen. . . . He carried his point by threatening to take away his picture and resign at once, unless they re-hung him, which they did. He told them his mind very freely, and said they were jealous of all rising men, and turned out or hung their pictures where they could not be seen."

Mark Anthony, the landscape painter, is described by Mr. W. M. Rossetti as "a fine genius, not adequately valued now."

The drawing by Hunt turned out of the Academy was "a life-size crayon of his father, admirably finished."

"Some new Davis" was William Davis, an Irish landscape painter, settled in Liverpool. Madox Brown wrote in May, 1856 :— "There is a little landscape by Davis, of Liverpool, of some leafless trees and some ducks, which is perfection. I do not remember ever having seen such an English landscape ; it is far too good to be understood, and is on the floor." Four months later he wrote :—"This Davis, who has been one of the most unlucky artists in England (now about forty, with a wife and family), is a man with a fine-shaped head and well-cut features, and his manners are not without a certain modest dignity, though crushed by disappointment. Miller is the only man who buys his pictures." He died in April, 1874. At the sale of Mr. Leathart's collection on June 19, 1897, a small picture of his entitled *An effect of Mist on the Mersey*, was sold for fifty guineas. He and Inchbold were a second time companions in misfortune. In May, 1865, Madox Brown wrote :— " By the *Daily Telegraph* this morning it would appear that Davis as well as Inchbold has been rejected *in toto*."

On *Orlando*, one of the two pictures kicked out of the Academy, Mr. Arthur Hughes had worked for some time in Rossetti's studio. He had long been painting scenes from *As You Like It*. This *Orlando*, he tells me, was done before he had attained sufficient mastery. How well he succeeded in the end is seen in the beautiful triptych illustrating scenes from Shakespeare's play, in Mr. Sing's collection in Aigburth, Liverpool. The "child in a flannel nightgown" was his nephew, Edward Hughes, now well known as an artist.

The "new man named Leighton" was Lord Leighton, the late President of the Royal Academy. His picture was entitled *Cimabue's Madonna carried in Procession through the Streets of Florence*. Twenty-seven years later, at the Academy banquet, speaking of two artists lately dead, after mentioning one, he continued :—"The other was a strangely interesting man, who, living in almost jealous seclusion as far as the general world was concerned, wielded, nevertheless, at one period of his life, a considerable influence in the world of art and poetry,—Dante Gabriel Rossetti, painter and poet."

Haworth Churchyard, in *Fraser's Magazine*, "signed 'A,'" was not by Allingham, but by Matthew Arnold, who wrote to his mother on April 25th of this year :—"There will be some lines of mine in the next *Fraser* (without name) on poor Charlotte Brontë." The stanza which contains "some *thorough* appreciation of poor *Wuthering Heights*, but raves of Byron," is the following :—

> "Round thee they lie—the grass
> Blows from their graves to thy own !
> She, whose genius, though not
> Puissant like thine, was yet
> Sweet and graceful ;—and she
> (How shall I sing her ?) whose soul
> Knew no fellow for might,
> Passion, vehemence, grief,
> Daring, since Byron died,

"That world-famed son of fire,—she, who sank
Baffled, unknown, self-consumed ;
Whose too bold dying song
Stirr'd, like a clarion-blast, my soul."

In his boyhood Rossetti had delighted in Byron. When he was sixteen years old, "some one told him," writes Mr. W. M. Rossetti, "that there was another poet of the Byronic epoch, Shelley, even greater than Byron. I do not think that he ever afterwards read much of Byron."

Rossetti's *Annunciation* was his *Ecce Ancilla Domini*; the "water-colour Dante" was *Dante drawing an Angel in Memory of Beatrice*. Of this picture Mr. W. M. Rossetti gives the following explanation :—

"Dante relates that, on the first anniversary of his lady's death, he was engaged in drawing an angel, in memory of her, when he found that certain persons had entered his chamber unperceived; and he then saluted them saying, 'Another was with me.'" On May 11, 1854, Rossetti wrote to his brother :—"I heard from MacCrac, who offers £50 for the water-colour, with all manner of soap and sawder into the bargain,—a princely style of thing." On this Mr. W. M. Rossetti remarks :—"That my' brother should have regarded £50 for the water-colour as 'a princely style of thing' shows how scanty was then the market for his productions."

"Combe of Oxford" was the printer to the Clarendon Press. He made a collection of Præraphaelite paintings; among them was Holman

Hunt's *Light of the World*, which his widow gave
to Keble College, Oxford, and this water-colour
of Rossetti's, which, with other pictures, she be-
queathed to the University Gallery.

"Charles Alston Collins," a brother of Wilkie
Collins, "was a young painter much under Millais's
influence, and though not a member of the ' Brotherhood,' practically a Præraphaelite."   He died early.
Why he and one or two others were never chosen
into the Brotherhood is shown in the following
quotation from Mr. Holman Hunt's article in the
Contemporary Review for May, 1886 :—" Outside
of the enrolled body [the P.R.B.] were several
artists of real calibre and enthusiasm, who were
working diligently with our views guiding them.
W. H. Deverell, Charles Collins, and Arthur
Hughes may be named.   It was a question whether
any of these should be elected.   It was already
evident that to have authority to put the mystic
monogram upon their paintings could confer no
benefit on men striving to make a position.   We
ourselves even determined for a time to discontinue
the floating of this red rag before the eyes of
infuriate John Bull, and we decided it was better
to let our converts be known only by their works,
and so nominally Præraphaelitism ceased to be.   We
agreed to resume the open profession of it later,
but the time has not yet come.   I often read in
print that I am now the only Præraphaelite.   Yet
I can't use the distinguishing letters, for I have
no ' B.' "

I have heard Mrs. Combe relate a story, told also by Mr. Holman Hunt in this same paper, how Millais and Collins, when very young men, once lodged in a cottage nearly opposite the entrance of Lord Abingdon's park close to Oxford. She learnt from them that they got but poor fare, so soon afterwards she drove over in her carriage, and left for them a large meat-pie. Millais, she added, one day said to Mr. Combe :—" People had better buy my pictures now, when I am working for fame, than a few years later, when I shall be married and working for a wife and children." It was in these later years that old Linnell exclaimed to him :—" Ah, Mr. Millais, you have left your first love ; you have left your first love."

"The Bernal humbug" was the sale for nearly £71,000 of Ralph Bernal's collection of glass, plate, china, and miniatures.

Of James Collinson the following account is given by Mr. Holman Hunt in the *Contemporary Review*:—" He had been a meek fellow student ; painstaking he was in all his drawings, and accurate in a sense, but tame and sleepy, and so were all the figures he drew. . . . It was a surprise to all when, in the year 1848, he appeared in the Exhibition with a picture called *The Charity Boy's Début*. . . . It transpired that he had roused himself up of late to enter the Roman Church, and that thus inspirited he had made the further effort to paint this picture. It was natural for all the students to blame them-selves for having ignored Collinson, but Rossetti

went further, and declared that 'Collinson was a
born stunner,' and at once struck up an intimate
friendship with him. When the Præraphaelite
Brotherhood was inaugurated he at once enrolled
Collinson as one who wanted only the enthusiasm
which we had to make him a great force in the
battle. . . . At our monthly meetings he invariably
fell asleep at the beginning, and had to be waked
up at the conclusion of the noisy evening to receive
our salutations. He never could see the fun of
anything, and I fear we did not make his life more
joyful. . . . Even in the day he was asleep over
the fire, with his model waiting idle, earning his
shilling per hour all the time. But at the last
moment he unexpectedly waked up, sent in his
resignation as a Præraphaelite Brother—ungrateful
man!—sold his lay figure and painting material by
forced sale, and departed to Stonyhurst to graduate.
At the end of a twelvemonth or so he abandoned
the idea of conventual or priestly life, again took
to painting, and, I believe, executed many very
creditable pictures of a modest character."

According to W. B. Scott, "at the seminary they
set Collinson to clean the boots as an apprenticeship
in humility and obedience. They did not want him
as a priest; they were already getting tired of that
species of convert, so he left, turned to painting
again, and disappeared."

Allingham's bust was by Munro. The lines in
The Academy Catalogue on that sculptor's *Lover's
Walk* are from Allingham's *Wayside Well* :—

> " Sweet shall fall the whisper'd tale,
> Soft the double shadow."

Mr. Hughes tells me that " the Patriotic Fund Exhibition was a collection of drawings and paintings chiefly by amateurs, got up for exhibition and sale for the benefit of the widows and orphans of the soldiers who fell in the Crimean War. I gave a little painting of a soldier returned minus an arm to his wife and baby, both of whom he managed to embrace, I remember, somehow with the remaining one. I quoted for it from *Spring is Come*:—

> ' Some voices answer not thy call
> When sky and woodland ring,
> Some voices come not back at all
> With primrose blossoming.' "

Patrick Macdowell was an Irish sculptor—a member of the Royal Academy.

" Rossetti was born on May 12, 1828, at No. 38, Charlotte Street, Portland Place, London, and was baptized at All Souls' Church, Langham Place, as a member of the Church of England."

To sit up till three in the morning was no uncommon thing with Rossetti. One of his comrades in his student days describes how " his cheeks were roseless and hollow enough to indicate the waste of life and midnight oil to which the youth was addicted."

XXI.

CLEVEDON, SOMERSETSHIRE,

June 25, 1855.

DEAR ALLINGHAM,

I'm thanking you here for your book received in London a week or so ago, and don't exactly know whether you are at New Ross or Ballyshannon now, and have a suspicion you'll soon be visible (and heartily welcome) in London, *whither I return to-day*, after a day or two only here ; and write now, having got up at 6 in the morning, and being too early to go to breakfast with Miss Siddal, whom I came to see here. She is rather better just now, and will probably go to winter somewhere abroad. Your volume has accompanied her and me on excursions, and been read at home too.

I have such a strong idea that I am to see you soon that I sha'n't enter so much into the poems as I otherwise should now, but my favourites among the new ones are the 2 *Harps, The Pilot's Daughter, St. Margaret's Eve, The Girl's Lamentation, The Sailor* (both these last most admirable), and *Would I Knew. The Nobleman's Wedding* I really don't think at all improved [Ah ! it is ! W. A.], and am not at all sure about the close of *The Pilot's Daughter. The Music Master* is full of beauty and nobility, but I'm not sure it is not TOO noble or too resolutely healthy.

ROSSETTI SITTING TO MISS SIDDAL.

(*By Dante Gabriel Rossetti.*)

[To face page 136.

LONDON, *July* 4.

I had to break off in the above, and go on with
it to-day, instead of beginning afresh, to prove that
I was not waiting for you to write, as I remembered well owing you two or three, though one of
mine had been lost for some time. Yours was very
welcome on Monday. Going on about *The Music
Master*, I see the sentence already written looks
very iniquitous, and perhaps is ; but one can only
speak of one's own needs and cravings : and I must
confess to a need, in narrative dramatic poetry
(unless so simple in structure as *Auld Robin Gray*.
for instance), of something rather " exciting," and
indeed I believe something of the " romantic " [1]
element, to rouse my mind to anything like the
moods produced by personal emotion in my own
life. That sentence is shockingly ill worded, but
Keats's narratives would be of the kind I mean.
Not that I would place the expressions of pure
love and life, or of any calm, gradual feeling or
experience, one step below their place,—the very
highest ; but I think them better conveyed at less
length, and chiefly as *from oneself*. Were I speaking to any one else, I might instance (as indeed I
often do) the best of your own lyrics as examples ;
and these will always have for me much more

---

[1] In the original *schoolgirl*, which preceded *romantic*, has been
scored out.

attraction than *The Music Master*. The latter, I think, by its calm subject and course during a longish reading, chiefly awakens contemplation, like a walk on a fine day with a churchyard in it, instead of rousing one like a part of one's own life, and leaving one to walk it off as one might live it off. The only part where I remember being much affected was at the old woman's narrative of Milly's gradual decline. Of course the poem has artistic beauties constantly, though I think it flags a little at some of its joints, and am not sure that its turning-point would not have turned in vain for me at first reading, if I had not in time remembered your account of the story one day on a walk. After all, I fancy its chief want is that it should accompany a few more stories of deeper incident and passion from the same hand, when what seem to me its shortcomings might, I believe, as a leavening of the mass, become *des qualités*. As I have stated them, too, they are merely matters of feeling, and those who felt differently (as Patmore, who thinks the poems perfect) might probably be at the higher point of view. P. was here last night with Cayley and one or two more. We sat all the evening on my balcony, and had ice and strawberries there, and I wished for you many times, and meanwhile put in your book as a substitute (having, you may be sure, torn out that thing of Dalziel's).

I have propagated you a little—among other cases, to a man named Dallas the other day, who has just come to settle in London, having written a book called *Poetics*, and being a great chum of A. Smith—*i.e.*, *the* Smith—and Dobell. After reading him much of you I enunciated opinions of a decisive kind as to the relative positions of our rising geniuses, and was rather sorry for argument's sake to find him not unsympathising.

I'm glad you've heard from Ruskin, and hope that you may find time in your week to arrange somehow a meeting with him. He has been into the country, and unwell part of the time, but is now set up again and very hard at work. I have no more valued friend than he, and shall have much to say of him. Of other friends, you'll find Woolner (27, Rutland St., Hampstead Road, his *house;* 64, Margaret St., Cavendish Sq., his *study*). Patmore, and Hannay get-at-able, besides Munro and Hughes, with whom you've been *en rapport*. *My rapports* you ask of with that "stunner" stopped some months ago, after a long stay away from Chatham Place, partly from a wish to narrow the circle of flirtations, in which she had begun to figure a little ; but I often find myself sighing after her, now that "roast beef, roast mutton, gooseberry tart," have faded into the light of common day. "O what is gone from them I fancied theirs?"

Have you seen *Eustace Conyers?* It is admirable in all Hannay's qualities, and a decided advance on *Fontenoy*. I congratulate you on your change of place, and myself on the prospect of your going farther, *i.e.*, London, so soon for a while, and I trust not faring worse. Mind, I have nothing to show worth showing. Ruskin has been reading those translations since you, and says he could wish no better than to ink your pencil-marks as his criticisms. He sent here, the other day, a stunner, called the Marchioness of Waterford, who had expressed a wish to see me paint in water-colours, it seems, she herself being really first-rate as a designer in that medium. I think I am going to call on her this afternoon. There, sir! R. has asked to be introduced to my sister, who accordingly, will accompany Miss S. and myself to dinner there on Friday.

That building you saw at Dublin is the one. I must have met Woodward, the architect of it, at Oxford (where he is doing the new museum), and talked of you to him, just at the time you were in Dublin, as I heard immediately after, and therefore did not send on to you his full directions how you should find him (or his partner, if he were away) and see all his doings there, which, however, can come off another time. He is a particularly nice fellow, and very desirous to meet you. Miss S. made several lovely designs for him, but Ruskin thought them too good for his workmen at Dublin to carve. One, however, was done (how I know not), and is there ; it represents an angel with some children and all manner of other things, and is, I believe, close to a design by Millais of mice eating corn. Perhaps though they were carved after your visit.

I haven't seen Owen Meredith, and don't feel the least curiosity about him. There is an interestingish article on the three " Bells " in *Tait* this month, where *Wuthering Heights* is placed above *Currer* for dramatic individuality, and it seems C. B. herself quite thought so.

I'll say no more, as I hope so soon to see you, but am ever your affectionate friend,

D. G. R.

Notes on XXI.

Rossetti had been at Clevedon with Miss Siddal, who had gone there for the sake of her health. Writing to his mother he said :—" The junction of the Severn with the Bristol Channel is there, so that the water is hardly brackish, but looks like sea, and you can see across to Wales, only eight miles ·off, I think. Arthur Hallam, on whom Tennyson wrote *In Memoriam*, is buried at Clevedon, and we visited his grave."

> "There twice a day the Severn fills ;
>   The salt sea-water passes by,
>   And hushes half the babbling Wye,
>   And makes a silence in the hills."

The poems mentioned by Rossetti are in *Day and Night Songs.* " Throughout his life," writes his brother, " the poetry of sentimental or reflective description had a very minor attraction for him." To Mr. Edmund Gosse Rossetti wrote in 1873 :— " It seems to me that all poetry, to be really enduring, is bound to be as *amusing* (however trivial the word may sound) as any other class of literature ; and I do not think that enough amusement to keep it alive can ever be got out of incidents not amounting to events." Rossetti here uses *amusing* much as Johnson used it when he wrote that "*Coriolanus* is one of the most amusing of our author's performances."

From his balcony Rossetti had a fine outlook on the Thames. The house was swept away when the river was embanked. It stood in front of the site now occupied by the eastern end of Keyser's Royal Hotel, so near to Blackfriars Bridge that a stone could have been pitched on to it from the balcony. One of the rooms facing southwards was very sunny. At the window he would loll sometimes for hours together, looking at the people passing over the bridge. To watch this living stream flow by had an endless fascination for him. He used to tell the story that, one day, he and another of the Brotherhood were thus lolling, when they both cried out,

" Why, there goes Deverell ! " At that hour Deverell died.

Eneas Sweetland Dallas published *Poetics, an Essay on Poetry*, in 1852. Mr. G. C. Boase in his article on him in the *Dictionary of National Biography*, says that for many years he was on the brilliant staff of John T. Delane, the editor of the *Times*. In 1868 he edited *Once a Week*. He died in 1879. " He had a singularly handsome presence and charming manners—his conversation was bright and courteous."

Of Alexander Smith there is further mention in Letter XXXII. Of Sidney Dobell's *Keith of Ravelston* Rossetti wrote in 1868 :—" I have always regarded that poem as being one of the finest, of its length, in any modern poet. What a pity it is that he generally insists on being so long-winded, when he can write like that ! "

The friendship between Rossetti and Ruskin did not last. " Gradually," writes Mr. W. M. Rossetti, " the intimacy between the two friends relaxed. Rossetti, as he advanced in years, in reputation, and in art, became less and less disposed to conform his work to the likings of any Mentor—even of one for whom he had so genuine an esteem as he entertained for Mr. Ruskin ; while the latter, serenely conscious of being always in the right, laid down the law, and pronounced judgment tempered by mercy, with undeviating exactness. At last the relations between the painter and critic became strained—one was so earnest to enlighten the other, and the other was so difficult to be enlightened out of his own perceptions and predilections ; and it may have been in 1865 or 1866 that Ruskin and Rossetti saw the last of one another—mutually regretful, and perhaps mutually relieved, that it should be the last."

" That ' stunner ' " was clearly the " Belle *pas Sauvage* " of Letters VII. and IX. In my undergraduate days at Oxford when not unfrequently I was in Rossetti's company, I one day heard him maintain that a beautiful young woman, who was on her trial on a charge of murdering her lover, ought not to be hanged, even if found guilty, as she was " such a stunner." When I ventured to assert that I would have her hanged, beautiful or ugly, there was a general outcry of the artistic set. One of them, now famous as a painter, cried out, " Oh, Hill, you would never hang a stunner ! "

" O what is gone from them I fancied theirs ? " is borrowed with a slight change from the last line of *Æolian Harp* in the second series of Allingham's *Day and Night Songs.*

" Gift books have rather poured in on me lately," wrote Rossetti to his mother a few days after the date of this letter ; " Hannay's new novel, *Eustace Conyers*, very first-rate in Hannay's qualities, and a decided advance on *Fontenoy.*"

A little earlier he had written to her :—" An astounding event is to come off to-morrow. The Marchioness of Waterford has expressed a wish to Ruskin to see me paint in water-colour, as she says

my method is inscrutable to her.   She is herself an
excellent artist, and would have been really great, I
believe, if not born such a swell and such a stunner."

Mr. Holman Hunt gives the following account of
a visit he received from her :—" With *The Light of
the World* standing nearly complete upon the easel,
I was surprised one morning by the sound of
carriage wheels driven up to the side door, a very
loud knocking, and the names of Lady Canning and
the Countess of Waterford preluding the ascent of
the ladies.   I think they said that Mr. Ruskin had
assured them that they might call to see the picture.
My room, with windows free, overlooking the river,
was as cheerful as any to be found in London ; but
I had not made any effort to remove traces of the
pinching suffered till the previous month or so, and
to find chairs with perfect seats to them was not
easy.   But the beautiful sisters were supremely
superior to giving trace of any surprise.   It might
have seemed that they had always lived with broken
furniture by preference."   An account of the sisters
has been lately written by Mr. Augustus J. C. Hare
under the title of *The Story of Two Noble Lives*.
There is no mention of these visits to the two
painters.

On Benjamin Woodward's death in 1861 Rossetti
wrote of him to Alexander Gilchrist :—" He built
the new Crown Insurance Office in New Bridge
Street, Blackfriars, close to my studio.   It seems to
me the most perfect piece of civil architecture of the
new school that I have seen in London.   I never

cease to look at it with delight. I must have been the last friend who saw him in England. . . . I am sitting now in the place, and I think in the chair he sat in, to write this. If I am ever found worthy to meet him again, it will be where the dejection is unneeded which I cannot but feel at this moment.; for the power of further and better work must be the reward bestowed on the deserts and checked aspirations of such a sincere soul as his."

Allingham wrote to Mr. W. M. Rossetti on May 28, 1855 :—" Yesterday in Dublin I saw but hastily the part-finished building in Trinity College, with numberless capitals delicately carved over with holly leaves, shamrocks, various flowers, birds, and so on. Ruskin has written to the architect, a young man, expressing his high approval of the plans ; so by and by all your *cognoscenti* will be rushing over to examine the Stones of Dublin."

My friend, Professor Dowden, tells me that he has looked in vain for the mice eating corn. Sir Thomas Deane, the son of Woodward's partner, is sure that neither Millais's nor Miss Siddal's design was used.

The second Lord Lytton, under the name of Owen Meredith, published this year *Clytemnestra, The Earl's Return and Other Poems.*

XXII.

Tuesday 17 [*July*, 1855].

Dear Allingham,

I think the enclosed is from Miss Bessie Parkes, and I have from the same lady a copy of her poems sent here for you. *Are* you coming up after all, or will the narrow gaugers clip your wings? I've been expecting and wishing much for you.

Scott has been in town and leaves to-morrow. I write this note in great haste. Am I to send the book on?

Your affectionate,

D. G. R.

Note on XXII.

" The narrow gaugers "—though perhaps it is hardly necessary to explain the pun—were Allingham's superior officers in the Customs, who were, Rossetti implies, ungenerous in their treatment of him. There is a reference of course to the narrow-gauge railways.

XXIII.

Chatham Place.

Saturday [*July,* 1855].

Dear Allingham,

Come here by all means. Bed, too, if you like.

If you have time and inclination while in Dublin to call on Woodward, his address is 3, Upper Merrion Street. If he were away, he told me his partner Sir Thos. Deane, or their managing man, whose name I forget, would with pleasure show you their works in hand.

All here will be glad to see you, and I not the least.

Your D. G. R.

Should I by any chance be out when you come here, feel for key of *centre door* under *right* hand door mat. In key's absence call at top of kitchen stairs for housekeeper, *Mrs. Burrell.*

Excuse dirty paper—only bit I could find.

XXIV.

Sunday [*July*, 1855].

DEAR ALLINGHAM,

How beastly of them Customs' 'ogs! I and every one had been on the look out for you. I wish I could come to the lakes with you, but it's quite out of the question just now, though nothing would delight me more. I think it seems possible I may be going on the Continent this autumn. Miss S. is going—to Florence possibly, and a lady, a cousin of mine, is to be with her most likely, so this might render my joining the party possible. She will in any case settle abroad for some time, in a climate less changeable than this—France or Italy. The wizard in the case being of course J. R. [John Ruskin] who you know is to have all she does for some time.

Thus, till this move is settled or quashed, *i.e.*, my part in it, I must bide at my work, such as it is. I don't find what I'm about at all amusing, and should have been peculiarly solaced by a sight of you—but it wasn't to be. Let's go on writing to each other instead at any rate.

Your affectionate D. G. R.

NOTE ON XXIV.

Dr. (now Sir Henry) Acland, who had been

consulted about Miss Siddal's health, " opined,"
writes Mr. W. M. Rossetti, " that her lungs were
nearly right, the chief danger consisting in ' mental
power long pent up, and lately overtaxed.' He
advised her to leave England before cold weather
set in ; and this she did towards the latter end of
September, having as companion a Mrs. Kincaird,
a cousin of ours, who knew something of French
and continental life."

* * *

XXV.

Sunday night,
29th [post-mark July, 1855].

DEAR ALLINGHAM,

"I had this pleasure" (Mac Crackice)
this morning, and this evening Seddon is wanting
to send a picture to Liverpool Exhibition, and
doesn't know how, and I undertook to communicate
for him with Mr. Oakes, who is, I believe, Sec.
to the L. Ex.   But I don't know Mr. O.'s address
(Allingham—"Well, do I ?") No ; but Mr. Miller
could no doubt put you in the way of it, and you
could put it on the envelope and seal and post
same in some Liverpool letter-box, or deliver, if so
inclined.

If Mr. Oakes should by chance be no longer in

the above capacity, would you (if you can without any awkwardness) ask Mr. Miller himself to read the letter (apologising for the liberty I should be taking), as I feel confident he could expedite Seddon's affair equally well.

If you *would* find this at all awkward, let me know at once of Mr. O.'s unavailability, and I'd write at once to Mr. M. Please do as much of all this as proves necessary and excuse trouble. . . .

I'm very sleepy. Good-night.

Your D. G. R.

Would you oblige me with a *prompt* word in answer.

Notes on XXV.

Of Mr. John Miller of Liverpool Madox Brown wrote on September 25, 1856:—" This Miller is a jolly, kind old man, with streaming white hair, fine features, and a beautiful keen eye like Mulready's; a rich brogue [he was Scotch not Irish] a pipe of Cavendish, and a smart rejoinder, with a pleasant word for every man, woman, and child he meets, are characteristics of him. His house is full of pictures, even to the kitchen. Many pictures he has at all his friends' houses, and his house at Bute is also filled with his inferior ones. His hospitality is somewhat peculiar of its kind. His dinner, which is at six, is of one joint and vegetables, *without* pudding—bottled beer for drink

—I never saw any wine. After dinner he instantly hurries you off to tea, and then back again to smoke. He calls it a meat tea, and boasts that few people who have ever dined with him come back again."

Mr. W. M. Rossetti describes him as " one of the most cordial, large-hearted and lovable men I ever knew." He was so strong in belief as to be a sceptic as regards the absence of belief. I once heard him say, in his strong Scotch accent, " An atheist, if such an animal ever really existed." What the suppositious animal would do I forget.

XXVI.

Friday [*August*, 1855].

DEAR ALLINGHAM,

I'm sending you on two letters to Mr. Miller's at I[sle] of Bute, as you told us, thinking you'll have left Edinb[urgh] by now. I'd have sent them on before this to Liverpool, but thought letters wouldn't reach you if you had left L., and had given up the idea of your getting mine for Mr. Oakes. As it is, pray thank Mr. Miller much from Seddon and self for the trouble we're putting him to. I'm sure he'd agree with me as to the advantage of securing S's picture for the L. Exhibition.

But now—further—I have a long parcel for Miss C. Allingham to W. A. Esq., care of D. G. R., dated July 30, and brought by carrier :—further—I have B. R. Parkes' volume for you ;—further—a Mr. Delap (I think) called for you, and I told him I'd tell you. Furthest—What am I to do with the two parcels?

Miss S. is here, and thanks you very much for your book with which she's delighted.

In haste,

Yours affect.

D. G. R.

NOTE ON XXVI.

The book for which Miss Siddal thanked Allingham was his *Day and Night Songs*.

XXVII.

Tuesday [*August*, 1855].

DEAR ALLINGHAM,

I've just got your note and sent on the long parcel, with Miss Bessie's book, to Chancery Lane.

I'm surprised you didn't know of Millais' marriage, as it was in the papers—the *Leader* had slipped it in somehow among the *Deaths!* He is going to live for a year at or near Perth, and wrote to some one the other day that he was "perfectly aghast at his own happiness."

That's a stupid enough notice of *The Music Master*, &c., in the *Athenæum*, in all conscience. I wonder who did it—some fearful ass evidently, from the way he speaks of Millais as well as of you. I saw some notes for a notice by William the other day, which of course is to be the Koh-i-noor of the lot. W. has just returned from a trip (walking chiefly), to Stratford-on-Avon, Kenil-worth, &c., which I made and revelled in two years back. He is going on immediately to Paris.

. . . Did I offer you the loan of Hannay's novel? It is engaged to one person yet, after which I'll send it if you like.

Write soon and so will I. This is written in a hurry, with a water-colour (which I hate) waiting for me.

Yours affectionately,

D. G. R.

I re-open the letter to enclose a little excite-ment which please return.

Notes on XXVII.

The following is the notice of Millais's marriage in the *Leader* of July 7, 1855 :—

" Deaths.

" Millais—Gray.   June 3, at Bowerswell, John
Everett Millais, Esq., A. R. A., to Euphemia
Chalmers, eldest daughter of George Gray, Esq.,
writer, Perth."

The "fearful ass" in the *Athenæum* of August
18, 1855, thus wrote of Millais :—"*The Fireside
Story* by the last-named gentleman, is a proof
that he can be in earnest without being absurd,
and reproduce nature without administering on
the occasion a dose of ugliness as a tonic."

XXVIII.

Sunday, 25 Nov., '55.

DEAR ALLINGHAM,

I'm quite ashamed of the long delay in
answering your letter—especially when I remember (as such things generally happen) that on
receiving it I sat down to answer on the spot,
and was only compelled by some accident to
postpone it—of course no further than the same
evening.   I believe that must be a good month
ago.

I have not 'the letter by me in beginning this
answer, but remember it opened with a question
about Routledge.   At that time I could only
have given a very bad answer on this head :

as some time after the publication of your vol. I had (hearing nothing from R. & Co.) sent in my "small account," but with no result up to the time of hearing from you, which was ever so long an interval; I having, on their showing no signs of life, let the matter go its way. Some short time ago, however, Hughes hearing this, in a fit of virtuous and friendly indignation, gave them a look up about it, and they have now paid me at the same rate as him, with which I am perfectly well satisfied. I know no further about Millais, and am very sorry you should have been worried about it all.

I have just come back from a ten day's trip to Paris, in pursuit of various things and persons. The Brownings are there for the winter, on account of the cholera at Florence, and had previously been some time in London, where I saw them a good many times, and indeed may boast of some intimacy with the glorious Robert by this time. What a magnificent series is *Men and Women.* Of course you have it half by heart ere this. The comparative stagnation, *even among those I see,* and complete torpor elsewhere, which greet this my Elixir of Life, are awful signs of the times to me—"and I must hold my peace!"—for it isn't fair to Browning (besides, indeed, being too much trouble) to bicker and flicker about it. I fancy we shall agree pretty well on *favourites*, though one's mind has no right to be quite made up so soon on such a subject. For my own part, I don't reckon I've read them at all yet, as I only got them the day before leaving town, and couldn't possibly read them then,—the best proof to you how hard at work I was for once,—so heard them read by William; since then read them on the journey again, and some a third time at intervals; but they'll bear lots of squeezing yet. My prime favourites hitherto (without the book by me) are *Childe Roland, B*[r.] *Blougram, Karshish, the Contemporary* [*How it Strikes a Contemporary*], *Lippo Lippi, Cleon,* and *Popularity;* about the other lyrical ones I can't quite speak yet, and their names don't stick in my head: but I'm afraid *The Heretic's Tragedy* rather gave me the gripes at first, though I've tried since to think it didn't, on finding the *Athenæum* similarly affected.

8 Jan., 1856.

A month and a half actually, dear A., since the last sheet, already long behindhand, yet which has lain in my drawer ever since, till it is too late now to wish you merry Christmas, too late to wish you happy New Year, only not too late to feel just the same towards you as if I were the best correspondent in the world, and to know you feel the same towards me. I am sure, too, you believe that, little as I do to deserve and obtain frequent letters from you, your letters are as great a pleasure to me as any I get,—*greater*, I think, than any, except certain ones which you'll be glad to hear come now dated *Nice*, their writer having left England three months ago, and benefiting already, I trust, by the genial climate she is now enjoying, which, while that bitter cold weather was ailing us here, remained as warm as the best English May.

Many thanks indeed for your new year's gift,— a most delightful one. Old Blake is quite as loveable by his oddities as by his genius, and the drawings to the Ballads abound with both. The two nearly faultless are the *Eagle* and the *Hermit's Dog*. Ruskin's favourite (who has just been looking at it) is the *Horse ;* but I can't myself quite get over the intensity of comic decorum in the brute's face. He seems absolutely snuffling with propriety. The *Lion* seems singing a comic song with a pen behind his ear, but the glimpse of distant landscape below is lovely. The only drawing where the comic element riots almost unrebuked is the one of the dog jumping down the crocodile.

As regards engraving, these drawings, with the *Job*, present the only good medium between etching and formal *line* that I ever met with. I see that in coming to me the book returns home ; having set out from No. 6 Bridge St., Blackfriars, just 50 years ago. Strange to think of it as then, new literature and art. Those ballads of Hayley—some of the quaintest human bosh in the world—picked their way, no doubt, in highly respectable quarters, where poor Blake's unadorned hero at Page 1 was probably often stared at, and sometimes torn out.

I broke off at the last sheet in mid-Browning. Of course I've been drenching myself with him at intervals since, only he gets carried off by friends, and I have him not always by me. I wish you'd let me hear in a *speedy* answer (there's cheek for you !) all you think about his new work, and it shall nerve me to express my ideas in return ; but since I have given up poetry as a pursuit of my own, I really find my thoughts on the subject generally require a starting-point from somebody else to bring them into activity ; and as you're the only man I know who'd be really in my mood of re-ceptiveness in regard to Browning, and as I can't get at you, I've been bottled up ever since *M. and W.* came out. By the bye, I don't reckon William —the intensity of fellow-feeling on the subject making the discussion of it between us rather flat. I went the other day to a 1d. reading-room,—a real blessing—which now occupies the place of Burford's Panorama, and where all papers and reviews whatsoever are taken in. There I saw two articles on Browning — one by Masson — really thoroughly appreciative, but *slow*—in the *British Quarterly*— and one by a certain Brimley, of Trin. Col., Cam., in *Fraser*,—the cheekiest of human products. This man, less than two years ago, had not read a line of Browning, as I know through my brother; and I have no doubt he has just read him up to write this article ; which opens, nevertheless, with accusations against R. B. of nothing less than personal selfishness and vanity, so plumply put as to be justifiable by nothing less than personal intimacy of many years. When I went to Paris, I took my copy of *Men and Women* (which had been sent me the day before) with me, and got B. to write my name in it. Did you get a copy? We spoke often of you,—he with great personal and poetical regard —I of course with loathing. I inclose herewith a note which reached me before the book, containing emendations. Copy them, if you please, and return the note. I spent some most delightful time with Browning at Paris, both in the evenings and at the Louvre, where (and throughout conversation) I found his knowledge of early Italian art beyond that of any one I ever met,—*encyclopædically* beyond that of Ruskin himself. What a jolly thing is *Old Pictures at Florence !* It seems all the pictures *desired* by the poet are in his possession

PIPPA PASSES.

(*By Miss Siddal.*)

[*To face page* 161

in fact. At Paris I met his father, and in London an uncle of his and his sister, who, it appears, performed the singular female feat of copying *Sordello* for him, to which some of its eccentricities may possibly be referred. However, she remembers it all, and even *Squarcialupe, Zin the Horrid,* and the *sad dishevelled ghost.* But no doubt you know her. The father and uncle—father especially—show just that submissive yet highly cheerful and capable simplicity of character which often, I think, appears in the family of a great man who uses at last what the others have kept for him. The father is a complete oddity—with a real genius for drawing—but caring for nothing in the least except Dutch boors,—fancy the father of Browning! —and as innocent as a child. In the New Volumes, the only thing he seemed to care for much was that about the Sermon to the Jews.

At B.'s house at Paris I met a miraculous French critic named Milsand, who actually before ever meeting Browning knew his works to the very dregs—and had even been years in search of *Pauline,*—how heard of I know not,—and wrote a famous article on him in the *Revue des Deux Mondes,* through which B. somehow came to know him. I hear he has translated some of the *Men and Women,* which must be curiosities. In London I showed Browning Miss Siddal's drawing from

Pippa Passes, with which he was delighted beyond measure, and wanted excessively to know her. However, though afterwards she was in Paris at the same time that he and I were, he only met her once for a few minutes : she being very unwell then and averse to going anywhere ; and Mrs. B. being forbidden to go out, and so unable to call. What a delightfully unliterary person Mrs. B. is to meet! During two evenings when Tennyson was at their house in London, Mrs. Browning left T. with her husband and William and me (who were the fortunate remnant of the male party) to discuss the universe, and gave all her attention to some certainly not very exciting ladies in the next room. . . . I made a sketch of Tennyson reading, which I gave to Browning, and afterwards duplicated it for Miss S. . . . He is quite as glorious in his way as Browning, and perhaps of the 2 even more impressive on the whole personally. . . .

Have you reviewed Browning anywhere, or shall you? Hannay has my copy for a similar purpose, but I see no fruit coming of it. In B.'s note enclosed, the portrait referred to is one of himself by Page, an American living at Rome, which he has confided to my care with some idea of its going to the R.A. After much delay I have only just got hold of it, and am much disappointed in it, so shall advise its non-exhibition, as a portrait of Browning oughtn't to be put out of sight or kicked out. I have done one in water-colours myself, which hangs now over my mantelpiece, and which every one says is very like. Next time I have the chance I shall paint him in oil, and probably Mrs. B. too, with him. Ruskin, on reading *Men and Women* (and with it some of the other works which he didn't know before), declared them rebelliously to be a mass of conundrums, and compelled me to sit down before him and lay siege for one whole night; the result of which was that he sent me next morning a bulky letter to be forwarded to B., in which I trust he told him he was the greatest man since Shakespeare.

Of other friends there is little news I think. Hughes is painting *Porphyrio and Madeline* in 3 compartments. Hunt is (I believe with better grounds than hitherto) expected back almost daily. Woolner has made some lovely sketches in clay. Patmore has just lost his father, and is on the eve of bringing out the *Espousals*. Ruskin's new volume will be in my hands I believe, on Tuesday. WHAT ARE YOU AT? I have just seen a capital sonnet of yours,—a star shot as rubbish into a dust-bin labelled the *Idler*. I've done lots of work lately (*i.e., for me*), but all in water-colours, and nearly all for Ruskin. Among the later of my drawings finished are *Francesca da Rimini* in 3 compartments ; *Dante cut by Beatrice at a marriage feast ; Lancelot and Guenever parting at tomb of Arthur :* at finishing of each of which, and of various others I have done, I have very much wished you were by to show them to. I'm sorry to say my modern picture remains untouched since last Xmas ; but this has really not been through idleness, as I have done more during the past year than for a long while previously, and I think I can myself perceive an advance in my later work. *Pray, again, what are you up to ?*

I've left no space for the French Exhibition, to which indeed I devoted only one of the 10 days I spent in Paris,—my head not being a teetotum nor my mind an old-clothes shop. Delacroix is one of the mighty ones of the earth, and Ingres misses being so creditably. There is a German, Knaus, who is perfection in a way something between Hogarth and Wilkie; Millais and Hunt are marvels and omens. Water-colour Hunt and Lewis are the only things in their department. The rest is silence ; or must be so for the present.

What do you think of Browning being able to read *The Mystake ?* Could you?

Yours affectionately,

D. G. ROSSETTI.

NOTES ON XXVIII.

Of this trip to Paris Munro wrote to W. B.

Scott :—" I have been to Paris to see the great exhibition with D. G. R. We enjoyed Paris immensely; in different ways, of course, for Rossetti was every day with his sweetheart, of whom he is more foolishly fond than I ever saw lover."

Mr. W. M. Rossetti, tracing his brother's early favourites among the poets, says :—" At last—it may have been 1847 [when he was nineteen years old]—everything took a secondary place in comparison with Robert Browning. *Paracelsus, Sordello, Pippa Passes, The Blot in the 'Scutcheon*, and the short poems in the *Bells and Pomegranates* series were endless delights; endless were the readings, and endless the recitations."

The letter from Nice was from Miss Siddal, who was spending the winter there in the vain hope of winning back health.

The book that " returns home; having set out from No. 6, Bridge Street, Blackfriars, just fifty years ago," was *Ballads by William Hayley, founded on anecdotes relating to animals, with prints, designed and engraved by William Blake.* Chichester, printed by J. Seagrave for Richard Phillips, Bridge Street, Blackfriars, London, 1805. On May 16, 1802, Hayley wrote of Blake :—" He is at this moment by my side, representing on copper an Adam of his own, surrounded by animals,—a frontispiece to the projected ballads." Gibbon wrote of Hayley on July 3, 1782 :—" He rises with his subject, and, since Pope's death, I am satisfied that England has not seen so happy a mixture of strong sense and flowing numbers." Porson thus ridiculed the mutual flattery of Hayley and Miss Seward :—

Miss Seward loquitur.
Tuneful poet, Britain's glory,
　Mr. Hayley, that is you.

Hayley respondet.
Ma'am, you carry all before you,
　Trust me, Lichfield Swan, you do.

Miss Seward.
Ode, didactic, epic, sonnet,
　Mr. Hayley, you're divine.

Hayley.
Ma'am, I'll take my oath upon it,
　You yourself are all the Nine.

It was in 1853 that Rossetti "first definitely decided to adhere to painting as his profession, to the comparative neglect of poetry." At a still earlier date, on August 13, 1852, he wrote to his brother, "I have abandoned poetry." Nevertheless, so late as August 12, 1871, he wrote to Madox Brown :—" I wish one could live by writing poetry. I think I'd see painting d——d if one could."

I remember seeing, about the year 1856, a pen-and-ink drawing by Rossetti, of Browning, with a look of angry scorn, tearing out from a magazine the pages in which his poems were criticised. I have little doubt that it was Brimley's article that was thus treated. We see a different side of this reviewer's character in the following extract from a letter by T. S. Baynes, published in *The Table-Talk of Shirley:*—"Only a day or two ago, in looking over some papers, I met with the note I received when with you last year from poor Brimley, in which he speaks so calmly, yet so despondingly, about his health. He died last week. For a long time he had worked on at his post in the immediate presence of death, waiting calmly amidst pain and toil for the moment of release and rest."

Six years before Rossetti "spent some most delightful time with Browning at the Louvre," he had visited it with Holman Hunt, as he thus describes in the last six lines of a sonnet :—

> " Meanwhile Hunt and myself race at full speed
>   Along the Louvre, and yawn from school to school,
>   Wishing worn-out those masters known as old.
> And no man asks of Browning ; though indeed
>   (As the book travels with me) any fool
>   Who would might hear Sordello's story told."

Squarcialupe is found on page 66, *The sad dishevelled form* (not ghost) on page 99, and *Zin the Horrid* on page 104 of *Sordello*, edition of 1885.

Hawthorne, who met Browning in the summer of 1856, describes him as "a younger man than I expected to see, handsome, with brown hair. He is very simple and agreeable in manner, gently impulsive, talking as if his heart were uppermost."

The following anecdote Mr. Arthur Hughes had from Rossetti, who in his turn had it from Brown-

ing's father.   Once when the poet was kept indoors a few days by illness his father, who was
living in another house, on going to visit him
was each day received boisterously and cheerfully with the words :—" I have done another
act, father."   He was writing *The Blot on the
Scutcheon*, and he finished it in five days.

Mr. Hughes described to me Browning's uncle
as "a good-looking, well-to-do city gentleman,
with a gray head."   He had met him at a party
and fell into talk with him.   "'No doubt you admire
your nephew's poetry very much,' I said.   'I like
my nephew,' he replied, 'but I do not know that
I appreciate poetry properly.   I cannot say that
I understand his.   What I say to him is this :—
" Poetry of a difficult character should be printed
on a large page with a wide margin at side, as
official documents are printed with a space for
notes.   Why do not you print your poetry in the
usual way, and then on the side say what it
means ? " ' "

J. Milsand reviewed Browning in the *Revue des
Deux Mondes* of August 15, 1851, the second part
of an article on *La Poésie Anglaise depuis Byron*;
and also in the *Revue Contemporaine* of September
15, 1856.   In 1864 he published *L'Esthétique
Anglaise, Etude sur M. John Ruskin*.   Of *Pauline*
for which " he had been years in search," the
following anecdote is told by Mr. W. M. Rossetti :—" In the British Museum my brother had
come across an anonymous poem entitled *Pauline*.

He admired it much, and copied out every line of it." He inferred that it was by Browning. On writing to the poet, he learned that his inference was right.

In 1863 Browning dedicated a new edition of *Sordello* "to J. Milsand of Dijon;" and later on he honoured his memory by the following dedication of *Parleyings with Certain People* :—

IN MEMORIAM

J. MILSAND

OBIIT IV SEPT. MDCCCLXXXVI

Absens absentem auditque videtque

Matthew Arnold, writing on November 9, 1866, says :—"I had asked Lake to dine quite alone with us; then a M. Milsand, a Frenchman and a remarkable writer, called unexpectedly, and I added him to Lake; then I found Milsand was staying with Browning, and I added Browning; I found that Lord Houghton was a friend of Milsand's, and so I asked him too. Everybody made themselves pleasant, and it did extremely well."

Last year £175 was given for a copy of the first edition of *Pauline,* a poem of which the author in the preface to the collected edition of his works says :—"The first piece in the series I acknowledge and retain with extreme repugnance, indeed purely of necessity."

On one of the two evenings which Tennyson spent at Browning's house Rossetti heard one poet read aloud his *Maud,* and the other his *Fra Lippo*

Lippi. Mr. W. M. Rossetti, describing this evening, says:—" My brother made two pen-and-ink sketches of Tennyson, and gave one of them to Browning. So far as I remember, the Poet Laureate neither saw what Dante was doing nor knew of it afterwards. His deep, grand voice, with slightly chaunting intonation, was a noble vehicle for mighty verse. On it rolled, sonorous and emotional." Rossetti, according to Mr. Hall Caine, spoke of the incident in these terms:—" I once heard Tennyson read *Maud*, and whilst the fiery passages were delivered with a voice and vehemence which he alone of living men can compass, the softer passages and the songs made the tears course down his cheeks." Patmore, in a letter to Allingham, dated September 12, 1855, speaking of Tennyson, who had read to him "a passage here and there in *Maud*," continues :—" His reading magnifies the merit of everything ; it is so grand."

Mr. W. M. Rossetti tells me that the portrait his brother drew of Browning, "after he took a fanciful prejudice against him he gave away."

The Espousals is the second part of *The Angel in the House.* " I am sorry," wrote Henry Taylor on February 7, 1856, "that Patmore is writing a second part. Nothing is more important to a light poem of that kind than to be rounded off briefly and lie in a ring fence."

" Ruskin's new volume " was, I think, the third volume of *Modern Painters.* On July 1st of this year Rossetti had written :—" Ruskin is very hard at work on the third volume of *Modern Painters*, who, I tell him, will be old masters before the work is ended." In the summer of 1856, Rossetti, as will be seen, was reading the fourth volume.

Allingham's sonnet is entitled *The Three Sisters* (the three Brontës). *The Idler* was edited by E. Wilberforce. It came to an end with its sixth number.

That Rossetti at this time did "nearly all" his pictures for Ruskin is explained by the following statement by Mr. W. M. Rossetti :—" From an early date in their acquaintance Mr. Ruskin undertook to buy, if he happened to like it, whatever Rossetti produced, at a range of prices such as he would have asked from any other purchaser, and up to a certain maximum of expenditure on his own part. . . . My brother availed himself of Ruskin's easy liberality without abusing it. In fact, he was made comfortable in his professional position."

The picture which he describes as *Dante cut by Beatrice at a marriage Feast* bears the title *Beatrice at a Marriage Feast denies Dante her Salutation.* His "modern picture" was *Found.*

Of Delacroix, whom he praises so highly in this letter, he wrote from Paris in 1849 :—" Delacroix (except in two pictures, which show a kind of savage genius) is a perfect beast, though almost worshipped here." Mr. Holman Hunt, who was Rossetti's companion in this visit to Paris, writes :—" Delacroix was to me only a very far removed old master of poor capacity."

Of Ingres Rossetti wrote :—" This fellow is quite unaccountable. One picture of his in the Luxembourg is unsurpassed for exquisite perfection by anything I have ever seen, and he has others there for which I would not give two sous." For his *Ruggiero and Angelica* he composed two sonnets.

The Mystake was Rossetti's perversion of *The Mystic*, by P. J. Bailey, published this year. That author's *Festus* he had in earlier years "read over and over again."

XXIX.

Thursday [*Endorsed March 7, 1856*].

DEAR ALLINGHAM,

I've been putting off writing to you in hopes of doing so at some length, but have been so busy that at length in despair I snatch a half hour before model comes this morning to do my bare duty to you, still deferring my pleasure.

Many thanks for Aubrey de Vere, whom I have hardly looked into yet, but will prove, I suspect, more in my line than yours—not that I either have quite given over backbone as unaccessary to human structure. But I have rather a weakness to the man, though this vol., as far as I see, doesn't seem up to the best of the *Proserpine* one.

I have had 3 parcels here for you—two Art

Union ones (!), which a considerate hand relieved me of (by your order as I understood) from the Office yesterday. I still have a largish parcel from some one whose name the bearer told me (beginning with S, I think). What shall I do with it? Or is it possible these are forerunners of your coming? May it be so. Now something else. Dalziel (very good naturedly, *considering*) called here the other day to enlist me for an illustrated selection of Poets which he has the getting up of, it being edited by Revd. Wilmott. That venerable parson had not, it seems, included Browning, for whose introduction I made an immediate stand, and said in that case I would illustrate him. I think it will probably be done, and I shall propose (I fancy as yet) *Count Gismond*,—"Say, hast thou lied?" —which I designed some years ago. But I should also like to do one from you, if anything illustratable of yours is included and you are not pre-engaged. *Something* of yours, I gathered from D., was to be in. Would you tell me *what?* *i.e.*, if you know. I told him I should not be able to do them for *several* months, as the Tennyson ones still hang on my hands; but he seemed to say that would do. I am to write to him about subject from Browning, so would you let me also hear of yours at once, if you can?

That notice in *The Oxford and Cambridge Mag.* was

the most gratifying thing by far that ever happened
to me—being unmistakeably [*sic*] genuine. I thought
it must be by your old acquaintance Fryer, of
Cambridge, he having called on me once about
those same things. But it turns out to be by a
certain youthful Jones, who was in London the
other day, and whom (being known to some of the
Working Men's Coll. council) I have now met.
One of the nicest young fellows in—*Dreamland.*
For there most of the writers in that miraculous
piece of literature seem to be. Surely this cometh
in some wise of the *Germ*, with which it might bind
up. But how much more the right thing—in kind
—than the *Idler!* I see it monthly. The new
No. has a story called *A Dream*, which really is
remarkable,[1] I think, in colour.

This brings me to my water-colours. I'm doing
a large one I'd like you to see—Dante's vision of
Beatrice dead, *Vita Nuova*—one of my very best.
I've done, too, lately, a monk illuminating and
other beginnings. I've got (I think) a commission to paint a reredos (altar-piece) for Llandaff
Cathedral—a big thing, which I shall go into
with a howl of delight after all my small work.
I fancy it will pay wellish, too.

Your affectionate

D. G. ROSSETTI.

---

[1] He had at first written " remarkable in some respects."

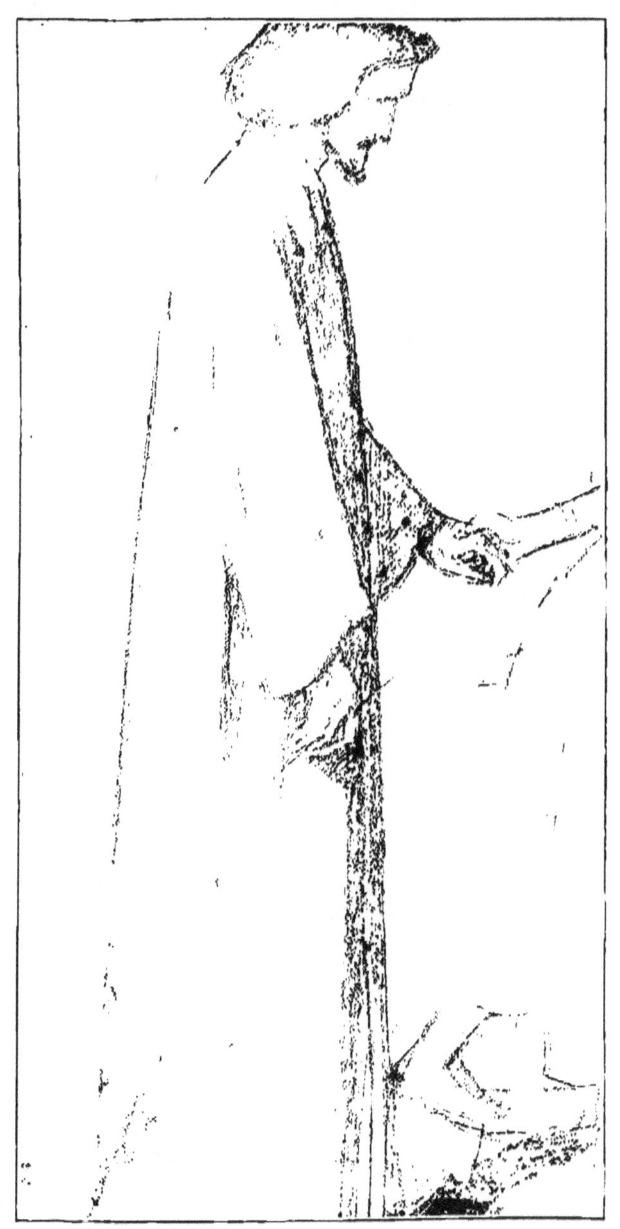

EARLY SKETCH FOR DANTE'S "VISION."

(By D. G. Rossetti.)

[*To face page* 174.

Notes on XXIX.

Four years later Rossetti described Aubrey de Vere as " surely one of the wateriest of the well-meaning." Sir Henry Taylor, writing to the poet on April 9, 1855, said: —" I have considered your volume a great deal, and written to you not a little upon it with the mind's pen, curious to know, if you be not a great poet, wherein you fail. Not in intellect, certainly, for therein you range with Coleridge and Wordsworth, and above Tennyson; not in art or the rhythmic sense, for in that you are equal to Wordsworth; not in fancy, of which you have more than any of them. Is it, then, in human and imaginative passion? That, I think, is the only question." In 1843 de Vere had published *The Search after Proserpine, Recollections of Greece, and other Poems.*

Rossetti was not enlisted for this " illustrated selection of poets," which, towards the end of the year, was published under the title of *The Poets of the Nineteenth Century,* selected and edited by R. A. Willmott.

To *The Oxford and Cambridge Magazine* Rossetti contributed *The Burden of Nineveh, The Staff and the Scrip,* and *The Blessed Damozel,* slightly altered from the form it bore in *The Germ.* The mention of this magazine brings back to my memory a little front parlour in a small lodging - house in Pembroke Street, Oxford, in which, in the Michaelmas term of

1855, I heard a knot of eager young men talk of the forthcoming first number. They were all my seniors in standing, some of them by two or three years. I was only in my second term. The two leaders were Burne-Jones and William Morris. Next to them was Richard Watson Dixon (now a canon of the Church of England), whom Rossetti "described, towards 1880, as 'an admirable but totally unknown living poet. His finest passages," he added, "are as fine as any living man can write.'" The most generally beloved in the little set was Charles Joseph Faulkner, scholar of Pembroke College, who, after winning the highest honours in examinations, became Fellow and Tutor of University College. It was a distinguished Common Room which he joined, numbering as it did among its members John Conington, Goldwin Smith, A. P. Stanley, and Canon Bright. "Most whist-loving of the sad socialist race, and affectionately remembered as 'Citizen Faulkner'"— so he is described in the recent *History of Pembroke College*. Till an insidious malady had begun to work its ruin on his fine mind he was the pleasantest of companions as he was always the truest of friends. He inherited a love of art from his father, who, he told me, in early manhood had been a designer in metal-work, and had once gained a prize offered by some Society of Arts. Being a poor artisan, he walked all the way from Birmingham to London to receive it, and back again. In the few days which he stayed in the town to see the sights he lived chiefly on dry bread and raisins. What the son could have done as an artist he showed by engraving the frontispiece in Miss Rossetti's *Goblin Market*. "The principal drawing," writes Mr. W. M. Rossetti, "was cut on the wood by Mr. Morris with uncommon spirit— I believe his first attempt in that line." It was by Charles Faulkner, and not by William Morris, that this drawing was cut. It was his first, and, I believe, his last attempt. He gave an early impression of it to my little daughter, his god-child. He was the third member in the art firm of Morris, Marshall, Faulkner & Co. To my long friendship with this most upright and truthful of men I owe more than I can tell. All of these men but Morris had been born, or at all events had been educated, in Birmingham. Another of the set, the late Edwin Hatch, afterwards became distinguished as a theological scholar. Between him and the others I never discovered any bond of sympathy but this common Birmingham origin. One evening, when I was absent, he described me as "the personification of all the intellectual vices of the age." I had been brought up a Utilitarian. I was, I fear, less pained by the vices which were laid to my charge than flattered by "intellectual" which qualified them.

I was introduced to this little fraternity by the future editor of the magazine, William Fulford, a poet of no mean power. It was, in fact, "a nest of singing birds," who, night after night, were

found together in the close neighbourhood of Dr.
Johnson's old college, often in the college itself.
It was a new world into which I was brought. I
knew nothing of art, and nothing of Tennyson,
Browning, and Ruskin. The subjects which I had
always heard discussed were never discussed here,
while matters on which I had never heard any one
speak formed here the staple of the talk. I recall
how, one evening, the nineteenth century was de-
nounced for its utter want of poetry. This was
more than I could bear, for the nineteenth century
was almost an object of adoration in my father's
house. I ventured to assert that it could boast, at
all events, of one piece of poetry—the steam-
engine. The roar of laughter which burst forth
nearly overwhelmed me. The author of *The
Earthly Paradise* almost overturned his chair as
he flung himself backwards, overpowered with
mirth. I was too much abashed to explain that
I was recalling the sight I had once had of an
engine rushing through the darkness along a high
embankment, drawing after it a cloud of flame
and fiery steam.

In the first number of the magazine, the editor,
in an article on Tennyson, praised the music to
which *Sweet and Low* had been set. I recall the
pleasure with which he read to us a letter from the
poet, asking for the name of the publisher of the
music, as no setting that he knew of pleased either
himself or his wife.

What the " youthful Jones " thought of Rossetti

getic withal to an extraordinary degree in Ruskin's style, but quite mild and feminine—10 hours at the top of a ladder to copy a Giotto ceiling being nothing to her. She has been travelling all over Italy with Layard, and they together have given one one's first real chance of forming a congruous idea of early art without going there—he having traced all he could get at by single figures and groups—and she having made coloured drawings of the whole compositions, and the chapels, etc., where they are painted on the walls. They have hundreds—whole reams of these things—of course more interesting than one can say. Benozzo Gozzoli was a god. It is fearful to hear them describe the havoc going on among the originals of their tracings, etc. In one instance, specially admiring a glorious fresco by Pietro della Fran-cesca—I was told that while the tracing was being made, some demons came with an order to knock it out of the wall to make a window—which was done! I believe some means will be taken to publish or show publicly all these things. A most glorious treat which I had yesterday is the sight of the Giotto tracings made for the Arundel Society, and now in the Crystal Palace. I hope you'll be in time for them. The woodcuts pub-lished give no idea.

I've just finished a largish drawing for one Miss

we learn from Canon Dixon, who wrote, "The great painter who first took me to him said, 'We shall see the greatest man in Europe.'"

The water-colour of Dante's vision, says Mr. W. M. Rossetti, "is the same subject as the large oil-picture now in the Walker Gallery at Liverpool, but not at all the same composition." "*The Monk Illuminating* is the water-colour named *Fra Pace*."

For the triptych for Llandaff Cathedral Rossetti was to receive £400. It was not finished till 1864.

<hr>

XXX.

Friday [April, 1856].

DEAR ALLINGHAM,

Many thanks for your "sunny memory" of me. The photograph interests me as in some degree embodying your whereabouts.

I have just been turning over the 3 parcels of books left for you with me, and a dismaller collection I never saw. Is it possible you read all that? The only one to my taste is a nice clean Mrs. Boddington. I have met lately with a lady—one Mrs. Burr—who always brings her to my mind—having the same tendency to poetic travelling, and being much what I fancy her in age and person—about 32, refined and very nearly beautiful, ener-

Heaton, of Leeds, of Dante's dream of Beatrice lying dead. It has taken me nearly 2 months, and is the best I have done. I fear it must go before you come, or I should like of all things to show it you.

Being short of news (and time) I enclose 2 or 3 notes of Browning's as a peace - offering. You ought to see *one* passage. His portrait by Page is accepted at R.A., but I dare say they'll gibbet it in some way, and it isn't good.

I agree partly about Ruskin as far as I've read the 4th vol., but there are glorious things, of course; *Calais Church* at beginning is one.

Really, the omissions in Browning's passage are awful, and the union with Longfellow worse. How I loathe *Wishi-washi,*—of course without reading it. I have not been so happy in loathing anything for a long while—except, I think, *Leaves of Grass*, by that Orson of yours. I should like just to have the writing of a valentine to him in one of the reviews.

Perhaps you've heard of Academy pictures—so I give you but a summary. Millais sends 5 : *Peace concluded*, a stupid affair to suit the day—but very big, and fetching him £900 ! without copyright, for which he expects £1,000 more ; *Children burning Autumn leaves*, very lovely indeed ; *Blind Girl and rainbow*, one of the most touching and perfect things I know ; *Church besieged in Cromwell's time,* with child lying wounded on knight's tomb, haven't seen ; *Boy looking at Leech's picture book.* Hunt sends only *Scapegoat*—a grand thing, but not for the public—and a few lovely landscape drawings. His big picture of *Christ and the Doctors in the Temple* is about the greatest thing, perhaps, he has done, but only half done yet. Hughes' *Eve of St. Agnes* will make his fortune, I feel sure.

Bessie P.'s [Parkes's] *Gabriel* is Shelley, I hear.

Your loving D. G. R.

NOTES ON XXX.

"Sunny memory" Rossetti perhaps borrowed from Mrs. Stowe's *Sunny Memories of Foreign Lands*, which had been brought out a year earlier.

Mary Boddington published a volume of poems in 1839. "I fancy," writes Mr. W. M. Rossetti, "that her name has now passed out of all remembrance. It may be as far back as 1847 that my brother (and myself) grew very familiar with a few specimens of poetry by her, and had a great liking for them. I could still repeat most of one poem about a lady who had drowned herself, beginning—

> ' They laid my lady in her grave,
> My lady with the deep blue eye.' "

This poem is given in Allingham's *Nightingale Valley*, page 184.

In 1868 Sir H. A. Layard published for the

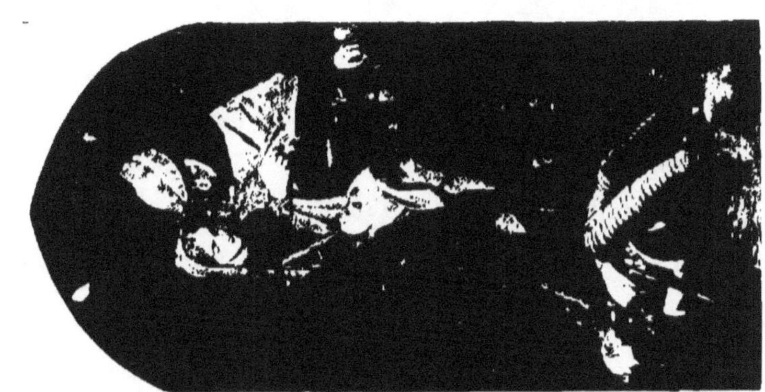

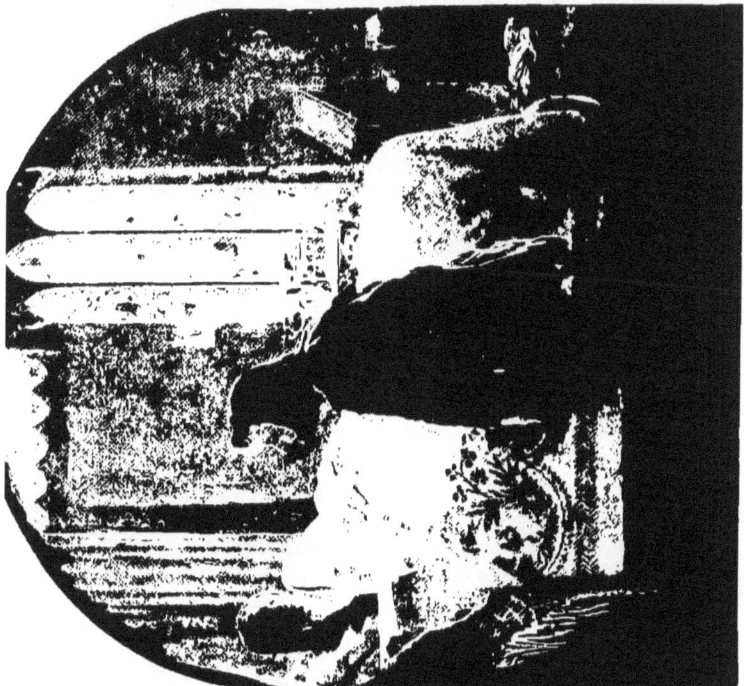

Arundel Society a monograph on The Brancacci Chapel, at Florence, in which he described the mosaics. This was his first publication on Italian art. "At Millais' house one night," writes Mr. Holman Hunt, "we found a book of engravings of the frescoes in the Campo Santo at Pisa. It was probably the finding of this book at this special time which caused the establishment of the Præraphaelite Brotherhood." "These engravings," says Mr. W. M. Rossetti, "give some idea of the motives, feeling, and treatment of the paintings of Gozzoli."

"The omissions in Browning's passage" were omissions in a quotation in *Modern Painters*, vol. iv. p. 377, from *The Bishop orders his Tomb at Saint Praxed's Church.* "The union with Longfellow" is in the following passage on the same page :—"Thus Longfellow in *The Golden Legend* has entered more closely into the temper of the monk, for good and for evil, than ever yet theological writer or historian, though they may have given their life's labour to the analysis ; and again, Robert Browning is unerring in every sentence he writes of the Middle Ages," &c.

Matthew Arnold, this same spring, described Ruskin's new volume as "full.of excellent *aperçus*, as usual, but the man and character too febrile, irritable, and weak to allow him to possess the *ordo concatenatioque veri.*"

Leaves of Grass must be Whitman's, poems ; though why Rossetti should describe the author as "that Orson of yours" I cannot understand.

The following extracts from two of Allingham's letters to Mr. W. M. Rossetti show that Allingham had not at this time read the book :—

March 15, 1857. "*Leaves of Grass* I have bought partly from what you say (7s. 6d., mind!), but not read. First glimpse shows something of a *got-up* air. Is 'Whitman' real? Do you know Thoreau's *Concord* and *Life in the Woods?* They are worth having."

April 10, 1857. "I've read *Leaves of Grass*, and found it rather pleasant, but little new or original; the portrait the best thing. Of course, to call it poetry, in any sense, would be mere abuse of language. In poetry there is a special freedom, which, however, is *not* lawlessness and incoherence."

On May 19 of the same year he returns to the subject :—

"I have been very flat and heavy lately, and out of humour with poetry-writing. The fact is I am dismal for want of some society. I'm weary of wandering about the fields—sermons in stones, and no good in anything. 'Rusty' is derived from 'rus.' I must get out of this desolate Ballyshannon village—and long for it again, perhaps, in another mood. But in any mood, case, or tense, I couldn't allow *Leaves of Grass* to be poetry. I wish we had some accepted word like 'poeticality.' The *Leaves* are suggestive, like the advertisement columns of a newspaper, or a stroll along Fleet Street and Thames Street, but poetry without form is—what shall I say? Proportion seems to me the most inalienable quality of a poem. From the chaos of incident and reflection arise the rounded worlds of poetry, and go singing on their way."

Rossetti, writing in 1878 about his brother's *Lives of Famous Poets*, says of Whitman :—" By the bye, I am sorry to see that name winding up a summary of great poets ; he is really out of court in comparison with any one who writes what is not sublimated Tupper ; though you know that I am not without appreciation of his fine qualities." The two brothers differed greatly in their estimate of Whitman. Mr. W. M. Rossetti wrote to Mrs. Gilchrist in 1869 :—" That glorious man Whitman will one day be known as one of the greatest sons of Earth, a few steps below Shakespeare on the throne of immortality."

About three of Millais' five Academy pictures Madox Brown thus wrote :—" I saw Millais' picture of the year, *Autumn Leaves*—the finest in painting and colour he has yet done, but the subject somewhat without purpose and looking like portraits. His large picture is, I believe, sold to Miller for a thousand guineas. I don't like it much ; the subject is stupidish and the colour bad, but some of the expressions beautiful and lovely parts. *The Blind Girl* is altogether the finest subject—a religious picture and a glorious one. It is a pity he has scamped the execution."

Mr. Holman Hunt had returned to England in February of this year. " For four years after my return," he writes, " I had to keep *The Finding of the Saviour* often with its face to the wall, while I was working at pot-boilers to get the means to advance it at all ; and frequently when I obtained a little money I could only work a week at the picture before the demand for rent, taxes, or some debt made itself heard.   Had we found a public showing only a reasonable amount of interest and independence of taste, and of faith that our countrymen could and should win glory for the nation, I know that my two companions [Rossetti and Millais] would have done greater things than can easily be imagined, and I can assert that what I now show of my life's work would be but a tithe of what there would be ; but even yet, I thank God, the day leaves me opportunity to work with my might."

Miss Parkes had published a poem under the title of *Gabriel*.

XXXI.

Monday [May, 1856].

DEAR ALLINGHAM,

Would you kindly, in coming to town, bring Miss S.'s *wood-block* of the old ballad.   She wants to *borrow* it of you, as she thinks of painting the subject at once, and has no other design of it.

I only write this word or two, as I am so soon to enjoy the sight of you.   The R.A. Ex. is full of

P.R. work this year. Hughes' *Eve of St. Agnes* is a real success. The finest thing of all in the place, to my feeling, is a picture by one Windus (of Liverpool), from the old ballad of *Burd Helen* another version of *Childe Waters*. It belongs, I hear, to your friend Miller.

Your D. G. ROSSETTI.

NOTES ON XXXI.

Madox Brown recorded in May, 1856 :—" Off solus to the Royal Academy. Hunt and Millais unrivalled except by Hook, who, for colour and indescribable charm is pre-eminent, even to hugging him in one's arms. A perfect poem is each of his little pictures. Millais' looks ten times better than in his room, owing to contrast with surrounding badness. Hunt's *Scapegoat* requires to be seen to be believed in. Only then can it be understood how, by the might of genius, out of an old goat, and some saline incrustations, can be made one of the most tragic and impressive works in the annals of art."

Gambart, the picture-dealer, "who had given Mr. Hunt a commission, when he went to the Holy Land, for a large picture similar to his *Light of the World*, complained to Linnell :—' I wanted a nice religious bicture, and he bainted me a great goat.' " After Mr. Hunt had painted these two pictures he received one vote when he stood for election to the Royal Academy.

Windus was a Liverpool painter. Madox Brown, writing about his picture on May 14 of this year said :—" Rossetti forced Ruskin to go with him to see it *instanter*, because he had not noticed it in his pamphlet, and extorted the promise of a postscript on its behalf." In the postscript to the third edition of *Notes on Pictures in the Royal Academy*, 1856, Ruskin says :—" Generally speaking, the arrangement of the pictures in the Academy this year is better than usual : but the errors which are usually notable in various parts of the room seem to have been all concentrated in the one crying error of putting No. 122 nearly out of sight. . . . I passed this *Burd Helen* by. . . . Further examination of it leads me to class it as the second picture of the year ; its aim being higher, and its reserved strength greater than those of any other work except the *Autumn Leaves*."

XXXII.

MRS. GREEN'S, 17, ORANGE GROVE, BATH.

[*Postmark, December* 18, 1856.]

MY DEAR ALLINGHAM,

Very glad was I of your undeserved letter. How long have I meant to write to you ! It was sent on to me here, where I have been a week or two, and may still be a week.

The piece of news freshest in my mind is *Aurora Leigh*,—an astounding work, surely. You said nothing of it. I know that St. Francis and Poverty do not wed in these days of St. James' Church, with rows of portrait figures on either side, and the corners neatly finished with angels. I know that if a blind man were to enter the room this evening and talk to me for some hours, I should, with the best intentions, be in danger of twigging his blindness before the right moment came, if such there were, for the chord in the orchestra and the proper theatrical start ; yet with all my knowledge I have felt something like a bug ever since reading *Aurora Leigh*. Oh, the wonder of it ! and oh, the bore of writing about it.

The Brownings are long gone back now, and with them one of my delights,—an evening resort where I never felt unhappy. How large a part of the real world, I wonder, are those two small people ?—taking meanwhile so little room in any railway carriage, and hardly needing a double bed at the inn.

Little Read has been in London lately, and I saw him once or twice—just the same as ever— with a new wife, I hear, but he did not say so. They are going on to Rome.

What of London friends ? Woolner is still doing his bust of Tennyson, and his medallion, you know, is to face the title of the new edition. His statue of Bacon, for the Oxford Museum, turned out a very first-rate thing, and is likely, I hope, to do him great good. There was an article on it in the *Daily News*, written by one Revd. Elliott, and an allusion, I hear, in the *Athenæum*. By the bye, your mowing song was one of your best. Hunt is going on with his great picture, and is painting at present in the Alhambra Court at the Crystal Palace, where he finds some architectural matters for his background. Hughes has 3 or 4 pictures in hand; but of these you are likely to have heard. Munro is still at work for Woodward. Brown has lately got the prize of £50 at Liverpool for his *Christ washing Peter's Feet*, which is proving of use to him. He has a 400 guinea commission from Mr. Plint, of Leeds, for a large modern picture which he began some time ago, called *Work*, and illustrating all kinds of Carlylianisms. It will be a most noble affair, and will at last, I should hope, settle the question of his fame, which is making some steps at last. Did you see his woodcut in *The Poets of the* 19*th Century?*—very fine still, though rather mauled. They have treated you snobbily enough there. I had engaged to do Browning; but what could have been done with *Evelyn Hope* or *Two in the Campagna? Count Gismond* now!—but they

yet seen by him in the Tennyson. Hunt's _Oriana_ & _Lady of Shalott_ are my favorites — both masterpieces. I have done as yet four — _Mariana in South_, _Sir Galahad_, & two to the _Palace of Art_. I hope to do a second to _Sir Galahad_, but am very uncertain as to any more. But these engravers! What ministers of wrath! Your drawing comes to them, like Agag, delicately, & is hewn to pieces before the Lord Harry. I took more pains with one block lately than I had with anything for a long while. It came back to me on paper the other day with Dalziel performing his cannibal jig in the corner, and I have really felt like an invalid ever since. As yet, I fare best with W. J. Linton. He keeps stomache aches for you, but Dalziel deals in fevers & agues.

By the bye, what do you think of Alex. Smith's Tennysonian poem in the _National Mag_? I think it an advance — indeed very fine in parts. Woolner met him & Dobell in Edinburgh lately — liked

<DALZIEL'S "CANNIBAL JIG.">

DALZIEL'S "CANNIBAL JIG."

[To face page 191.

wouldn't. How truly glorious are both of Millais'
drawings! Among his very finest doings, I think,
and preferable to any I have yet seen by him in
the Tennyson.

Hunt's *Oriana* and *Lady of Shalott* are my
favorites, both masterpieces. I have done, as
yet, four,—*Mariana in South*, *Sir Galahad*, and
two to the *Palace of Art*. I hope to do a
second to *Sir Galahad*, but am very uncertain as
to any more. — But these engravers! What
ministers of wrath! Your drawing comes to them,
like Agag, delicately, and is hewn in pieces before
the Lord Harry. I took more pains with one block
lately than I had with anything for a long while.
It came back to me on paper, the other day, with
Dalziel performing his cannibal jig in the corner, and
I have really felt like an invalid ever since. As yet,
I fare best with W. J. Linton. He keeps stomache
aches for you, but Dalziel deals in fevers and agues.

By the bye, what do you think of Alex. Smith's
Tennysonian poem in the *National Mag.?* I
think it an advance—indeed, very fine in parts.
Woolner met him and Dobell in Edinburgh lately—
liked Smith much, who inquired a great deal about
you, on whose head he heaps coals of appreciation.
Read told me that the *Angel in the House* has had
a wild success in America.

How about *Blackwood*, where you say your poem

is probably to come out? I knew not that you had diggings in that direction. Stokes and Ormsby I see sometimes, and dine with them at the "Cheshire Cheese" at intervals—good fellows both—I will not forget your remembrances.

You will see no more of the poor *Oxford and Cambridge*. It was "too like the Spirit of Germ, Down, down!" and has vanished into the witches' cauldron. Morris and Jones have now been some time settled in London, and are both, I find, wonders after their kind. Jones is doing designs which quite put one to shame, so full are they of everything—*Aurora Leighs* of art. He will take the lead in no time. Morris, besides writing those capital tales, writes poems which are really better than the tales, though one or two short ones in the Mag. were not of his best. By the bye, though, *The Chapel in Lyoness* was glorious,—did you not think so? In his last tale—*Golden Wings*—the printer, after no doubt considering himself personally insulted all along by the nature of those compositions, wound up matters with an avenging blow, and inserted some comic touches, such as prefixing *old* to *woman* or *lady* in several instances, and other commissions and omissions. Morris's facility at poetising puts one in a rage. He has been writing at all for little more than a year, I believe, and has already poetry enough

for a big book.   You know he is a millionaire, and
buys pictures.   He bought Hughes's *April Love*,
and lately several water-colours of mine, and a
landscape by Brown,—indeed, seems as if he would
never stop, as I have 3 or 4 more commissions
from him.   To one of my water-colours, called
The Blue Closet, he has written a stunning poem.
You would think him one of the finest little fellows
alive—with a touch of the incoherent, but a real
man.   He and Jones have taken those rooms in
Red Lion Square which poor Deverell and I
used to have, and where the only sign of life,
when I found them the other day, on going to
enquire, all dusty and unused, was an address
written up by us on the wall of a bedroom,—so
pale and watery had been all subsequent inmates,
not a trace of whom remained.   Morris is rather
doing the magnificent there, and is having some
intensely mediæval furniture made—tables and
chairs like incubi and succubi.   He and I have
painted the back of a chair with figures and
inscriptions in gules and vert and azure, and we
are all three going to cover a cabinet with pictures.

Morris means to be an architect, and to that end
has set about becoming a painter, at which he is
making progress.   In all illumination and work
of that kind he is quite unrivalled by anything
modern that I know—Ruskin says, better than

anything ancient.   By the bye, it was Ruskin made me alter that line in *The Blessed D.*   I had never meant to show him any of my versifyings, but he wrote to me one day asking if I knew the author of *Nineveh,* and could introduce him—being really ignorant, as I found—so after that the flesh was weak.   Indeed, I do not know that it will not end in a volume of mine, one of these days.   But first I want to bring out those translations, which I have not found time yet to get together for Macmillan, so busy have I been.   Do you not think Vernon Lushington's *Carlyle* very good in *O. and C. Mag.?*   His things and his brother's, Morris's, and the one or two by Jones (who never wrote before or since) are the staple of that magazine. The rest—had better have been—silence.   Another matter which shall be silence—mainly—on my part is your picture at Tom Taylor's—merciful silence, O! W. A.! were it better, wouldn't I tell its faults!

A lady, to whose doings you once inferred a comparison of the above, has been, you will be sorry to hear, most terribly ill a month or two ago, but is now somewhat better again.   She has begun an oil picture from that wood-block subject, though a good deal altered, but it seems as if her health could set all her efforts at naught.   There were some thoughts of her going this winter to Algiers (whither Barbara Smith and her sick sister are gone) but Miss Siddal seems to have no fancy for the place. Medical men are recommending it this winter, but earthquakes seem rather a shy feature of the entertainments.

Have you heard of the Howitts? I have seen them, though not very lately, and fear that Miss H. is anything but well. *Spiritualism* has begun to be in the ascendant at the Hermitage, and this to a degree which you could not conceive possible without witnessing it. Do not say anything to anybody, though. I elicited from W. Howitt, before his family, his opinion of it with some trouble, and found it to be a modified form of my own, which of course I give without reserve—but the ladies of the house seem to take but one view of the subject, and, astounding as it may appear, Mrs. Browning has given in her adherence. I hope *Aurora Leigh* is not to be followed by " that style only." Browning, of course, pockets his hands and shakes his mane over the question, with occasional foamings at the mouth, and he and I laid siege to the subject one night, but to no purpose.

Here we are in the 3rd sheet and 3rd hour, A.M. Goodbye for the present. Do let us keep it up now.

Yours ever affectionately,

D. G. ROSSETTI.

P.S.—Do you know that poor Boyce has been at Death's door out in the Pyrenees? I hope he is better now, and believe he is likely to be soon back.

Notes on XXXII.

Rossetti was at Bath on a visit to Miss Siddal, who was there for the sake of her health. Ten weeks earlier Madox Brown recorded :—" Painted at William Rossetti from 8 at night till 12. Gabriel came in, and, William wishing to go early, Gabriel proposed that he should wait five minutes, and they would go together ; William being got to sleep on the sofa, commenced telling me he intended to get married at once to Guggum, and then off to Algeria ! and so poor William's five minutes lasted till half past 3 A.M." On March 17, 1857, Brown recorded :—" All day with Gabriel, who is so unhappy about Miss Siddal that I could not leave him."

" *Aurora Leigh*," wrote Mr. W. M. Rossetti to W. B. Scott, " was sent to Gabriel, and also to Woolner, by Mrs. Browning herself, and both are unboundedly enthusiastic about it." Mr. Rossetti tells me that his brother, " towards 1845–47, was a semi-idolater of Mrs. Browning ; but in more mature years he saw very clearly the defects (along with the beauties) of her tendencies and style."

His friendship with Mr. Browning came to an end through a wild suspicion that in some lines in *Fifine*

Miss Siddal.

after a drawing in pencil by D. G. Rossetti.

at the Fair he was attacked. "On one or two occasions," writes Mr. W. M. Rossetti, "when the great poet, the object of my brother's early and unbounded homage, kindly inquired of me concerning him, and expressed a wish to look him up, I was compelled to fence with the suggestion, lest worse should ensue."

On April 11, 1856, Madox Brown wrote:— " Woolner's bust of Tennyson is fine, but hard and disagreeable. Somehow there is a hitch in Woolner as a sculptor. The capabilities for execution do not go with his intellect."

Hawthorne recorded on July 30, 1857:—"Going into the saloon of the old masters [at the Manchester Exhibition] we saw Tennyson there, in company with Mr. Woolner, whose bust of him is now in the Exhibition. Gazing at him with all my eyes I liked him well, and rejoiced more in him than in all the other wonders of the Exhibition. I would most gladly have seen more of this one poet of our day, but forebore to follow him ; for I must own that it seemed mean to be dogging him through the saloons, or even to look at him, since it was to be done stealthily, if at all." What a fine subject is there here for a painter—the old masters on the wall looking down on the poet, with his sculptor by his side, and the shy dreamer of beautiful dreams from the other side of the wide sea looking at him by stealth !

Rossetti wrote to his brother on August 2, 1856:—"I have been twice to see Ristori, with a

Rev. William Elliott, a friend of Patmore and Woolner, who is a tremendous Browningian."

The Mowers is given on page 58 of Allingham's *Flower Pieces.*   The following stanza is perhaps the prettiest in the poem :—

> " White falls the brook from steep to steep
>   Among the rocks and heather—
> A scythe-sweep and a scythe-sweep,
>   We mow the dale together."

Madox Brown's picture of *Christ washing Peter's Feet*, now in the National Gallery, contains portraits of four of the P. R. B.—Holman Hunt, D. G. Rossetti and his brother, and F. G. Stephens.   In the Royal Academy it had been hung near the ceiling.   "When Grant, the future President, came to offer his congratulations, Brown, whose eye had only just fallen on it, turned his back in speechless indignation, and walked out of the building."   Of *Work*, which is in the Manchester Public Gallery, he made the first studies in June, 1852 ; it was finished in August, 1863.   It was in November, 1856, that Mr. Plint, giving him the commission for it, wrote :—" I hope we may both, in God's mercy, be spared to see it happily finished."   Only half the prayer was granted.   The liberal patron of art died nearly two years before the last touch was given.   The long delay was mainly due to the need the painter was under, to borrow Johnson's words, "of making provision for the day that was passing over him."   That his fame was slow in " making steps " was owing in some measure, writes Mr. W. M. Rossetti, to "the absolute silence which Mr. Ruskin in all his published writings preserved as to his works." Rossetti was the warm friend of both men. "Brown soon got to hate the very name of Ruskin. So Rossetti had, in some degree, to steer a middle course between his warm feelings for Brown on one side, and for Ruskin on the other."

Allingham had only a single poem in *The Poets of the Nineteenth Century—An Autumnal Sonnet.* Rossetti contributed no illustration.

Dalziel's "cannibal jig" was his signature in very unequal letters at the bottom of the engraving, of which Rossetti gives Allingham an imitation.

In a letter to W. B. Scott, two months later, Rossetti again brought in Agag : "After a fortnight's work, my block goes to the engraver, like Agag, delicately, and is hewn to pieces before the —Lord Harry."

Alexander Smith's poem in the *National Magazine* for December, 1856, was entitled *The Night before the Wedding.* The "coals of appreciation" heaped by Smith are explained by the following passage in Allingham's letter to Mr. W. M. Rossetti, dated March 15, 1857 : "Don't waste sympathy on Alexander Smith. I hear he is coming out with Macmillan shortly ; but if he ever produces a *good* book I undertake to eat it, literally, as St. John did, miraculously, I suppose, that one in the Revelation. Smith, Dobell, Festus, and all

that sort of thing is a mere passing hubbub."
Matthew Arnold, in one of his letters, says of
Smith : " It can do me no good to be irritated with
that young man, who has certainly an extraordinary
faculty, although I think he is a phenomenon of a
very dubious character : but il fait son métier—
faisons le nôtre."   Matthew Arnold is quoting the
words of the usurer in the eighth chapter of *Le
Diable Boiteux*, who, after listening to an eloquent
sermon against usury, says to a young spendthrift :
" C'est un savant homme ; il a fort bien fait son
métier, allons-nous-en faire le nôtre."

Stokes is Mr. Whitley Stokes, C.I.E., LL.D.
Rossetti wrote to Miss Rossetti in January, 1861 :—
" Last night I read some of your poems to Stokes
—a very good judge and conversant with publishers."   " Mr. Ormesby," writes Mr. W. M.
Rossetti, " a bright writer on the press, died some
years ago."

Rossetti at one time used to dine frequently at
that famous old Fleet Street tavern, the " Cheshire
Cheese."   He mentions it twice in his letters to
Alexander Gilchrist.

Golden Wings was published in the December
number of the *Oxford and Cambridge Magazine*.
The printer's " comic touches" are found in the
following passages :—" Old knights who fought in
that battle, and who told me it was all about an
old lady," &c.   " I put my shield before me and
drew my sword, and the old women drew together
aside and whispered fearfully."

Morris's first book, *The Defence of Guenevere and Other Poems*, was dedicated to Rossetti. Of "his facility at poetizing" I can give the following instance: Charles Faulkner, coming to my house from Morris's, told me that on the previous day the poet had written seven hundred lines of *Jason*. Rossetti's statement that he was "a millionaire" was the wild exaggeration of a poor painter.

"The subject of *The Blue Closet*," Rossetti wrote, "is some people playing music." Mr. W. M. Rossetti tells us that when Mr. Rae "inserted in a catalogue of his pictures certain quotations from Morris's poems as illustrating *The Tune of Seven Towers* and *The Blue Closet*, Rossetti remarked, 'The quotations should have been left out, as the poems were the result of the pictures, but do not at all tally to any purpose with them, though beautiful in themselves.'" John Parker, the editor of *Fraser's Magazine*, wrote to "Shirley" on May 14, 1860:—"I saw Morris's poems in manuscript. Surely 19-20ths of them are of the most obscure, watery, mystical, affected stuff possible. The man who brought the manuscript (himself well known as a poet) said that 'one of the poems which described a picture of Rossetti was a very fine poem; that the picture was not understandable, and the poem made it no clearer, but that it was a fine poem, nevertheless.'"

It was on the first floor of No. 17, Red Lion Square, that first Rossetti and Deverell, and afterwards Burnes-Jones and Morris, had their rooms.

In June, 1857,[1] I rowed down the Thames from Oxford to a village on the outskirts of London in company with William Morris and Charles Faulkner. With the improvidence of youth, by the time we reached Henley we had spent all our money except just enough to enable Faulkner to buy a return-ticket to Oxford, where he had to attend a college meeting. He was to bring back a supply in the evening. The weather was unusually hot. Morris and I sauntered along the river-side. I have not forgotten the longing glances he cast on a large basket of strawberries. He had always been so plentifully supplied with money that he bore with far greater impatience than I did this privation. At last the shadows had grown long and the heat was more bearable. We went with light hearts to the railway station to meet our comrade. "Well, Faulkner," cried out Morris cheerfully, "how much money have you brought?" Our friend gave a start. "Good heavens!" he replied, "I forgot all about it." Morris thrust both his hands into his long dark curly hair, tugged at it wildly, ground his teeth, swore like a trooper, and stamped up and down the platform—in fact,

---

[1] Most of the following narrative will be found in my *Talks about Autographs*, page 136. Now that unhappily, by the death of William Morris, I am the sole survivor of the boat's crew, I can without impropriety add one or two circumstances which I had omitted. By a blunder I had given the date as 1858. I made another mistake in saying that Rossetti occupied the room with Burne-Jones. He must have been a visitor that night like myself.

behaved just like Sinbad's captain when he found that his ship was driving upon the rocks. His outbursts of rage, I hasten to say, were always harmless. They left no sullenness behind, and as each rapidly passed away he was ready to join in a hearty laugh at it. Faulkner, who was not the most patient of men, noticed that passengers, stationmaster, porters, engine-driver, and stoker were all gazing in astonishment. He, too, lost his temper, and, though in a far lower key and with far fewer gesticulations, stormed back. Morris soon quieted down, and a council of war was held. He fortunately had a gold watch-chain, on which he raised enough money to pay all needful expenses. I remember well how the rest of our journey we rowed by many a tavern on the bank as effectually constrained as ever was Ulysses not to listen to its siren call. It was through no Earthly Paradise that the young poet and artist passed on the afternoon of our last day. When we reached the landing-stage where we were to leave our boat, our common stock of money amounted to just one penny. We were still six or seven miles from our destination; but by neither train nor omnibus would our empty pockets allow us to travel, so we hired a cab. We were in some alarm lest we should come to a turnpike-gate. At last we reached Red Lion Square, where we found Burne-Jones and Rossetti. At night five mattresses were spread on the carpetless floor, and there I slept amidst painters and poets.[1]

[1] There may have been one or even two bedsteads in the room. Most of us, I am sure, slept on mattresses laid on the floor.

Next morning I watched Burne - Jones painting some lilies in the garden of the Square. It was, I believe, the first time he painted in oils.

The following is Ruskin's letter to Rossetti :—

" DEAR ROSSETTI,—I am wild to know who is the author of *The Burden of Nineveh*, in No. 8 of *Oxford and Cambridge*. It is glorious. Please find out for me, and see if I can get acquainted with him."

On Rossetti's mention of Spiritualism in this letter, his brother remarks : " He here speaks scornfully of it. In later years (beginning, say, in 1864) he believed in it not a little."

Madox Brown wrote on April 9, 1868 : " Blank gave a spirit *soirée*, at which Rossetti attended, and flowers grew under Blank's hands out of the dining-table and eau de Cologne was squirted over the guests in the dark ; but Gabriel, growing irreverent, and addressing the S.'s by the too familiar appellation of ' Bogies,' they squirted plain (it must be hoped *clean*) water over those present and withdrew. So the report runs—I was not there."

" Our daughter," wrote Mrs. Howitt, " had, both by her pen and pencil, taken her place amongst the successful artists and writers of the day, when, in the spring of 1856, a severe private censure of one of her oil-paintings by a king among critics so crushed her sensitive nature as to make her yield to her bias for the supernatural and withdraw from the ordinary arena of the fine arts. In the spring of 1856 we had become acquainted with several most ardent and honest spirit-mediums. I was invited to a *séance* at Professor De Morgan's, and was much astonished and affected by communications purporting to come to me from my dear son Claude. With constant prayer for enlightenment and guidance we experimented at home. I felt thankful for the assurance thus gained of an invisible world, but resolved to neglect none of my common duties for spiritualism."

Hawthorne, who had met Mrs. Browning in the summer of this year, recorded in his note-book: "She introduced the subject of spiritualism, which, she says, interests her very much; indeed, she seems to be a believer. Mr. Browning, she told me, utterly rejects the subject, and will not believe even in the outward manifestation, of which there is such overwhelming evidence."

A year or two earlier I was present at an evening party at Professor De Morgan's, where a German exhibited a plan of ancient Jerusalem, which he had drawn, he said, by the aid of clairvoyance.

XXXIII.

14, CHATHAM PLACE, BLACKFRIARS.

[*End of* 1856.].

DEAR ALLINGHAM,

I wish, in writing again to me (which of course you're yearning to do by this time) you'd

tell me whereabouts it was in the Brit. Mus.
Print Room, that you saw an indescribable print
which you described to me at the time—Early
German, I believe, and in several compartments,
if I remember rightly.   I am going sometimes
there now, and having made some fruitless searches
after that print, which excited me at the time I
thought I wouldn't be licked, if a note by you
would help.

What sort of Xmas weather have you out there?
Is it any good wishing you merriment out of it?
To-day here is neither a bright day nor a dark day,
but a white smutty day,—piebald,—wherein, accordingly, life seems neither worth keeping nor getting
rid of.   The thick sky has a thin red sun stuck
in the middle of it, like the specimen wafer stuck
outside a box of them.   Even if you turned back
the lid, there would be nothing behind it, be sure,
but a jumble of such flat dead suns.   I am going
to sleep.

Are you to write the next great modern epic?
If so, you may put the above into blank verse.
I give it you.   And meanwhile, be sure to talk
to me about *Aurora Leigh*.

I have little news for you.   One sad piece though,
by the bye, for which you'll be sorry.   Poor Tom
Seddon died last month at Cairo.   He had been
married, and had a boy since last returning thence,

and went back there to pursue the path he had struck out, and is dead.   I am pretty sure you knew him.

Ruskin wants me very much to enter the old water-colour society, and says John Lewis will do anything to facilitate my entrance.   This would be a great advantage to the sale of my water-colours, but I fear it might chance to bonnet my oil-painting for good.   I don't know what to do.

Your friend,
D. G. ROSSETTI.

P.S.—I'll certainly claim your photograph.   I enclose you one in return from one of my blocks —*St. Cicely* (*Palace of Art*).   It is a horrid bad photograph, but as D——l has had the settling of the thing since it becomes of some interest.

NOTES ON XXXIII.

"Thomas Seddon," writes Mr. W. M. Rossetti, "died of dysentery very soon after his arrival at Cairo, and a life full of brightness, and a career full of high promise, were suddenly cut short at the early age of thirty-five."   His health, which had long been delicate, had suffered much on the voyage from Marseilles to Alexandria.   The weather was rough and the accommodation and food were bad.   On his arrival he gave himself no rest.   He was attacked by dysentery, which soon carried him off. Over his pure spirit the gloom of Sabbatarianism was cast. From his deathbed he wrote to his wife :—" This is a sharp curb, just as I felt ready to set to at my work ; but God has humbled me, and I trust proved me, and I believe punished me for a want of sufficient attention to his Sabbath, for if instead of walking about all day before and after church I had spent both Sundays quietly at home I might have been spared this." Mr. Holman Hunt tells me that of this inner gloom little was known even by his intimate friends. He was fond of playing practical jokes—somewhat cruel ones, too.

Rossetti never entered the Old Water-Colour Society.

Towards the end of 1856 Madox Brown wrote :— " Rossetti has been here nearly a fortnight, coming about twelve, and working or not working at his drawing on wood for *St. Cecilia.* It is jolly quaint but very lovely."

XXXIV.

14, Chatham Place, E.C.

Friday [*Postmark Jan.* 31, 1857].

Dear Allingham,

Will you be on the Committee as per enclosure? And will you answer at once—as I fancy the list may be making out.

I enclose also a little poem, pitched on—where?
—in *Reynolds' Miscellany!* and the authorship of
which I want to find out.   Do not you?

I shall write again soon, and trust to have another
photograph for you.

Your D. G. R.

Some people say here you wrote A. S.   Of course
I have undeceived some, *and did not spread the
report.*   I believe (*entre nous*) Maclennan did, being
a great friend of Smith.   I like *Abbey Easaroe.*

NOTES ON XXXIV.

The Committee was that of the Seddon Subscription Fund.   In a resolution moved by Holman
Hunt and seconded by D. G. Rossetti, Thomas
Seddon was described as "an artist, who, having
proposed to himself the application of absolute truth
in landscape to scenes of high historic and sacred
interest, undertook two journeys to the East, in
which he unflinchingly grappled with difficulties
previously deemed insurmountable, and the second
of which terminated his life at an early age."

With the money which was raised his "admirably
faithful view of Jerusalem" was purchased for the
National Gallery.

The following is "the little poem pitched on in
Reynolds' Miscellany,"—vol. xvii. p. 360.

15

A LOVER'S PASTIME.

Before the daybreak I arise
And search, to find if earth or air
   Hold anywhere
The likeness of thy sweet, sweet eyes.

   In nature's book,
Where semblances of thee I trace,
I mark the place,
With flowers that have a pleading look,
   For pity, gentleness and grace,
     With lilies white ;
And roses that are burning bright
I take for blushes : then I catch
The sunbeams from the jealous air,
   And with them match
The amber crowning of thy hair.

The dews that shine on withering wood,
   Or thirsty lands,
Quietly busy doing good,
   Are like thy hands.
The brown-eyed sunflower, all the day
   Looking one way,
I take for patience, made divine
By melancholy fears like thine.

   Ere break of day
I'm up and searching earth and air,
   To find out where,
   If find I may,.
Nature hath copied to her praise
The beauty of thy gracious ways.

   The wild sweet-brier
Shows through the book in many a place,
But for the smiling in thy face
   She would not have her good attire.

Sometimes I walk the stubbly ways
  That have small praise,
But spy out ne'ertheless,
Some patch of moss, all softly pied,
Or rude stone, with a speckled side,
  Telling thy loveliness.
I make believe the brooks that run
  With pleasant noise,
From sun to shade, and shade to sun,
  Mimic thy murmured joys.

  So, dearest heart,
I cheat the cruelty
That keeps us all so long apart,
  With many a poor conceit of thee.

  The songs of birds,
Floating the orchard tops among,
Echo the music of thy tongue ;
And fancy tries to find what words
  Come nestling to my breast
With melody so excellently dressed.

  Before the daybreak I arise,
And search through earth, and sky, and air,
But find I never anywhere
  The likeness of thy sweet, sweet eyes,
My modest lady, my exceeding fair."

The authorship of these lines I have not been able
to discover.

Abbey Asaroe (not *Easaroe*) is printed in Allingham's *Irish Songs and Poems*, p. 45.

XXXV.

[Undated.   Water-mark of letter paper 1858.]

My dear Allingham,

. . . I have one of the Magdalene photo-
graphs for you—but do not know how to reach
you with it. If I knew I would accompany it
with one of the Henry Taylor photos (Quoth
tongue &c.) of which I expect an instalment.
. . . I think you told me long ago that you had
recovered those proof sheets of my Italian Poets
(on whose loss, by the bye, I hope you have not
really based my lazy silence, which was pure lazi-
ness) and that they contain some notes of yours.
If so, I should like to have the benefit of these,
and would be glad to see them. I expect soon to
have copied all of my own verses which I care to
copy, with a view to printing some day. I have
often benefited by your criticism, and if you would
not find it a bore I would send you the MS. book,
and ask you to annotate it freely, and to tell me
of any pieces therein contained which you would
omit altogether. A good number of my perpe-
trations I have already excluded. Of course you
know our common race too well to think that I
should *always* benefit by a warning though one
rose from the grave—but I am sure I should get
something out of you. If I can be of any use at

all in your dealings with Bell & Daldy, through
their being such near neighbours of mine, pray
tell me.

And believe me,
dear Allingham,
yours affectionately
D. G. ROSSETTI.

NOTES ON XXXV.

"The Magdalene photograph" was of the pen-
and-ink drawing of *Mary Magdalene at the door
of Simon the Pharisee.*

"The Henry Taylor photograph" is of another
pen-and-ink drawing, *Hesternæ Rosæ.* "It represents," to quote the words of Mr. W. M. Rossetti,
"a tent occupied by a group of men and women—
the men throwing dice, one of the women sadly
reminiscent of the vanished days of her innocence;
and it bears the motto of Sir Henry Taylor's verses
in *Philip van Artevelde* (Part ii., act v.).

> "'Quoth tongue of neither maid nor wife
>   To heart of neither wife nor maid,
>   Lead we not here a jolly life
>   Betwixt the shine and shade?
>
>   Quoth heart of neither maid nor wife
>   To tongue of neither wife nor maid,
>   Thou wagg'st, but I am worn with strife,
>   And feel like flowers that fade.'"

XXXVI.

Thursday, [shortly before Christmas, 1859].

My dear Allingham,

Many thanks for your volume just received. I was agreeably surprised to see my sister's name on your list,—deservedly, I think.

The book is all the welcomer that it leads me to hope I was mistaken in a conclusion I had begun arriving at, that I must unwittingly have incurred the displeasure of one of my oldest and most valued friends, no other than yourself. Your silence before going and since I wrote to you had led me to fear this possibility. Now, if it is so, will you tell me downright, and the why? But perhaps you are only paying me out in my own coin,—if utter absence of answer can be considered payment in any sense,—in which case I must confess I could only cry, *Mea Culpa !*

By the bye, that is the title of a queer little poem, evidently modern, in your collection, with no name to it. Whose is it? Or where got you it?

A merry Christmas and " warious games of that sort " to you.

Yours affectionately,

D. G. Rossetti.

Notes on XXXVI.

In Allingham's *Nightingale Valley, a Collection of Choice Lyrics and Short Poems,* just published, Christina Rossetti's *An End* was included.

"Warious games of that sort" would seem to have been a favourite quotation with Rossetti, for this was the second time he made it in his correspondence with Allingham.

XXXVII.

[*Christmas,* 1859.]

My dear Allingham,

I was very glad to hear from you at last, but sorry and surprised to hear that your ailments have not quite left you even yet. I had understood from William that you were very much better when he saw you shortly before you went back. May health come to you as the chief pleasure of the season, and all the others with it.

Apart from the defect found by Ruskin in N. V. [*Nightingale Valley*]—and more apparent (sincerely) to him than to me, as I should wish almost any printed poem of mine to appear when next printed with certain revisions—there are various holes I have to pick in the book. I will turn

over my copy now I have read it and marked it,
and pull you up by it. First then, I have scored
the following as doubtful " Choicest English
Poems "—2 ?'s denoting double doubt.

> ? ? Wake, Lady. [Joanna Baillie.]
> Fair Ines. [Thomas Hood.]
> The Seven Sisters. [William Wordsworth.]
> The Amulet. [R. W. Emerson.]
> Abou Ben Adhem. [Leigh Hunt.]
> ? ? Ode to the Cuckoo. [John Logan.]
> ? ? Season for Wooing. [W. C. Bryant.]
> The Idle Voyager. [Hartley Coleridge.]
> The Last Day of Autumn. [From the
>   German.]
> To Mary in Heaven.[1] [Robert Burns.]
> The Northern Star. [Anonymous.]
> To Lucasta. [R. Lovelace.]
> The Fugitives.[2] [P. B. Shelley.]
> ? ? Song from the Spanish. [W. C. Bryant.]
> Adieu. [Thomas Carlyle.]
> To a Sky Lark. [William Wordsworth.]
> Ned Bolton (hardly as good as Dibden's

----

[1] The Heavens nevertheless as yet not falling on me.

[2] Nor the mountains hitherto covering me. This always seems
to me a desperately loose piece of writing,

> " In the court of the fortress,
> Beside the pale portress "—

Fancy a fortress with a portress to keep the thieves out, &c ,
&c. [Note by Rossetti.]

best. Why is not *Tom Bowling* in at this rate?). [William Kennedy.]

An Angel in the House. [Leigh Hunt.]

Disdain Returned. [Thomas Carew.]

Inscription for Fountain. [Barry Cornwall.]

The Exile. [Thomas Hood.]

Lord Ullin's Daughter. [Thomas Campbell.]

? ? ? The Hour of Prayer. [Felicia Hemans.]

Song from Lady of Lake. ["Soldier rest! thy warfare o'er." Walter Scott.]

To a Cold Beauty.

Evening. [Alfred Tennyson.]

Phillida and Corydon. [Nicholas Breton.]

The Knight's Tomb (the only good lines, at the end, being old). [S. T. Coleridge.]

The Angel (hardly Blake's best).

The Skylark. [James Hogg.]

Ballad. ["She's up and gone." Thomas Hood.]

Down on the Shore (more than 2 thirds of this author being better). [William Allingham].

May and Death (not B.'s best). [Robert Browning.]

I don't mean to say that, taking all the lump of British Poetry, I mightn't have even further substitutions to propose (absentees occurring at the moment, Herbert—Byron—Henry Taylor!!), but those marked above I think misplaced even apart from the question of varying taste—most on absolute artistic grounds—the others as compared with their writers' powers.

Now I really think, to continue, there's much too much Wordsworth. He's good, you know, but unbearable. I don't pretend to have read all you've put in of his, but noticed with sorrow that he has two more pieces in the book than Tennyson, who comes next, and 6 more than Shakespeare—one morceau of Wordsworth, which I had not met with anywhere· else (*To my Maiden Sister, sent by my Dear Wife's (and my own) darling boy,—* or something like that), drew my pencil, I confess, to the margin in a moment, with the compound adjective " puffy-muffy," not inapplicable to much I have found in the same excellent writer.

Then of the Shakespeare sonnets inserted, the only one which, to my thinking, ranks among his very first is the *Love's Consolation.* In *The Wife of Usher's Well*, I do not think the inserted stanza indispensible [*sic*] to the sense, and don't you agree with me that modern additions are best avoided, if possible?

Barthram's Dirge is, I believe, undoubtedly by Surtees. *Sic Vita*, you probably know, is often printed with two or three more stanzas of the same length as the one you give, but these perhaps you reject as spurious. I do not bear them in mind.

In *Ulalume* you have omitted two lines at the close of stanza 6 I believe. Ought it not to run thus ?

> " In terror she spoke letting sink her
>   Plumes till [Wings until] they trailed in the dust,
>   *In agony sobbed letting sink her*
>   *Wings* [Plumes] *till they trailed in the dust,*
>   'Till they sorrowfully trailed in the dust."

Au reste, you have cut out that abominable *vista*.

So there I have made enough objections,—humbly, mostly, I beg you to believe,—and not said a word yet of all the praise the book deserves—full as much as Ruskin gives it. Your preface is most excellent, and will show the wise ones that the editor is " somebody " besides Giraldus. And why Giraldus ? And why, I would almost say, *Nightingale Valley*, had I not almost said too much already.

Mea Culpa I described as a queer poem, in my last, lest by any possibility it should be written by any one I hated. The fact, as I thought then and think now, is that it is an extremely fine one —I think one of your very finest. I half suspected you, but it is not very recognizable as yours. What a splendid version you have of Auld Robin Gray! Is it altered at all by W. A.?

Yours affectionately,

D. G. R.

Notes on XXXVII.

"The defect found by Ruskin" in *Nightingale Valley* was, it seems probable, Allingham's revision of some of the poems.

Rossetti's admiration of Henry Taylor's poetry in his early manhood is mentioned by Mr. Holman Hunt in the following passage:—"Rossetti delighted most in those poems for which the world then had shown but little appreciation. *Sordello* and *Paracelsus* he would give by forty and fifty pages at a time, and what were more fascinating, the shorter poems of Browning. Then would follow the grand rhetoric from Taylor's *Philip van Artevelde*, in the scene between the herald and the Court at Ghent with Philip in reply."

The "*morceau* of Wordsworth" is entitled, *To my Sister. Written at a Small Distance from my House, and sent by my Little Boy.* Matthew Arnold included it in that selection of the poet's works of which he writes: "The volume contains, I think, everything, or nearly everything, which may best serve him with the majority of lovers of poetry, nothing which may disserve him." According to Mr. Hall Caine, as quoted by Mr. W. M.

Rossetti, " Rossetti thought Wordsworth was too much the high priest of Nature to be her lover." Mr. Caine speaks also of " Rossetti's grudging Wordsworth every vote he gets." His indifference to the beautiful poet was perhaps due to his having spent all his childhood and youth, and most of his manhood, in London.

It was no doubt by mistake that the two lines had been omitted in *Ulalume*. " That abominable *vista*" is found in the eighth stanza :—

> " Thus I pacified Psyche and kissed her,
>   And tempted her out of her gloom—
>   And conquered her scruples and gloom ;
> And we passed to the end of the vista,
>   But were stopped by the door of a tomb."

Allingham edited Poe's *Poems* for Routledge in 1857. In the preface he says : " In our private copy of *Ulalume* we have taken the liberty to expunge the rhyme of *vista* in the eighth stanza, reading the line thus :—

> " And we passed from the shade as I kissed her."

It was this emendation, introduced in *Nightingale Valley* without acknowledgment, that Rossetti praised. This poem and others of Poe's " were a deep well of delight to Rossetti in his early years," as his brother tells us. The ordinary reader may perhaps be forgiven if he looks upon *Ulalume* as highly melodious rant. If the cockney rhyme which Rossetti found abominable seemed

correct to Poe's ear, it was perhaps due to the
five years he spent in his boyhood in a school at
Stoke Newington. Rossetti, it will be remembered, had himself made *calm* rhyme with *arm*,
so that he had little reason to be offended.

"Ruskin," as Allingham told Mr. W. M.
Rossetti, "wrote a warm little note to the 'editor
of *Nightingale Valley*,' calling it the best collection
he ever saw." On the title-page it is described
as "edited by Giraldus."

Allingham's *Mea Culpa* is as follows :—

"At me one night the angry moon,
  Suspended to a rim of cloud,
  Glared through the courses of the wind.
  Suddenly there my spirit bow'd,
  And shrank into a fearful swoon,
  That made me deaf and blind.

We sinn'd—we sin—is that a dream?
  We wake—there is no voice nor stir;
  Sin and repent from day to day,
  As though some reeking murderer
  Should dip his hand in a running stream,
  And lightly go his way.

Embrace me fiends and wicked men,
  For I am of your crew. Draw back,
  Pure women, children with clear eyes.
  Let scorn confess me on his rack,—
  Stretch'd down by force, uplooking then
  Into the solemn skies!

Singly we pass the gloomy gate;
  Some robed in honour, full of peace,

Who of themselves are not aware;
Being fed with secret wickedness,
And comforted with lies; my fate
Moves fast; I shall come there.

All is so usual, hour by hour,
Men's spirits are so lightly twirl'd
By every little gust of sense;
Who lays to heart this common world?
Who lays to heart the Ruling Power,
Just, infinite, intense?

Thou wilt not frown, O God.   Yet we
Escape not Thy transcendent law;
It reigns within us and without.
What earthly vision never saw
Man's naked soul may suddenly see,
Dreadful, past thought or doubt."

XXXVIII.

PARIS, *Wednesday*, [*June*, 1860].

MY DEAR ALLINGHAM,

Have you heard yet that I'm married?
The news is hardly a month old, so it may not
have reached you, though I have meant to write
you word of it all along, as you are one of the
few valued friends whom Lizzie and I have in
common as yet; nor, as the circle spreads, will she

be likely to feel a warmer regard for any than she does for you.

Of her health all I can say is that it is possible to give rather better news of it than I could have given a month ago. Paris seems to agree so well with her that I am fearful of returning to London (which, however, we must do in a day or two) lest it should throw her back into the terrible state of illness she had been in for some time before. But in that case I shall make up my mind to settle in Paris for a time, as I could no doubt paint here well enough. In any case I expect a move, as winter comes on, will be necessary.

You know I have been meaning to inflict my vol. of MS. rhymes on you for some time, but have been so busy lately and wanted to copy a little more first. I shall try and send them yet. When shall we be likely to see you again in London? Jones is married, too, only a week ago. He and his wife (a charming and most gifted little woman) were to have met us in Paris, but he has not been well enough to travel with pleasure.

With love from both of us I remain,

Your affectionate

D. G. ROSSETTI.

NOTES ON XXXVIII.

Rossetti was married to Miss Siddal at Hastings

on May 23, 1860. On April 13, in a letter to his mother about the approaching event, he wrote :—" Like all the important things I ever meant to do, —to fulfill duty or secure happiness,—this one has been deferred almost beyond possibility." Ruskin, writing to congratulate him, said :—" I think Ida should be very happy to see how much more beautifully, perfectly, and tenderly you draw when you are drawing *her* than when you draw anybody else. She cures you of all your worst faults when you look at her."

Mr. W. M. Rossetti, speaking of Lady Burne-Jones, says : " Two of her sisters are Mrs. [now Lady] Poynter, wife of the director of the National Gallery [now President of the Royal Academy], and Mrs. Kipling, mother of Mr. Rudyard Kipling."

It was during this visit to Paris (according to Mr. William Sharp) that Rossetti completed his drawing called *Dr. Johnson and the Methodistical Young Ladies at the Mitre Tavern.* Among the very few works of history and biography that he had read " Boswell's *Johnson* held a high place."

The following anecdote of the end of Rossetti's wedding trip I have from Mr. Arthur Hughes :—" It was from Munro I had the story that D. G. R., having spent his honeymoon and all his money in Paris, was returning, when he read in the first paper he got on the way, of the sudden death of a friend (not a great friend at all, I think), a writer named Brough, one of the class of which James

Hannay was a prominent type—a young man with a wife and two little children. Rossetti knew that ways and means would be doubly deficient to the widow in such circumstances. He had spent all his own now; but a certain portion of that existed in jewelry upon Mrs. Rossetti, who no doubt fully sympathised with the trouble in question, so that when they reached London they did not go straight home, but drove first to a pawnbroker, and then to the Brough lodgings, and after that home, with entirely empty pockets; but, I expect, two very full hearts."

XXXIX.

SPRING COTTAGE, DOWNSHIRE HILL, HAMPSTEAD,

[*July* 31, 1860].

MY DEAR ALLINGHAM,

I was very sorry to miss you, and very glad to hear from you. At the time you were still in town I was so harrassed [*sic*] with house-hunting and my wife was so unwell that I found it daily impossible to see you till the time was past. I hope it may come again as soon as possible, and at a more propitious time. I have succeeded in getting no permanent quarters yet, but we have a very nice little lodging as above, and I am obliged to go in and out every day to my work, which I could postpone no longer. I have the Blackfriars rooms till Michaelmas in any case—so before then I hope we may be settled down elsewhere. It must be hereabouts, as no other part near London would be half so suitable to my wife. The difficulties are manifold :—all houses to let are either too large, or else must be taken on too long a lease for us who do not know whether we may not be forced away altogether, or at any rate for every winter.

Lizzie is getting a little stronger now after a very bad attack of illness ; but she is still so weak that the least excitement knocks her up again, and always so obstinately plucky in illness that there is no keeping her down if she can only be up and doing. The other day she saw Ned and his wife for the first time, and we all went with the Browns to the Zoological Gardens, but it was more than she ought to have done. To-day is the last day of the Academy, and we are still uncertain this morning whether it will be wise for her to go, though I have cut my day's work for the purpose. It is very provoking to be unable to take her to see so many kind friends, all so pressing and anxious, or even to let them come to us.

I am anxious about the Sawdust Poem, but am not sure that that product is better adapted for wholesome spiritual bread than it is for the bodily. Sawdust, more or less, however, is the fashion of

the day; ——'s wooden puppet-show of enlarged
views instead of Veronese's flesh, blood, and slight
stupidity. Give me the latter, however,—or even
Millais' when Veronese's is not to be had. But O
that Veronese at Paris!

As to Ruskin's ten years' rest, I do not know
about his writing, but I will answer for my reading,
if he only writes like his article in the *Cornhill* this
month. Who *could* read it, or anything about such
bosh!

Ruskin, by the bye, carried off that MS. book of
mine some little while before he left England, and
has not returned it; but I am trying to get it
through the servants at his place, and still trust to
send it you, though indeed I sincerely suspect it
would be better for me to stick to painting only
and let it be. However, I do not mean to let it
interfere at all with that, and then, if it is rot, it
will not matter much. You tell me you are in
Part 2 of your Poem, but not when Part 3 and
publication seem likely. I know no more than
yourself of the matter of Browning's Poem, though
he told me of it (and of an additional series of *Men
and Women* in progress!) when he wrote to me
lately, and sent the portraits. I had given him
a splendid cast of Keats's head, which I got from
Donovan (the same I once had before and broke, if
you remember). I had a mould taken by Munro

before I sent the cast off, so can let you have a copy, if you care to be put in mind of mere strawberry-merchants. . . .

By the bye I remember sending you a little book of bogy poems in emblematic green cover, and hearing from you that you had one already. If you still have mine, would you oblige me by sending it back, as I sometimes think of it when I want to be surprised.

Do write to me again, and I'll try to be a better correspondent, now I'm married and settled. My wife and I are

Yours affectionately,

D. G.
E. E. } Rossetti.

Notes on XXXIX.

Spring Cottage has disappeared. It was within two or three minutes' walk of the house in which Keats had lodged some forty years earlier.

Some time in the following year Rossetti wrote to Madox Brown :—" Dear Brown, Lizzie and I propose to meet Georgie and Ned [Mr. and Mrs. Burne-Jones] at 2 P.M. to-morrow at the Zoological Gardens—place of meeting the Wombat's Lair." The wombat had a strange attraction for Rossetti. On September 15, 1869, he wrote to his brother :—" Will you thank Maggie for her most complete information about the Passover,

Also Christina for the Shrine in the Italian taste which she has reared for the wombat. I fear his habits tend inveterately to drain architecture." Six days later he wrote:—"The Wombat is 'A Joy, a Triumph, a Delight, a Madness.'" Madox Brown used to tell how at Rossetti's house one day at dinner, the wombat, "who occupied a place of honour on the épergne, descending unobserved during a heated discussion, devoured the entire contents of a valuable box of cigars."

"The Sawdust Poem" is probably described in the following letter of Allingham's, dated March 12, 1860 :—"I am doing something occasionally at a poem on Irish matters, to have two thousand lines or so, and can see my way through it. One part out of three is done. But alas! when all's done, who will like it? Think of the Landlord and Tenant Question in flat decasyllables! Did you ever hear of the Irish coaster that was hailed, 'Smack ahoy! what's your cargo?' 'Timber and fruit!' 'What sort?' 'Besoms and potatoes!' I fear my poem will no better fulfil expectations." This poem was first published in *Fraser's Magazine*, 1862–3, under the title of *Laurence Bloomfield, or Rich and Poor in Ireland.* In the preface Allingham says :—" A man who was neither English nor Irish, Ivan Tourganief, after reading the book, said to a friend of the author (who may be forgiven for recalling the words), 'I never understood Ireland before.'"

Rossetti, a month earlier, had seen Veronese's

Marriage in Cana. He described it as "the greatest picture in the world, beyond a doubt." His brother writes that "later on, 1871, he had got to think Veronese (and also Tintoret) 'simply detestable without their colour and handling.'"

The August number of the *Cornhill Magazine* contained the first part of Ruskin's *Unto this Last.* Mr. Collingwood, writing of Ruskin's stay at Chamounix in July, 1860, says :—" He was far from well; feeling, for the first time to a serious degree, the morbid depression which some of the letters of the period indicate ; and turning over in his mind the thoughts he was embodying in a new series of *Essays on Political Economy.* These new papers, painfully thought out and carefully set down in his room at the Hotel de l'Union, he sent to his friend Thackeray. His reputation as a writer and philanthropist, together with the friendliness of editor and publisher, secured the insertion of the first three from August to October. Thackeray then wrote to say that they were so unanimously condemned and disliked that, with all apologies, he could only admit one more. So the series was brought hastily to a conclusion in November ; and the author, beaten back as he had never been beaten before, dropped the subject and 'sulked,' as he called it, all the winter."

Donovan was a phrenologist of King William Street, who was known by the casts he used to take of murderers as soon as they were hanged. The cast of Keats's head is reproduced in Mr. Buxton Forman's *Letters of John Keats.*

Of " the little book of bogy poems " I give an account in a note on Letter XLVII.

Mrs. Rossetti's Christian names were Elizabeth Eleanor.

XL.

[*September or October*, 1860.]

MY DEAR ALLINGHAM,

I am sending you them things at last, *i.e.*, the MSS. which Ruskin has only just returned me ; I having asked him to send one— viz. *Jenny*, to the *Cornhill* for me—he of course refusing to send that, offering to send some of the mystical ones that I don't care to print by themselves.

My delay has been partly through this, and partly through wanting to add more before sending them to you. But they'd better e'en go now, for no more will get done for the nonce. The only one very unfinished, both in what is written and unwritten (I think), is *The Bride's Chamber*. I wish you'd specially tell me of any you don't think worth including. You will find that your advice has been followed often (if you remember what you gave), and so it is not time wasted to advise me. When I think how old most of these things are, it seems like a sort of mania to keep thinking of them still; but I suppose one's leaning still to them depends mainly on their having no trade associations, and being still a sort of thing of one's own. I have no definite ideas as to doing anything with them, but should like, even if they lie at rest, to make them as good as I can.

And what are you doing? How goes the sawdust poem you spoke of? And is it to be visible that wine is packed therein, or is a pure surface of sawdust, betraying *no* wine, the duty of the modern bard? So may the Shade of Wordsworth smile on him and repay him by reading all his (W.'s) Poems through to him when the kindred Spirits meet.

I wish you were in town, to see you sometimes, for I literally see no one now except Madox Brown pretty often, and even he is gone now to join Morris, who is out of reach at Upton, and with them is married Jones painting the inner walls of the house that Top built. But as for the neighbours, when they see men pourtrayed by Jones upon the walls, the images of the Chaldeans pourtrayed (by *him!*) in Extract Vermilion, exceeding all probability in dyed attire upon their heads, after the manner of no Babylonians of any Chaldea, the land of any one's nativity,—as soon as they see them with their eyes, shall they not account him doting, and send messengers into Colney Hatch?

Lizzie has been rather better of late, I hope— certainly not subject to the same extent to violent fits of illness. She is at Brighton just now for a few days, but I know I may send you her love with mine. We are sorely put to it for a *pied-à-terre*, every house we try for seeming to slip through just as we think we have got it. For one in Church Row, Hampstead, which has just escaped us, my heart is in doleful dumps; it having a glorious old-world garden worth £200 a year to me for backgrounds.

Do let me hear from you (to Blkfrs [Blackfriars]) when you have got the book which goes with this, and believe me

Yours affectionately,
D. G. ROSSETTI.

William is gone to Florence to old Browning.

NOTES ON XL.

Jenny was begun as early as 1847, was almost finished about 1858, and was published in 1870. "Mr. Ruskin," writes Mr. W. M. Rossetti, "sent a letter criticising the poem, one of his objections being that 'Jenny' is not a true rhyme to 'guinea,' as in the opening couplet:

> ' Lazy, laughing, languid Jenny,
>   Fond of a kiss and fond of a guinea.'

This I regard as the stricture of a Scotchman."

Bride-Chamber Talk was begun as soon as *Jenny*, but was not published till 1881, when its title was changed to *The Bride's Prelude*.

Rossetti took part in painting Morris's house. In the record of his work for 1858–59 his brother mentions the "*Salutatio Beatricis, representing Dante meeting Beatrice in Florence, and in the garden of Eden*, painted in oil in a week on a door in Mr. Morris's residence, The Red House, Upton, near Bexley Heath, Woolwich." I remember the beautiful paintings on the doors and furniture in this pleasant house. I have not forgotten, moreover, a long and eager talk on pigments between my host and Charles Faulkner, of which I did not understand a single word. Towards the close of 1865 Madox Brown recorded :—" Morris leaves his house, and takes up with the Firm in a large house in Queen Square."

Morris in his Oxford days, and indeed long afterwards, was always known by the name of Topsy or Top, given him after the girl in *Uncle Tom's Cabin*.

Colney Hatch is a lunatic asylum near London.

The house in Church Row with its garden worth £200 a year for backgrounds recalls the anecdote of Linnell's purchase of Redstone Wood. "His solicitor told him the price asked was excessive. Linnell's reply was : 'Never mind, the land will prove a good investment; it will give me foregrounds—indeed, most of the materials I need for my pictures.'"

XLI.

BLACKFRIARS,
1st November [1860].

DEAR ALLINGHAM,

I'm wanting to copy and illustrate some poem of mine in the album of a kind and good lady —Mrs. Dalrymple—whether known or unknown to you I am not sure. Now do not hurry any consideration you may mean to bestow on my MSS., as I feel sure they will benefit thereby; but when you *can*, let me have them again, without their losing such advantage. I have thus much need of them as I have no other copies now.

And what do you think of *Faithful for Ever?* And have you seen Ruskin's letter to the *Critic* about it, in answer to a spiteful attack there? I was very sorry to hear what you wrote me about the Author's wife—poor thing—but I hope she may be mending as one hears no more. I wrote to Patmore after reading his book, which he sent me, saying all that I (most sincerely) admired in it, but perhaps leaving some things unsaid; for what can it avail to say some things to a man after his third volume? "Of love which never finds its published close, what sequel?" And how many?!

A man (one Gilchrist, who lives next door to Carlyle, and is as near him in other respects as he can manage) wrote to me the other day, saying he was writing a life of Blake, and wanted to see my manuscript by that genius. Was there not some talk of *your* doing something in the way of publishing its contents? I know William thought of doing so, but fancy it might wait long for his efforts; and I have no time, but really think its contents ought to be edited, especially if a new *Life* gives a "shove to the concern" (as Spurgeon expressed himself in thanking a liberal subscriber to his Tabernacle). I have not yet engaged myself any way to said Gilchrist on the subject, though I have told him he can see it here if he will give me a day's notice.

By the bye, talking of Blake, did I (I think I did) solicit from you one of the two copies you have, or had, of a certain greenish Book of Bogies, one whereof was once sent you by the present applicant, who lately found out from the Ghost's publisher that the literary character is quite out of print and has no further views on the British press?

And again—how am I to send a certain photograph which lies here inscribed to you? Or shall I keep it till you come?

Lizzie has been rather stronger lately, and we have resolved (after much vain house-hunting about Hampstead and Highgate) to weather out the winter here at Blackfriars, taking the 2nd floor in the next house in addition to these rooms (the landlord of both being the same, and he offering us the floor at a moderate rent). We could have a door opened between the two floors—a plan adopted throughout the two houses—and feel at home, and settled for the time being.

You know William is back from Florence, etc.—having found the Brownings at Siena—the great one exuberant as ever. I had a request the other day to illustrate *Aurora Leigh*, from, or rather on the part of, the publisher, but really I don't think I could make much of it. However, if it were done by various hands, I should like to make one among them. R. B. was not very explicit to William on the subject of his present labours.

Have you seen a new vol.,—however, I'm not quite sure the copies are all out yet,—viz., 2 plays by Algernon Swinburne and did you meet him in London? He is very Topsaic, with a decided dash of *Death's Jest Book*, if you have read that improving book. But there's no mistake about some of his *poems*—much more, indeed, than these published plays. The other day Ned. Jones, his wife, my wife, and I went to Hampton Court and lost our-

selves in the maze. I wish you had been one of
the party, and so would Jones have wished, I know,
as you are on his select list, which is not too large.
Really I still believe you ought to come to London.
At the end of the winter the Jones's and we mean
to take a house together, if we can find one to our
liking.

With kindest remembrances from both of us,

I am,

Yours affectionately,

D. G. ROSSETTI.

What of your poem ?   Do tell.

NOTES ON XLI.

Mrs. Dalrymple was sister of Mrs. Cameron,
famous for her photography, and of Mrs. Prinsep
(the mother of the Royal Academician).

Patmore wrote to Allingham on November 25,
1861 :—" *The Victims of Love* is the completion of
Faithful for Ever, which was abandoned by me in
an unfinished state when my wife's condition of
health seemed quite hopeless. I hope you will not
read it till it appears as part of the second and
revised edition of *Faithful for Ever*, which will
probably appear in the spring."

In a letter in *The Critic*, October 27, 1860,
Ruskin wrote :—" The poem is, as I said, to the
best of my belief, a finished and tender work of
very noble art."   To this the editor replied :—" If

we be not very much mistaken, Mr. Ruskin said that he preferred *Aurora Leigh* to any poem since Milton. . . . A re-perusal leads to the belief that the ' poem ' is about as jejune, puerile, and inartistic a piece of writing as it would be possible to produce." He goes on to quote '' Mr. Patmore's never-to-be-forgotten couplet :—

> " ' A gentlewoman's twice as cheap,
>   As well as pleasanter to keep.' "

Rossetti, in the line which he incloses in quotation marks, applying it so humorously to Patmore's *Angel in the House*, parodies Tennyson's *Love and Duty :*—

> " Of love that-never found his earthly close,
>   What sequel ? "

Allingham, in a letter to Patmore dated March 29, 1856, had told him that he was writing at too great length. The poet replied :—" You horrify me with your talk about pruning. The poem wants at least one third more to make it a complete statement of the matter." An amusing instance of his vanity is shown in the following passage in a letter he wrote to Allingham on September 12, 1855 :—" What do you think of the gratuitous slight put upon you and me in Kingsley's notice of *Maud ?* I would not change *Tamerton Church Tower* [one of his own poems] nor, if I was the author of it, *The Music Master* for fifty *Mauds*."

"One Gilchrist" was Alexander Gilchrist, author of *Lives of Etty and Blake*. "For him," writes Mr. W. M. Rossetti, "the feeling of Rossetti was one of genuine friendliness. He liked the writer and his writings, and had a high regard for his insight as a critic of art." Gilchrist's sudden death in the following November came as "a staggering blow" to his friend. When, a few months later, Rossetti lost his wife, he wrote to Mrs. Gilchrist: —"I feel forcibly the bond of misery which exists between us, and the unhappy right we have of saying to each other what we both know to be fruitless." He and his brother helped the widow to complete her husband's *Life of Blake*.

The manuscript by Blake had been offered Rossetti in 1847 for ten shillings. "Dante's pockets," writes his brother, "were in their normal state of depletion, so he applied to me, urging that so brilliant an opportunity should not be let slip, and I produced the required coin. His ownership of this volume conduced to the Præraphaelite movement; for he found here the most outspoken (and no doubt, in a sense, the most irrational) epigrams and jeers against such painters as Correggio, Titian, Rubens, Rembrandt, Reynolds, and Gainsborough. These were balsam to Rossetti's soul, and grist to his mill. At the sale of his library the Blake manuscript sold for £110."

Mr. W. M. Rossetti, describing to W. Allingham his trip to Italy, says :—" The Brownings were not at Florence, but at their summer haunts, the Villa

Alberti, Marciano, near Sienna. Old Browning jolly and lovable beyond description, looking very healthy and alive ; Mrs. Browning moderately well."

"Mr. Swinburne," writes Mr. W. M. Rossetti, "dedicated to Rossetti his first volume, *The Queen Mother, and Rosamund.* His brilliant intellect, his wide knowledge of poetry and astonishing memory in quotation, his enthusiasm for whatsoever he recognised as great, his fascinating audacity and pungency in talk, and the singular and ingenuous charm of his manner to any one whom he either liked or respected made him the most welcome of comrades to Rossetti."

Rossetti wrote to "Shirley" in 1865 :—"You will find Swinburne's *Atalanta* a most noble thing ; never surpassed, to my thinking."

Thomas Lovell Beddoes wrote to a friend from Pembroke College, Oxford, on June 8, 1825 :— "Oxford is the most indolent place on earth. I have fairly done nothing in the world but read a play or two of Schiller, Æschylus, and Euripides. I am thinking of a very Gothic-styled tragedy, for which I have a jewel of a name—*Death's Jest Book.* Of course no one will ever read it."

XLII.

[November 22, 1860.]

MY DEAR ALLINGHAM,

I know I'm wrong to be nervous, but as your letter of the 13th talks of my MSS. coming back in a day or two (I have no copies besides), it looks as if something *might* have happened; but no doubt, after all, it hasn't.

I'm going to take the photograph with me as you direct the very first time I pass that way at any leisure, which is seldomer than would seem in the rational order of things; but it shall soon reach you now. There are several questions in your letter which I'll proceed to answer.

1. I have no copy of the letter of Ruskin's about Patmore in *The Critic*, or would have sent it you.

2. Swinburne's volume is in print certainly, as I have one; but I doubt if yet issued, or even all printed, as I believe he purposed some corrections. On second thoughts, I'll send you mine; but please return it at earliest, as I haven't yet read the first play, and may get found out. He read it me in MS.

3. I will enquire at Trübner's forthwith about your Yankee edition.

4. I suspect such an Opie as you describe cannot be worth much, but am not quite sure about it. Am much too ignorant to make a guess.

5. I never to my knowledge promised to get you a Tennyson portrait, and fear one is hardly get-at-able now; as I have been trying myself to get one of the slouch-hatted ones (I have the other from Mrs. Cameron), but judge they are all distributed, as it does not turn up. I am having a 4 - vol. Tennyson of the Tauchnitz edition bound for my wife, and wanted to face the 4 titles with the 2 photos and Woolner's 2 photo-portraits, but fear I shall be one short. Have you seen the Tauchnitz Tennyson? It contains all—even to the Idylls.

By the bye, if you have one, I wish you would send me one of those photos of yourself, as we are hanging pictures in profusion about our rooms here, and would hang you, if we could get you.

But mine seems lost (the one you gave long ago), as I can find it nowhere. If you haven't another to give, can one still be got at Bond Street?

About the Poems, I never meant, I believe, to print the Hymn (which was written merely to see if I could do Wesley, and copied, I believe, to enrage my friends) nor the Duke of Wellington. *The Mirror* I will sacrifice to you, and have no prejudice myself in favour of *Ave*, but should be smothered by certain friends it has if it did not go in. Are your objections to it on poetic or dogmatic grounds? and does *Dennis Shand* displease you for anything but its impropriety? But perhaps I shall find my answers in the margins. The one of any length I most thought of omitting myself is the *Portrait*, which is rather spoon-meat; but this, I see, you do not name, and perhaps I may leave it. My chief reason for including as much as I could would be to make the volume look as portly as may be from such a middle-aged novice. I would throw the *Bride's Chamber* over altogether if I could muster energy to supply an equal amount of new matter, but fear I shall have to finish it off somehow if I rush into print, as I almost think of doing now.

Your accusation of the *cause* of my anxiety about your poem is a little bit of genuine ill-nature now, is it not, to scold a reader of yours as I am—eh, now?

I am sorry to learn that in all these years you have had no better specimen of London at Ballyshannon than Aubrey de Vere, who is surely one of the wateriest of the well - meaning. I wish Lizzie and I could turn up some time in your neighbourhood for a change, or see you here, if not there, till when and ever,

I am and we are,

Yours affectionately,

D. G. ROSSETTI.

P.S.—We have got one of our rooms completely hung round with Lizzie's drawings, which I should like to show you.

NOTES ON XLII.

"I believe I have this Hymn somewhere," Mr. W. M. Rossetti informs me. "It was never published. I can remember that some years after Rossetti's death it was produced to me as being his, and I pronounced it spurious; but since then I have seen reason to alter my opinion. *Wellington's Funeral* was finally published by him; *The Mirror*, not by him, but by me, in the Collected Works." *Dennis Shand*, Mr. W. M. Rossetti describes as "a ballad of a rather light kind, not published."

About *The Portrait* Rossetti wrote to his mother in 1873: "I remember that, for the family *Hotch-Potch*, long and long ago, I first wrote *The Blessed Damozel*, and also a poem about a portrait. Have you these ancient documents, and could you let me have the same if in my own handwriting?" " *The Hodgepodge*," says Mr. W. M. Rossetti, "was a sort of manuscript family magazine, never passing beyond the range of the family circle, which was concocted during some months or weeks of 1847, or possibly 1846."

XLIII.

[*Postmark, November* 29, 1860.]

My dear Allingham,

The book comes safe. I've not yet had time to look well through your suggestions, but am glad to see there are fewest in the things done later. Some of the others I know can never be set quite right, but I dare say I shall find some help thereto in your notes. Would you tell me as regards *Jenny* (which I reckon the most serious thing I have written), whether there is any objection you see in the treatment, or any side of the subject left untouched which ought to be included? I really believe I shall print the things now, and see whether the magic presence of proof-sheets revives my muse sufficiently for a new poem or two to add to them.

Indeed, and of course, my wife *does* draw still. Her last designs would, I am sure, surprise and delight you, and I hope she is going to do better than ever now. I feel surer every time she works that she has real genius — none of your make-believe—in conception and colour, and if she can only add a little more of the precision in carrying out which it so much needs health and strength to attain, she will, I am sure, paint such pictures as no woman has painted yet. But it is no use hoping for too much.

I quite agree with you in loathing *Once a Week*, illustrations and all. Meredith's novel, however, has very great merit of a wonderfully queer kind, I thought. Did you? But through your poem (how long have such little commodities as 500-line poems been lying by with you?) I should like greatly to open a connection even with *Once a Week*, though it is only once a century that I feel disposed to "illustrate." (I had an application through Chapman, the other day, about doing *Aurora Leigh* all through [as I understood], but couldn't, though I should like to join with others, if feasible, for a block or two, for Browning's sake.)

I wish you would let me know what the subject is in your poem. If modern, so much the better ; only, if Irish, I fear failing in character and truth. But I am not so despairingly dilatory quite now, I think, as I used to be in those famous old days, and might not perhaps turn your poem into a posthumous one.

As for Swinburne's Plays, I don't think they will be to your liking. For my own part, I think he is much better suited to ballad-writing and such like, but there are real beauties in the plays too.

I have been to-day to Trübner and asked for your book from America. They showed me Ticknor & Fields' last list, wherein *it is not;* but said also that they were seeing Mr. Ticknor every day, and would enquire. I left them your address and my own,

Yours affectionately,

D. G. ROSSETTI.

The *Magdalene* shall soon reach you.

NOTES ON XLIII.

On May 24, 1870, Rossetti wrote to his maiden aunt :—" I just hear from mamma, with a pang of remorse, that you have ordered a copy of my Poems. You may be sure I did not fail to think of you when I inscribed copies to friends and relatives ; but, to speak frankly, I was deterred from sending it to you by the fact of the book including one poem *(Jenny)* of which I felt uncertain whether you would be pleased with it. I am not ashamed of having written it (indeed, I assure you that I would never have written it if I thought it unfit to be read with good results), but I feared it might startle you somewhat. . . .

My mother likes it, on the whole, the best in the volume, after some consideration."

Mrs. Gilchrist, writing to Rossetti about his poems, after speaking of *The Blessed Damozel*, goes on to say of *Jenny* —" There is another poem—other, indeed !—which moves me even to anguish : one which comes upon a woman with appalling force after she has been standing gazing into the very Sanctuary of Love where womanhood sits divinely enthroned. For she knows that if, looking up joyfully, the brightness shining on her also, she may say, 'my sister,' she must also, though shame should rise up and cover her, look down and say, 'O, my sister.'"

Mr. George Meredith's novel in *Once a Week* was *Evan Harrington*.

I cannot find any poem by Allingham in *Once a Week* about the time Rossetti wrote this letter.

XLIV.

[*January*, 1861.]

Dear Allingham,

I hope you've had all the luck of the Season, and that it's to last all the year. I write this more specially to say that I sent off the Magdalene photograph some time back by Green, and that I hope it reached you safely.

manufacture
made by a paper hanger
Somewhat as below . I
Shall have it printed
on common brown packing
paper and on blue
grocer's paper to try
which is best

DESIGN FOR WALL PAPER.

[To face page 251.

Lizzie is pretty well for her, and we are in expectation (but this is quite in confidence, as such things are better waited for quietly) of a little accident which has just befallen Topsy and Mrs. T. who have become parients [*sic*]. Ours however will not be (if at all) for 2 or 3 months yet.

We have got our rooms quite jolly now. Our drawing-room is a beauty, I assure you, already, and on the first country trip we make we shall have it newly papered from a design of mine which I have an opportunity of getting made by a paper-manufacturer, somewhat as below. I shall have it printed on common brown packing-paper and on blue grocer's-paper, to try which is best. [Here follows, in the original letter, a design of the wall-paper.]

The trees are to stand the whole height of the room, so that the effect will be slighter and quieter than in the sketch, where the tops look too large. Of course they will be wholly conventional: the stems and fruit will be Venetian Red, the leaves black—the fruit, however, will have a line of yellow to indicate roundness and distinguish it from the stem; the lines of the ground black, and the stars yellow with a white ring round them. The red and black will be made of the same key as the brown or blue of the ground, so that the effect of the whole will be rather sombre, but I think rich, also. When we get the paper up, we shall have the doors and wainscoting painted summer-house green. We got into the room in such a hurry that we had no time to do anything to the paper and painting, which had just been done by the landlord. I should like you to see how nice the rooms are looking, and how many nice things we have got in them.

However you have yet to see a real wonder of the age—viz., Topsy's house, which baffles all description now.

We are organising (but this is quite under the rose as yet) a company for the production of furniture and decoration of all kinds, for the sale of which we are going to open an actual shop! The men concerned are Madox Brown, Jones, Topsy, Webb (the architect of T.'s house), P. P. Marshall, Faulkner, and myself. Each of us is now producing, at his own charges, one or two (and some of us more) things towards the stock. We are not intending to compete with ——'s costly rubbish or anything of that sort, but to give real good taste at the price as far as possible of ordinary furniture. We expect to start in some shape about May or June, but not to go to any expense in premises at first.

Here is the last piece of news, and other there is none available I think. Description of pictures in hand is barren work. I am making use of your notes on my Poems and bettering some of them, I hope. I am now going to print all those written except the *Bride's Chamber*, and those you advised omitting. When printed, I shall see how much more is needed for a volume, and try to do it in the evenings, while the printed sheets wait, and then bring the book out. I am actually continuing the printing of the *Translations* now, and hope to get both books out together.

What became of the Poem you meant to send to *Once a Week*? Did you send it? I have not seen the paper regularly, but should have nosed it out nevertheless, I fancy, if it had appeared.

Write me as soon as you can, and believe me, with love from Lizzie and self,

Your affectionate

D. G. ROSSETTI.

NOTES ON XLIV.

"Our rooms" were the old quarters by Blackfriars Bridge, somewhat enlarged.

Mr. W. M. Rossetti, describing "the foundation of the decorative firm, which, known at first as 'Morris, Marshall, Faulkner & Co.,' is now named 'Morris & Company,'" continues :—"The Præraphaelite Brotherhood introduced into painting something that might well be called a revolution, and the firm introduced into decoration something still more revolutionary for widespread and as yet permanent effect. The first suggestion for forming some such firm," adds Mr. Rossetti, " came from Mr. Peter Paul Marshall, an engineer, son-in-law of Mr. John Miller of Liverpool." However true this may be, nevertheless, as Mr. Arthur Hughes points out to me, the germs of it are to be found in " the intensely mediæval furniture " which Morris had made for his rooms in Red Lion Square, and in the cabinet which he, Rossetti, and Burne-Jones covered with pictures. A further development is seen in the decorations of Morris's house at Upton.

Morris had of course to learn by experience. Mr. Hughes remembers a sofa designed by him, with a long bar beneath projecting six inches at each end, so that it tripped up some one who hastily went round it. Amid loud laughter each projection was at once shortened by three inches with a saw ; but even then there was danger to the passer-by. My study table was one of the earliest productions of the firm. Neither it nor an arm-chair which they made for me was such a thorough piece of workmanship as they would have produced later on. They were at first, as Faulkner told me, sometimes tricked by their men. How earnest Morris was in mastering every trade which he undertook the following anecdote shows. One day on my way to Oxford I fell in with him at Paddington and we travelled together. His hands were deeply stained with blue. He told me that he was working at a dyer's in the Midland Counties, as he meant to make carpets and hangings.   What he had already learnt showed him that the usual processes were very imperfect.

He used frequently to lunch at Faulkner's house in Queen's Square, coming in the French blouse in which he worked from the business-place of the firm —" the shop " as they always called it—close by.   Faulkner told me that the servant thought he was a butcher whom her master for some unaccountable reason had to lunch.

XLV.

[*Endorsed London, May* 10, 1861.]

My dear Allingham,

I have had to thank several people for expressions of sympathy, but few can be so worthy of thanks as yours, which I well know to be sincere. My wife is progressing very well, all things considered, and got over her confinement much better than we had ventured to hope.   The child had been dead for 2 or 3 weeks before, and you may imagine that my forebodings were none of the brightest.

I had delayed writing to you for some time till I could send you my book—*i.e.,* the *Translations,* which is now just finished printing, and will reach you in a few days I hope, if I can get at a copy ;

but I must be chary of what I do till I know whether it is to be my own or a publisher's. However I trust to send one to you now, as I am anxious to have your advice in case of prolonged negotiations with publishers. I try Macmillan first, as he has been again expressing wishes about it, but am not very sanguine of him. For one thing, I have been obliged to introduce, in order to give a full view of the epoch of Poetry, some matter to which objections may probably be raised; but I should not have cared to do the work at all unless completely from a literary point of view. I have also had to put in a good deal of my own prose, and, as far as I know, there is nothing more which could be added to the book, which makes nearly 500 pages.

It has interfered a good deal with my painting till lately, I am sorry to say. My own original *Pomes* (de Terre et de Ciel) must stand over as yet. But as I shall certainly not get the first book out till November, the second may possibly be ready too. I am going to do one, or perhaps two, etchings for the first.

Now, there is a world of words about myself when I had to tell you about your work; that is, *Morley Park*—which I read and found full of beauties,—best where most impassioned, as all poetry is and must be. The monologue of the deserted woman seemed to me most sustained in this respect—and you will say truly ought to be. In the rest I must say I found a certain degree of constraint in style—a rather wilful stiffness of expression (of which the opening couplet affords as good an example as any), and I thought also too much dwelling here and there on minute objects in nature—particularly in the bridegroom's speech to the bride. I have it not by me, so am speaking from memory. Moreover, the speeches struck me sometimes as having rather too literary—or clever —a turn. I recall as an instance what the main speaker says to his returned friend about his grown-up sweetheart, towards the end. The work is quite yours, however, and *really* a work, and would harmonize much better with a volume of your poems than with Macmillan's Macademy of stones for bread. By the bye, I dare say you liked my sister's little pennyworths of wheat prominent among the pebbles.

The Academy is rather seedy, only has a refreshing look through being more fairly hung than usual. Leighton might, as you say, have made a burst had his pictures not been very ill placed mostly—indeed one of them (the only very good one, *Lieder ohne Wörte*) is the only instance of very striking unfairness in the place. Hughes has got a good place, and looks very well indeed with a picture of a Laborer's return to his family. Hook's pictures are among the best, but one seems to have seen them before. Hunt's *Lanthorn maker* may be really the best picture there, spite of several decided shortcomings. Watts has two very good portraits (or more like pictures), one of Alice Prinsep. Mrs. Wells (Boyce's sister) has some first-rate things, and her husband (who has been driven from miniature to oil by the progress of photography) is not far behind her. There is a Scotchman named Archer, who has a picture I like as well as anything of a lady " Playing at Queen," with her quaint children holding her train and trotting after. But really there is not a single work of importance in the place which belongs to quite the first rank.

Pardon great hurry in this letter which is written before breakfast, and believe me (with love from wife),

Your affectionate
D. G. ROSSETTI.

I will give your love to —— and wife. They have a nice pretty elder sister of Mrs. ——'s in town. There might be a chance for you!! Only a little elder!!!

NOTES ON XLV.

On April 20, 1861, Rossetti had written to Alexander Gilchrist :—" My great anxiety about

CHRISTINA ROSSETTI.

(From a tracing of a sketch by Dante Gabriel Rossetti.)

[To face page 259.

my wife lasts still. She has too much courage to be in the least downcast herself."

On October 3, 1862, Mrs. Gilchrist, writing to Mr. W. M. Rossetti about the republication of Blake's *Daughters of Albion* says :—" It was no use to put in what I was perfectly certain Macmillan (who reads all the proofs) would take out again. He is far more inexorable against any shade of heterodoxy in morals than in religion."

The title of *Morley Park* was changed first into *Southwell Park*, and finally into *Bridegroom's Park*. It is included in a volume called *Life and Phantasy* in the last edition of Allingham's works. The opening couplet is as follows :—

> " Friend Edward, from this turn remark
> The sweep of woodland.   Bridegroom's Park
> We call it."

" ' My sister's little pennyworths of wheat ' " (Mr. W. M. Rossetti tells me) "were poems by Christina in *Macmillan's Magazine*.   One of them (the first) was *Up-Hill*, now of considerable celebrity."

It was in Cairo, Mr. Holman Hunt tells us, that he began " the little picture called *The Lantern Maker's Courtship*.   It was of an incident I saw in the bazaar."   Madox Brown recorded on July 28, 1856 :—" Saw Hunt's *Lantern Maker*, which is lovely in colour and one of the best he has painted, but like much he has done of late, very quaint in drawing and composition, but admirably painted."

Mrs. Wells died in the summer of this year.

" She was," writes Mr. W. M. Rossetti, " a painter of exceptional talent, from which my brother and many more hoped much.   He took a portrait of her as she lay in death."

J. Archer's picture was *Playing at a Queen with a Painter's Wardrobe.*

XLVI.

Monday [*summer of* 1861].

MY DEAR ALLINGHAM,

I am sending you by *book post* with this a sewed copy of my book.   I have only just got a few, and do not offer it you *en permanence* in this state, as I am going to make an etching, or perhaps two, for it, and there is another index to come at the end, but had 6 copies sent me now to use in getting a publisher, etc.   My first offer of it will be to Macmillan, with whom I have had some talk.

What I want chiefly to get rid of is the printer's bill, but I am led to think by some friends that I ought to expect *something* in money also.   What think you?   Will you tell me, and say all you have time to say in the way of criticism?   *Cancels* are still possible.   There are 5 *cancel* leaves already in the book (chiefly on score of decorum!), which you will notice by their being in the rough as yet.

My wife progresses well, I am glad to tell you. With her love to you,

I am, yours affectionately,

D. G. R.

NOTES ON XLVI.

" My Book" was *The Early Italian Poets*, now called *Dante and his Circle.* No etchings were included in it, though one was made, now in Mr. Fairfax Murray's collection. Macmillan did not publish the work, but Smith and Elder.

For the "*something* in money" which his friends led him to think he ought to expect he had to wait eight years. By 1869, about six hundred copies having been sold, he received, Mr. W. M. Rossetti says, " a minute dole of less than nine pounds."

—

XLVII.

[*Near the end of* 1862.]

MY DEAR ALLINGHAM,

. . . You will remember my troubling you once or twice about that *Bogie* poem book of Wilkinson's. I am wanting it now to mention in a passage on Blake's poetry which I am writing for the *Life* never quite completed. Could you kindly

let me have the loan of yours as soon as you
can. . . .

Yours affectionately,
D. G. ROSSETTI.

NOTES ON XLVII.

"That Bogie poem" was *Improvisations from
the Spirit*, by Dr. J. Garth Wilkinson, the homœopathist who was Miss Siddal's physician in 1854.
Hawthorne, whose children he attended in December, 1857, wrote of him:—"He is a homœopathist,
and is known in scientific or general literature; at
all events, a sensible and enlightened man, with an
un-English freedom of mind on some points. For
example, he is a Swedenborgian and a believer in
modern spiritualism. He showed me some drawings that had been made under the spiritual influence by a miniature-painter who possesses no
imaginative power of his own, and is merely a good
mechanical and literal copyist; but these drawings,
representing angels and allegorical people, were
done by an influence which directed the artist's
hand, he not knowing what his next touch would
be, nor what the final result." Hawthorne con-
cludes: "This matter of spiritualism is surely
the strangest that ever was heard of; and yet I
feel unaccountably little interest in it—a sluggish
distrust and repugnance to meddle with it—inso-
much that I hardly feel as if it were worth this
page or two in my not very eventful journal." It

does not appear that the doctor ever compounded his draughts and his pills under spiritual influence, though it seems hard that his patients should not have had the benefit of this supernatural aid.

Rossetti thus described this "bogy book" in the supplementary chapter he wrote for Gilchrist's *Life of Blake* :—" A very singular example of the closest and most absolute resemblance to Blake's poetry may be met with (if only one *could* meet with it) in a phantasmal sort of little book, published, or perhaps not published but only printed, some years since, and entitled, *Improvisations of the Spirit*. It bears no author's name, but was written by Dr. J. Garth Wilkinson, the highly-gifted editor of Swedenborg's writings, and author of a *Life* of him, to whom we owe a reprint of the poems in Blake's *Songs of Innocence and Experience*. These improvisations profess to be written under precisely the same kind of spiritual guidance, amounting to abnegation of personal effort in the writer, which Blake supposed to have presided over the production of his *Jerusalem*, &c. The little book has passed into the general (and in all other cases richly-deserved) limbo of the modern 'spiritualist' muse. It is a very thick little book, however unsubstantial its origin ; and contains, amid much that is disjointed or hopelessly obscure (but then, why be the polisher of poems for which a ghost, and not even your own ghost, is alone responsible ?) many passages and indeed whole compositions of a remote and charming beauty, or sometimes of a

grotesque figurative relation to things of another
sphere, which are startlingly akin to Blake's
writings—could pass in fact for no one's but his.
Professing as they do the same new kind of authorship, they might afford plenty of material for comparison and bewildered speculation, if such were
in any request."

Dr. Wilkinson in a note at the end of his *Improvisations* says :—" Suffice it to say that every
piece was produced without premeditation or pre-
conception : had these processes stolen in, such
production would have been impossible. The pro
duction was attended by no feeling and by no
fervour, but only by an anxiety of all the circum-
stant faculties to observe the unlooked-for evolution
and to know what would come of it."

According to W. B. Scott, " Emerson said
' Wilkinson was most like Bacon of all men
living.' " Scott adds that " Wilkinson was as tall
and as straight as a spear, and looked steadily at
you from behind his spectacles as if he saw your
thoughts as distinctly as your nose, while Tennyson cared little and noted little of either."

Rossetti had helped Mr. Gilchrist in editing
Blake's poems. He wrote to him :—" I am glad
you approve of my rather unceremonious shaking
up of Blake's rhymes [*i.e.*, the correction of Blake's
grammar]. I really believe that is what ought to
be done." Later on Mr. W. M. Rossetti was
reproached with these emendations. His brother
wrote to him on October 8, 1874 :—" I know you

would not quite have coincided with my method of treatment, nor should I now have adopted it to the same extent." Mr. W. M. Rossetti in a letter to Allingham about a proposed edition of Shelley, after speaking of " Shelley's mixing up you and *thou* in dialogue," continued :—" Gabriel said, ' Make everything uniform ; ' but I have not the remotest idea of doing that."

XLVIII.

16, CHEYNE WALK, CHELSEA,
Tuesday [1863].

MY DEAR ALLINGHAM,

My friend Taylor (of H.M. Theatre) writes me that he will reserve for me his two pit tickets for *Mirella* to-night (being unable to get better places for a new attraction). I shall not be able to go myself, but I write him word with this that you perhaps may, alone or with a friend. If you can go, ask any official about the place for Mr. Taylor, and he will do the needful. You need not think there is any awkwardness about it, as my plan with him, at his own request, has always been to send friends if I wished, instead of going myself?

When am I to see you again? I shall be going on Friday to Hughes's with Madox Brown and Ned Jones. They are to be here at 6, and I hope dine with me before going. Will you do the same, if you like to go on to Hughes's?

Yours affectionately,

D. GABRIEL R.

NOTES ON XLVIII.

Warrington Taylor, Mr. W. M. Rossetti tells me, was a man of good family who had come down in the world and was a check-taker at the Opera. He had a great love of music and art. Rossetti got for him the post of book-keeper in the firm of Morris & Co., where he did very well, having a good head for figures. Within four years after receiving the appointment he died of consumption.

Mirella or *Mireille* was an opera by Gounod. According to Mr. Holman Hunt, "Rossetti regarded music as positively offensive." Mr. W. M. Rossetti tells me that while his brother would never have willingly listened to an oratorio, or indeed to any music of that kind which Dr. Johnson, when he was told that it was very difficult, wished were impossible, nevertheless he was fond of the opera. He would moreover listen with pleasure to the singing of a simple ballad.

XLIX.

August, 1863,
16 CHEYNE WALK, CHELSEA.

MY DEAR ALLINGHAM,

I have been meaning to write any day since last seeing you, though in truth without much to say, but I am anxious to hear in return how you get on in your new quarters. I have not been out of London since seeing you, except for a couple of days to Brighton; and indeed, though I have earned this year more than any previous one, I seem never to have a penny wherewith to run away for a little, like other people. Perhaps I may yet, though, in another month, and who knows but I may see Venice? But I suppose it will not be.

Have you seen a new volume of poems by one Jean Ingelow? Really there seems a good deal in it.

This house goes on getting more settled, and I more restless. I do not know where it will take me to and how soon. I see hardly any one. Swinburne is away. Meredith has evaporated for good, and my brother is seldom here. There is only one more to unite with me in good wishes to you.

I would begin another sheet, however, but for

the little to say. So to make something I will direct your attention to the headings of these sheets, which are a combined effort of self as designer and Knewstub's (my pupil's) brother's firm as executants—he insisting on making me a present of a small stack of paper headed in various colours, which stuff up every drawer in my studio, and will last half my lifetime—or indeed perhaps head the news of my death when that occurs, before the black-edged paper has arrived. The above morbidity reminds me of the green bogie book, which you know you promised to send up when it came to hand.

You are somewhere near the New Forest, are you not? Or is this, as highly probably, a topographical bull which is opening your eyes and mouth at this moment. If so, it is only one of a large family of mine. But if you *are* near there, I really ain't sure that I sha'n't come and see you, and walk about for a day or two, if you can. Could you, supposing such a case? I am awfully done up for want of a change of some sort.

By the bye, Ned Jones said he should be in your neighbourhood before long, and should look you up. He is a dear old chap, and said much at same time which I was glad he should say, both for your and his sake.

Have you seen the blue book on the Royal

Academy—and would you like to see it? If so, I will send it you as a good cupboard skeleton in return for your bogies. There is abundance of rotten and decayed matter shovelled up in it, with much overfed sweltering thereby engendered, gorged creatures and starved anatomies, with some will-o'-the-wisps and the ghosts of various reputations. The only evidence of the lot which is worth reading as original thought and insight is Ruskin's. Him I saw the other day, and pitched into, he talked such awful rubbish ; but he is a dear old chap, too, and as soon as he was gone I wrote my sorrows to him. Browning was here at same time, very jolly indeed, and stayed and walked many times round the room, and many times stood still, with his hands in his pockets and his eyes wide open.

My love to you, and believe me ever yours

D. G. ROSSETTI.

Would you like me to send to you Blake's *Life?* Not out yet, but I have one in sheets.

NOTES ON XLIX.

Rossetti lost his wife on February 11, 1862. He had no heart to go on living in his old home by Blackfriars Bridge, and removed up the river to Chelsea. There he took a large house, in which his brother, Mr. Swinburne, and Mr. George Meredith were to have rooms, as sub-tenants.

That he should never have seen Venice, that he who was a Florentine of the Florentines should never have passed a single day in Florence, seems strange indeed. To borrow the words Mr. Holman Hunt used of him, he held that "people had no right to be different from the people of Dante's time." He cared for none of the discoveries of modern science. "What could it matter," he said, "whether the earth moved round the sun, or the sun travelled round the earth?" Why, with the large income that he was making, he seemed "never to have a penny wherewith to run away," why he never saw Venice, was due to his reckless expenditure. "Money," writes Mr. W. M. Rossetti, "dripped from my brother's fingers in all sorts of ways, unforecast at the time, and not always easily accounted for afterwards." Of this "dripping" an instance is given in the following passage in his letter to his brother, dated April 23, 1864 : "I have seen the owner of the zebu, and undertaken to buy him for £20,—£5 payable on Monday, and the rest within a fortnight. I shall then have plenty, but just now have none. Could you pay your £5 as the first installment?" The zebu was a small Brahmin bull, who chased his new master round a tree, and was at once resold.

Of Jean Ingelow's new volume of poems Matthew Arnold wrote :—"She seemed to me to be quite 'above the common,' but I have not read enough of her to say more. It is a great deal to give one true feeling in poetry, and I think she seemed to be able to do that; but I do not at present very much care for poetry unless it can give me true *thought* as well. It is the alliance of these two that makes great poetry, the only poetry really worth very much."

"The headings of these sheets" are thus described by Mr. W. M. Rossetti: "My father owned a largish seal marked with a cross,—a tree having the motto 'Frangas non flectas,'—and he said this was regarded as his crest. Mr. Knewstub, my brother's art assistant, who was connected with the firm of Jenner & Knewstub, got that firm to present to Gabriel a die with the crest and a monogram."

Allingham was living at Lymington, a little south of the New Forest, and over against the Isle of Wight.

The Blue Book was *The Report of the Commissioners appointed to inquire into the Present Position of the Royal Academy in Relation to the Fine Arts.*

"Mr. Ruskin," writes Mr. W. M. Rossetti, "took keen delight in Rossetti's paintings and designs. He praised freely and abused heartily both him and them. The abuse was good-humoured and was taken good-humouredly. . . . They took in good part, with mutual banter and amusement, whatever was deficient or excessive in the performance of the painter or in the comments of the purchaser and critic." Rossetti wrote to Madox Brown on

January 19, 1873 :—" I do not call John Ruskin's work criticism, but rather brilliant poetic rhapsody."

L.

16, CHEYNE WALK, CHELSEA.

[*23rd Sept.*, 1863.]

MY DEAR ALLINGHAM,

My serious thoughts of coming to you have come to nothing as yet, as I need not tell you. The fact is, while I was still revolving the idea, but almost too seedy to move at all, William dropped in with a request that I would accompany him to Belgium for a week. Finding that all was ready for this start on his part, which half helped me to be so too, and remembering that the other depended all on myself, and so was more problematical, I was induced to go with him, to very moderate results as regards enjoyment, but still to some benefit in that way as well as in health ; though having come back to finish the very nauseous job I ran away from—viz., some copies, only doing for filthy lucre's sake from some things of my own—I feel already quite as bad again as before I went. But whether I shall have the chance of another trip I am far from sure. If I should see you, after all, it will, I know, be with true pleasure ; but the year is getting late and the dun is at the door. Moreover, I make no doubt of reviving when I get to more likeable work, and being tolerably well rooted to it.

But present or absent believe me always,

Truly your friend,

D. G. ROSSETTI.

A man asked me the other day if I would do Blake for the *Westminster*. I said, no ; but ventured to name you as possible. Would you, if I hear more?

LI.

16, CHEYNE WALK, CHELSEA.
Saturday [probably 1863].

DEAR ALLINGHAM,

If fine, I expect to start for Lymington on Monday at 5.10 P.M. This intention however renders rain so probable that it is not certain you will see me then after all, as in case of bad weather looking likely to last I should put off coming till it was finer.

Ever yours D. G. ROSSETTI.

P.S.—However, on the whole I expect to come, and if not will telegraph.

19

LII.

[*Christmas*, 1865.]

MY DEAR ALLINGHAM,

Several months ago I got a good letter of yours asking me to come and see you. This had been uppermost in my mind to do, had I found myself able to do anything of the sort, even before getting your letter. However, it seemed quite hopeless already at the time of your writing, and proved more and more so afterwards. Yet I forbore answering *No*, in the hope of *Yes* for some time. Now on Christmas Eve *No* seems the word and no mistake. I have not had a single day out of London this year except once to Greenwich with Boyce, and once walking to Tottenham. For all that I've not done half I meant to do. Now the only thing left is to wish you all luck next year, and myself the luck of coming to see you then.

I heard of your being in town but for a flying visit, in which I am sorry you did not find time to look me up. However, if I scramble once more through the fogs and duns of a London Christmas, I'll hope to meet you again yet.

Worse, however, than not having yet thanked you for a pleasure offered is my omission to do so for one actually bestowed and enjoyed ; namely, the gift of your *Fifty Poems*. I remember they fared well with me, for I read them one evening right through when I felt much in want of other voices than plaguey ones from inside and outside ; and I found them full of good words and true. Every one is a study—not work thrown away, or no-work shovelled together ; those new to me were to the full as good as the old ones, and many of the old gained greatly on reacquaintance. So here come my late but real thanks to you.

Ever affectionately yours,
D. G. ROSSETTI.

NOTES ON LII.

Rossetti wrote to his uncle on November 15th of this year :—" Referring to my diary, I find there have been only twelve days during the five months ending with the close of October which have not been spent by me in work at my easel. I have completely missed all exercise and change of air this year, yet have no reason to complain as regards health."

On October 1st of the same year Madox Brown recorded :—" Walked to Tottenham with P. P. Marshall and Rossetti." Mr. Marshall lived at Tottenham, where he has left a memorial of his art in the small building above a well near the High Cross. The village—for a village it still was —was also the home of two men who bought

Præraphaelite pictures, Colonel Gillum and Mr. Goss.

Allingham wrote to Mr. W. M. Rossetti on March 19, 1865:—"My volume of *Fifty Modern Poems* is just coming out. Most of the pieces have been in magazines, etc. The whole is to myself already a thing of the past and not very interesting. I am occupied with other ideas. One quality the book has (implied in 'Modern'),—it is in harmony with the best minds of our day as to religion, being at once reverent and anti-dogmatic."

LIII.

16, CHEYNE WALK, CHELSEA,
                    [*Nov.* 8, 1866].

MY DEAR ALLINGHAM,

Herewith I send you a set of the photos, hitherto made from Lizzie's sketches—many mere scraps, but all interesting. I shall have the water-colours photo'd in due course, but this is a trouble-some job, as a first negative will be necessary, then a touched proof, and then a second negative, or the effect will be all false. I shall also print descriptions of each design. Room is left in the port-folio I think to contain these additions when ready.

One of these days I hope to see you at home. I

was obliged to run away from the gallery on Saturday last, as I had an appointment to catch a train.

Your affectionately

D. G. ROSSETTI.

NOTE ON LIII.

Mr. W. M. Rossetti tells me that these descriptions of Mrs. Rossetti's designs were never printed.

LIV.

22 March, [1867].

MY DEAR ALLINGHAM,

I inclose an answer to Aidé, which will tell you my mind, except that I may add to you that £1400 is £1400 to me, or rather to anybody rather than me as I never see it at all, and that my plan is to rent, not to buy. I have been pot-boiling to an extent lately that does not hold out much hope of estate buying or even renting. Moreover, as I haven't been outside my door for months in the daytime, I shouldn't have had much opportunity of enjoying pastime and pleasances. I have accordingly no news whatever, except of my easel, which is too mean a slave to small needs to be worth reporting on. I do not see a fellow of any sort really much oftener than you do, I imagine.

I lately heard from Aubrey de Vere, with a request to my sister and self to contribute something to a verse collection. We looked up scraps, and were promised proofs, but these come not; and I imagine that the result when in type will be the usual incentive to blasphemy. I wonder do you sail in the same boat—or "funny," as it is likely to prove according to my experience.

Yours always,

D. G. ROSSETTI.

NOTES ON LIV.

There should have been no need for "pot-boiling." In this year Rossetti made "little or not at all less than £3000."

His habit of not going outside his door in the daytime is thus accounted for by his brother : " He rose late ; painted all day, as long as light served him ; then dined ; and whether winter or summer, all was darkness, tempered by gaslight or moonlight, by the hour he left the house."

Mr. Aubrey de Vere could not have completed this "verse collection." In 1893 he published *The Household Poetry Book*, but it contains nothing by Rossetti or his sister.

A "funny" is the name given to a boat so frail that it oversets very easily.

LV.

Monday, [*September* 30, 1867].

My dear Allingham,

Do by all means come up—not for a day. but for as long as you can.   I am most wishful to return with you for another spell of country air and exercise, but must tell you that since returning to town I have found the confusion in my head and the strain on my eyes in working decidedly rather on the increase than otherwise, and am getting really anxious about it.   I mention this quite in confidence, as it w^{d.} be injurious to me if it got about.   The only 2 to whom I have named it are Brown and Howell, and I do not mean to say more about it.   To-morrow I shall finish a drawing I have been at work on, and on Wednesday shall probably go to Bowman, the oculist.   I must take his advice about going away, but am rather under the impression at present that the light rooms and sunlight outside at Lymington did me more harm than good.   I saw Howell yesterday, who is prepared to come to Lymington if I do.   It would give me much pleasure indeed to see you here if you can come, so do at once.

Yours ever,

D. Gabriel R.

NOTES ON LV.

"About this time Rossetti's eyesight began to fail. Sunlight or artificial light became increasingly painful to him, producing sensations of giddiness."

Howell had been Ruskin's secretary. Later on he was employed by Rossetti " to transact the sale of uncommissioned work. As a salesman he was unsurpassable."

LVI.

Thursday [*October* 10, 1867].

In case I don't see you to-day I write word that, as I expected you to-day, blokes are coming to-morrow to meet you at dinner at 7.

I went to Bowman, who gave me the information that if it didn't get better it might get worse.

Your D. G. R.

NOTES ON LVI.

Rossetti wrote to Brown in 1861 :—" Dear Brown, a few blokes and coves are coming at 8 or so on Friday evening to participate in oysters and obloquy."

He makes the following mention of the famous

oculist, Sir William Bowman, in a letter to his mother nearly two years later :—" I suppose I told you of my seeing Bowman before I left London, and that instead of taking a guinea fee (which he refused) he proposes to pay me one hundred and fifty for a little water-colour."

LVII.

16, CHEYNE WALK,
28 August, 1868.

MY DEAR ALLINGHAM,

I've been very seedy, and still am rather so, but doctors have been doing me some good.

I'm going to start away somewhere, but fancy seaside. There's a deadly-lively or very quiet place called Southwold, in Suffolk, where the Morris's, Howells, and others have been lately, and I think perhaps of going there. I don't know exactly what my moves may be ; but would it be in the nature of things for you to take a trip with me anywhere at present ? I think we rather used up the walks about Lymington last year, and seaside is desirable, and certainly no impending female photographers or even poets laureate.

I merely ask you the question as a guide in my

plans. We might go to several places even—say including a new visit to Stratford-on-Avon and neighbourhood, which will bear seeing often.

Will you kindly answer *at once*, as I ought to start at once.

Your affect.,
D. Gabriel R.

Notes on LVII.

"The terrible affliction of sleeplessness," writes Mr. W. M. Rossetti, "which was the origin of all the breaking-up of my brother's health, had already been going on some while before the autumn of 1868." He paid the visit to Stratford-on-Avon in September, and later on in the month he went to Penkill Castle, Ayrshire, where he stayed some weeks.

"The line about 'impending female photographers or even poets laureate' refers," Mr. W. M. Rossetti tells me, "to Tennyson at Freshwater, in the Isle of Wight, and to his near neighbour, Mrs. Cameron, a lady of good position and a very cordial friend of Rossetti. She had taken to photographing, and produced many remarkable things of broad pictorial effect."

LVIII.

Wednesday [*Christmas*, 1868].

MY DEAR ALLINGHAM,

Many are Xmas nuisances, and here comes another—accompanied, however, by all affectionate wishes.

I have been looking up a few old Sonnets, and writing a few new ones, to make a little bunch in a coming number of the *Fortnightly*—not till March, however, as they are full till then.

Among them are the enclosed two, about which I want an opinion. It seems to me doubtful whether the 2nd adds anything of much value to the first, and whether it (the 2nd) is not in itself rather far-fetched and obscure. I wish you would tell me what you think. I would excise the 2nd if the first is best by itself.

I suppose you heard that I have been queer with my eyes—this has caused inaction and the looking up of ravelled rags of verse. I am now at work again, however.

Affectionately yours,

D. G. ROSSETTI.

P.S.—Isn't there a chance of your coming up this Xmas ? Come and stay with me.

P.P.S.—How do you like the *Ring and the*

Book? It is full of wonderful work, but it seems to me that, whereas other poets are the more liable to get incoherent the more fanciful their starting-point happens to be, the thing that makes Browning drunk is to give him a dram of prosaic reality, and unluckily this time the "gum-tickler" is less like pure Cognac than 7 Dials gin. Whether the consequent evolutions will be bearable to their proposed extent without the intervening walls of the station-house to tone down their exuberance may be dubious. This *entre nous.*

NOTES ON LVIII.

Rossetti describes these sonnets in a letter to his mother, which begins :—" I send you my sonnets, which are such a lively band of bogies that they may join with the skeletons of Christina's various closets and entertain you with a ballet."

Mrs. Gilchrist wrote to a friend :—" I dined with the Rossettis on Thursday [April 19, 1869]. Gabriel Rossetti told a good story, which Carlyle, I believe, tells of himself—how he met Browning and *meant* to say something to please about *The Ring and the Book*, but somehow ultimately found himself landed in the reverse of a compliment :— ' It is a wonderful book, one of the most wonderful poems ever written. I re-read it all through—all made out of an Old Bailey story that might have been told in ten lines, and only wants forgetting.'

G. D. R. seemed himself to lean a little to this view, and to think there was perversity in the choice of the subject, though of course redeemed by superb treatment."

LIX.

16, CHEYNE WALK, CHELSEA.

21 *February*, 1870.

MY DEAR ALLINGHAM,

As you expressed a willingness for a little more scratching and sifting at my poetic diggings, I trouble you on a rather abject dilemma regarding a very old piece of work,—*Sister Helen*, enclosed.   The family name used in it was originally "Keith."   This I altered because of Dobell's ballad, *Keith of Ravelston* which bears also on faithless love and supernaturalism.   (I may add, however, that D.'s ballad was never published till some years after mine had been originally in print, but still I hate coincidences of the kind.)   This I have changed to "Holm," which is objected to now, from *I think a quarter* worth considering, as not being a well-sounding territorial name.   My reason for asking you about it is that (the Boyne being mentioned in the poem) an Irish name might perhaps do best. Would " Neill " do?—and would it fit in with " Eastholm," " Westholm," and " Neill of Neill " ? Would you give me a hint or a suggestion of some better name or system of nomenclature, if such occurs to you ?   The father being " of that ilk " should stand, I think, as elucidatory.   I write in great hurry, as I am trying to get the thing off for a new revise, and should be much obliged, therefore, if you could answer my question without delay.

I suppose you saw the evidently personal on-slaught on William's *Shelley* in the *Athenæum,*—by Buchanan, I believe.   I suppose I may expect to fare likewise, if nothing interferes.

Ever yours,

D. G. ROSSETTI.

NOTES ON LIX.

Rossetti, writing on January 3, 1854, " says that he had consigned the ballad of *Sister Helen* to Mrs. Howitt, ' for an English edition of a German something or other, which will be coming out now.' This German publication was named *The Düsseldorf Annual.*   The ballad appeared in it, without the author's name, but only with the initials ' H. H. H.' attached."

Of *Keith of Ravelston* Rossetti wrote in 1868 :—

"I have always regarded that poem as being one of the finest, of its length, in any modern poet; ranking with Keats's *La Belle Dame sans Merci*, and the other masterpieces of the condensed and hinted order so dear to imaginative minds." Of Dobell's poem the following is the first stanza :—

> "The murmur of the mourning ghost
>   That keeps the shadowy kine,
> O Keith of Ravelston,
>   The sorrows of thy line."

In 1866, Mr. Buchanan, in a burlesque poem, had made "a gratuitous and insolent attack upon Mr. Swinburne." Mr. W. M. Rossetti, in a review of Swinburne's poems, retaliated by saying that "the advent of so poor and pretentious a poetaster as Robert Buchanan stirs storms in teapots." Mr. Buchanan replied by his "personal onslaught" on Mr. W. M. Rossetti's edition of *Shelley*, which he followed up a little later by a severe review of Dante Rossetti's *Poems*. This he enlarged and published under the title of *The Fleshy School of Poetry and other Phenomena of the Day*. "I have," writes Mr. W. M. Rossetti, "more than once been told by friends that the animus against my brother apparent in the article should be regarded as a vicarious expression of resentment at something which I myself had written." On Dante Rossetti, who was already in a nervous state of health, Mr. Buchanan's attack had a disastrous effect.   "He was a changed man, and so continued till the close of his life."

I venture to quote, without first obtaining Mr. W. M. Rossetti's leave, the following passage from a letter in which he informs Allingham of the proposal made to him that he should edit *Shelley*: "Is it not a glorious chance, this *Shelley* editing and biographizing? Willingly would I not only be doing it for pay, but do it for nothing, or pay to do it."

LX.

28 *February*, 1870.

Dear Allingham,

Thanks for attending so promptly to my bewilderments.   I have adopted *Weir*, which seems to answer well. *Kerr* has not emphasis enough —runs too much off the tongue—for the poise of the verse.

As for that kind, good, overwhelming Lady A., she has written to me from at least 6 different parts of the British Islands during the past year, asking me to come down instantly and meet a sympathising circle.   But such things are quite impossible to me at the pitch of brutal bogyism at which I have arrived. *You* seem somehow to

keep your own man, but I am hardly my own
ghost.   I saw Ned the other evening, and he
seemed well on the whole, though rather collywobblyish.   I shall get into the country somewhere
—where,' I don't yet know—within a few days and
for a few weeks, to try if there is any marrow left
in me that can be squeezed out in the form of
rhyme before I go finally to press.   I mean to
be out in April—latter end, I suppose,—and should
like a few more pages if possible.   I want to get
near three hundred if I can, but have been
obliged to give up the idea of finishing several
things I had in hand for the purpose; and for all
that, having done no work to speak of in painting,
with this divided mind.   I must cart the things
off now, and then get to my easel again.

Ever yours,

D. G. ROSSETTI.

Christina has done a book of Nursery Rhymes,
and is publishing with Ellis, who offers her much
better terms than Mac. [Macmillan] does.   She
will leave Mac. altogether.

NOTES ON LX.

" Lady A." was, I conjecture, Lady Ashburton.
Rossetti wrote to his aunt in 1874 :—" Lady A.

20

[Ashburton] spoke of you in a friendly, even an affectionate way."

Far and wide as Dr. Murray has cast his nets for the great *Oxford English Dictionary* he has not caught *collywobblyish*.

LXI.

SCALANDS, ROBERTSBRIDGE,

HAWKHURST, KENT

[*March* 7, 1870].

DEAR ALLINGHAM,

You will be surprised at my address, which is Barbara's Cottage, not far from Hastings (but in Kent, as I find, or at least the above seems the proper form). I have been here a few days in company with Stillman, Wm's. American friend; having come for the purpose of recruiting and " working off" my book with the conscientious decency of Mr. Dennis the hangman. I shall have it out before the end of April. Stillman and I have this house to ourselves, and he is an utterly unobstructive man. Had your letter reached me in town I might probably have come down to you at once, and discussed the plan you propose, which seems promising—only I don't know whether such near seaside is likely to suit my eyes, to which, I believe, sea air is not suitable. However I must take the matter into consideration, and suppose I might even, if convenient to you, close at once with the proposal of joining you in rent for half a year, as it seems this wd only involve me in an expense of £15. So be it so, if you like —I shd reckon on probable advantage in a summary move to Lymington at some moment before that time is out, but if this should by possibility not come to pass, must stipulate beforehand that there be no question as to my being liable for my share, as I can only undertake it on those terms. [1]

There is really no news I know of since last writing. Barbara does not indulge in bell-pulls, hardly in servants to summon thereby—so I have brought my own. What she does affect is any amount of thorough draught—a library bearing the stern stamp of " Bodichon," and a kettle-holder with the uncompromising initials B. B. She is the best of women, but I fear from what I last saw of her that her health is failing, like my own.

Ever yours,
D. G. ROSSETTI.

[1] " Means that he will pay, come or not come." Note in Mr. Allingham's handwriting.

P.S.—By the bye, I fell back on *Keith*, after all, in that ballad. I couldn't quite please myself otherwise.

NOTES ON LXI.

Scalands, it will be remembered, was the house of Madame Bodichon (Miss Barbara Leigh Smith of earlier letters), who had been the kindest of friends to Rossetti's wife. She was also a warm friend of Allingham. "I love William Allingham," she was one day heard to say.

Of Mr. Stillman, Mr. W. M. Rossetti writes :—"Few men could have been better adapted than he, none could have been more willing, to solace Rossetti in his harasses from insomnia and other troubles ; but it is a fact that a remedy worse than the disease was the result of his friendly ministrations. Chloral as a soporific was then a novelty. Mr. Stillman had heard of its potency in procuring sleep, and he introduced the drug to Rossetti's attention. My brother was one of the men least fitted to try any such experiment with impunity. He began, I understand, with nightly doses of chloral of ten grains. In course of time it got to one hundred and eighty grains!" It wrecked his mind, and at last destroyed his life.

On May 4th Rossetti wrote to his mother:—"Dear Old Darling of 70. You will be glad to hear that the first edition is almost exhausted, and that Ellis is going to press with the second thousand. It

will have brought me £300 in less than a month."
Of these *Poems* his brother says :—" This date,
1870, should be borne in mind by any amateurs of
Rossetti's work ; for the volume named *Poems* of
1881, though partly a reissue of the book of 1870,
is very far from being identical with it."

LXII.

SCALANDS, ROBERTSBRIDGE.

[*Postmark, March 7, 1870*].

DEAR ALLINGHAM,

I now just hear casually that my book
has been applied for to the *Athenæum* by one of
its critics, I believe with friendly intentions. So
I ought to let you know after my suggestion.
Of course I should be very sorry if I had
missed you.

Ever yours

D. G. ROSSETTI.

NOTE ON LXII.

On February 3rd Rossetti had written to John
Skelton :—" I am anxious that some influential
article or articles by the well-affected should
appear *at once* when the book comes out. Swin-

burne wishes to 'do' it in the *Fortnightly*, and
Morris elsewhere ; and if these and yours, with
perhaps another or so, could appear *at once*,
certain spite which I judge to be brewing in at
least one quarter might find itself at fault." On
March 22nd he wrote to his mother :—" I shall
certainly get the book out before the end of April,
as three or four kindly hands are already at work
on it for the May periodicals."

LXIII.

Tuesday [August, 1870].

DEAR ALLINGHAM,

I'm sorry to have missed you yesterday.
Surely my letter went out to you before 5. Could
you come to-morrow (Wed^{y.}) instead? 7 o'clock
dinner.

Have you seen the last *Blackwood*? If you
have not, and need a relish before dinner, try it
instead of gin and bitters. What Brother Bard
but must find an added zest in the meat dispensed
by the hand of detected mediocrity?

Ever yours

D. G. ROSSETTI.

Notes on LXIII.

Blackwood's Magazine for August of this year contained a severe criticism of the *Poems*. I do not find in it, as I half expected, the words "detected mediocrity." The review is written in the following style :—" There is something in the character and temper of a painter so contemptuous of common public opinion that he refuses to exhibit his pictures—and of a poet who keeps his productions for some twenty years in the dark before he condescends to unfold them to the common eye —which in the first place attracts the imagination. Such a man walks serene at a height inaccessible to the common din, the comments and criticisms of lower earth. Such a man is too far removed from us to desire to be understood upon our level ; he addresses himself to the choice souls—the world within a world—the select of humanity." The reviewer says towards the close :—" In none of these poems, however, is there the least indication of a new poet arisen to bless us."

Rossetti's friend, John Skelton, the " Shirley " of *Blackwood*, had not been able to help him, at all events in that periodical.

LXIV.

[About November, 1870].

DEAR ALLINGHAM,

I can put your books on my basement floor—(stone-paved servants' hall)—where they will not be in the damp, I believe, and can stand clear of the floor if thought necessary. Or if you think it absolutely needed, I can clear space in a lumber-room upstairs.

Ever yours,
D. G. ROSSETTI.

LXV.

16, CHEYNE WALK,
Friday [about November, 1870].

DEAR ALLINGHAM,

I'm very sorry to tell you the high tide yesterday got into my basement floor, and that 3 of your boxes were a foot or more deep in water for some time. It is most vexatious to think what may have happened to the books. Will you look in to-day at dusk and stay to dinner at 6? I am only sorry that I have to go out about 7.

Ever yours,
D. G. ROSSETTI.

Note on LXV.

"On the basement of Rossetti's house at Chelsea," writes his brother, "there were spacious kitchen-rooms and an oddly complicated range of vaults, which perhaps had at one time led directly off to the river-side." The Thames Embankment had not as yet been raised in front of Cheyne Walk. In one of the boxes deposited on the basement floor it chanced that Allingham had placed the letters he had received from Rossetti. Some of them still bear marks of the flood ; two or three have been much injured, and one has been rendered illegible.

With this brief note the correspondence between the two men came to an end. Their friendship, once so strong and close, was not to last till death should come to give the final separation. So early as 1864 Allingham recorded in a note, "Our intimacy is a thing of the past." It must have revived to a certain extent, for in 1867 Rossetti passed some time with him at his house in Lymington. With the lapse of years, the letters, as has been seen, became less frequent and far briefer. So late as Christmas, 1868, we find the great painter signing himself, "Yours affectionately" ; after that date he is merely, "Ever yours." Warm hearted though he was in his friendships, nevertheless few of them lasted to the end of life. "It is a fact," writes his brother, "and a melan-

choly one, that Dante Rossetti, as the years
progressed, lost sight of all his Præraphaelite
Brothers, except only of Stephens at sparse intervals—'dear stanch Stephens, one of my oldest
and best friends,' as he wrote of him." He became
estranged from Ruskin and Browning. Between
him and Allingham, happily, there was no open
and direct breach. The long friendship slowly
died away.

THE END.